AN IDEAL WAY TO DIE

An Ed McCorkel Price Hill Mystery

ROY HOTCHKISS

Published by Edgecliff Press

in partnership with the

Price Hill Historical Society & Museum

Cincinnati, Ohio

An Ideal Way to Die

By Roy Hotchkiss

Published by Edgecliff Press, LLC.,
and the Price Hill Historical Society & Museum
Cincinnati, Ohio

www.edgecliffpress.com
www.pricehill.org

CIP Info
ISBN Number 978-0-9844622-8-5

Library of Congress Control Number: 2011936451
Copyright © 2011 by W. Roy Hotchkiss

Designed and edited by Julie Hotchkiss
Cover photograph © 2011 by Julie Hotchkiss

10   9   8   7   6   5   4   3   2   1

Published in the United States of America

To My Four Girls

ACKNOWLEDGMENTS

This book was produced from my manuscript as a project of the Price Hill Historical Society's Publications Committee, and the author gratefully acknowledges their support. Although it is a work of fiction, it has some historical perspective—at least that's how I'll put it. It is also the first novel the Price Hill Historical Society has published, but I hope it won't be the last, because I have already written a few others.

I would like to thank Betty Wagner and Joyce Meyer for telling me they enjoyed reading this book in manuscript, and also for suggesting that I might want to fix some of the mistakes they found in it. Any mistakes that remain, the author takes credit for.

Arnold's Bar & Grill also has my thanks for allowing their back bar to stand in for the 1940s Ideal Café in the cover photo.

Thanks also to all the denizens of the real Ideal Café, wherever they are now, who provided me with the inspiration for this story. However, all of the characters and many (though not all) of the locations in this story are fictitious and purely figments of my imagination. If these characters and places remind you of anyone, the resemblance is completely coincidental.

—W.R.H.

CHAPTER 1

"Do not turn around, Missster McCorkel. I vill kill you unlessss my ordersss are carried out. Firssst, giff me your gat."

"What?"

"I said, do not turn ..."

"No, no, I got that part. What was it you wanted me to give you?"

"Do not play ze gamesss viz me, McCorkel, giff me your gun."

"I don't have any gun. What's this all about?"

"I sssee ve vill haff to do dis der hard vay. Valk sstraight ahead, undt no funny bussssiness."

I did as I was told. We started down Sixth Street toward Walnut, then came to an alley.

"Turn in here." About half way down the alley, the voice said, "Diss iss far enough. Pleassse ssshtop here undt turn around, very slowly."

I slowly turned as I was told. The light in the alley was very dim but I could make out my assailant. He was a small man, with black hair plastered down on his head, wearing an ill-fitting brown double-breasted suit. And he did indeed have a gun in his hand.

"Look pal, I think you got the wrong guy. My name's Ed McCorkel and I'm just an insurance man, from Price Hill. I'm not carrying a gun, I don't even own one."

"Do not play me for der fool. You are Edvard McCorkel, der detective. Detectives carry gunss, I haff read all der booksss. Pleassse to raissse your handsss ofer your head." The little man patted my pockets and felt around my waist. "You are not armed. Diss iss wery ssstrange. You vill now lower your armss a little but do not try anything."

"Who are you? What the heck is going on here?"

What the heck is going on here, I thought to myself as I was saying out loud. Can this have anything to do with the Henry Holthaus business? I thought about how that affair began ...

THE COFFEE POT WAS PERKING. I TURNED DOWN THE GAS and finished knotting my tie, took the thermos bottle off of the counter and filled it from the coffee pot. I turned off the gas on the stove, took a box of cookies out of the cupboard, put on my jacket, and left the apartment on the third floor of the Covedale Building. I picked up an Enquirer on the corner and crossed the street to the Ideal Café.

I got to the door just as Charlie, the bartender, was unlocking it. It was about seven on a beautiful Saturday morning in early September, 1942. "Good morning, Charlie," I said to him. "The Reds beat Brooklyn twice yesterday. That makes four in a row."

"Mmmph," Charlie replied. "They're still in fourth place." Charlie was a little grouchy early in the morning. A faint whiff of stale beer greeted us as we walked into the bar. I sat at the first table as Charlie went around turning on lights, flushing the beer taps, and running fresh rinse water.

I looked at the front page of the paper. "Looks like the Japs are sending fresh troops into the Solomon Islands." I read the paper and ate my breakfast every morning at the Ideal. It was a better place than my lonely apartment.

I had just poured myself a cup of coffee when Charlie went to open the back door.

"SON OF A BITCH!" Charlie's voice exploded from the kitchen. I jumped up and ran back just in time to see him kick open the screen door and somebody go sprawling into the back yard.

"What happened?"

"That damn Henry Holthaus must have passed out on the back stoop," replied Charlie. "Look, that spill didn't even wake him up."

"He isn't moving, Charlie."

"He sure isn't."

"Charlie, there's a gun lying there by his hand and that looks like a bullet hole in his head."

"He must of been a lousy shot," replied Charlie. "There's three bullet holes in his hat."

"I think he's dead," I said.

"Yeah, we better call the cops."

"What must one do to be served?" came a voice from the doorway.

"Uh oh, it's the Prince."

The man in the doorway was tall, dark, and wore a long black cape. He was one of the local loonies. Actually, most people meeting him for the first time might not have considered him strange at all. He spoke very good English with the slightest Italian accent. It wasn't until you listened to him for some time that you realized he was talking about aliens from outer space, or some other complete nonsense. He thought he was an aristocrat driven out of Italy by the Fascists, but he was really the son of the local greengrocers. His given name was Anthony DiGiaccomo and he had been born in the United States.

"What has happened?" asked the Prince.

"I'll go call the cops," Charlie said, as he pushed past DiGiaccomo. "Ed, you stay here and keep an eye on the body."

"What has happened?" repeated DiGiaccomo.

"It looks like Henry Holthaus has had an accident," I replied.

"Ah," the Prince mused, "it is that new priest over at the church."

"No, it's Henry Holthaus."

"I meant that it was the priest who killed him," explained the Prince.

"Why would a priest want to kill old Hairless Hank?" Then I remembered I was talking to the Prince, and immediately regretted asking the question.

DiGiaccomo replied, "The priest is an assassin, sent by Mussolini."

"Why would Mussolini send someone to kill Henry Holthaus? Besides, the priest's name is O'Toole." I should have known better than to try to reason with the Prince.

"Of course, the name O'Toole is a sobriquet," the Prince explained to me. "His real name is Mustaccolli, and he mistook Holthaus for me. It is I that the Fascists are after."

"Prince, you are over six feet tall, you have got a full head of bushy black hair. Henry is bald and can't be more than five feet eight. You always wear a long black cape, Holthaus is wearing a shiny blue suit. How could it be mistaken identity?"

DiGiaccomo raised himself to his full height, pulled his cape protectively across his face and said, "It cannot be explained logically, because the Fascist pig O'Toole really is a priest."

"Oh," was the only reply I could come up with. By now other people had come into the Ideal and were at the back door trying to see what was going on.

"What's going on?" asked Brownie, the custodian of the Covedale Building, who had stopped for his morning eye opener. "Did Charlie throw him out?"

"That's where I slept last Tuesday," said Billy Boy Hanes, who came in to wait for his partner, Cyril Jackson.

I was becoming pretty exasperated, trying to guard the scene of what I suspected was a crime. Finally I saw a police officer at the door.

"Thank God you finally arrived."

"Well, I didn't actually arrive. I mean, I'm not really here. I mean, I'm not supposed to be here. I mean . . . I mean, I'm Patrolman Newmann. This is my beat, I just stopped in to talk to Charlie. I didn't know a thing about this . . . I'm definitely not here officially."

While the policeman tried to explain why he was where he was, another man came bounding through the door brandishing a revolver and screaming, "Nobody moves!"

Patrolman Newmann grabbed the newcomer by the collar and hit him on the head with his night stick and threw him out the back door.

"Who's this guy?" he asked.

"That's Arnie Chiggerbox," said Charlie, who had returned to see what was going on. "He's a cop."

"I may be in trouble!" exclaimed Newmann.

Just then the wail of a siren and the screeching of brakes announced the arrival of the official investigator. Sergeant William Stutter strode into the bar with an air of authority. He immediately spotted the pinball machine. "Is that an illegal gambling device?" Stutter asked.

"No," answered the Prince, who was sitting at a table eating my cookies and drinking my coffee. "It is a Martian sanitizing machine. It was left here by aliens in 1912 and is emitting rays that are slowly emasculating all the unprotected males in the area. I personally wear a metal cup."

"Are you trying to be funny?" asked the sergeant. "I can't stand comedians early in the morning."

"No, no, *mon capitan*, if I were trying to be funny I would have told you it was a cow."

Stutter ignored him. "Don't you go away, I'm going to want to talk to you later," Stutter called to me over his shoulder as he walked to the back. He surveyed the scene from the back door noting the two bodies lying in the yard.

"What the hell happened here, an early morning duel?"

"Uh, no, sir," Patrolman Newmann spoke up. "The person in the blue suit was found on the site and is presumed dead. The other person came on the scene later and became unconscious. He is presumed to be not dead, I hope. I'm Officer Joseph Newmann. This neighborhood is my regular patrol. I don't know if anyone checked to see if the victims were dead or alive and I don't know if an ambulance was called. I got here just before you arrived and didn't have time to do much."

"Except brain Chiggerbox," said a voice from the doorway.

"What, what was that?" said Stutter.

"Doc Scanninybit just came in, he'll be able to tell if they're alive or dead," came from someone else in the bar.

"Get him out here and have him examine these two," the sergeant called.

A man in his late fifties came through the back door. He was wearing a white t-shirt and black pants. He carried a chaser glass with four ounces of whiskey in it. The man's hand shook, but he did not spill any of the whiskey. He walked over to the first body—Arnie Chiggerbox—took a sip of his drink, nudged Arnie with his foot, stooped down, and pried open his mouth. He stood up, rinsed his finger in his whiskey, licked the finger, and said, "This one is alive but he has a bad cavity in one of his molars that needs attention." He took another sip of his drink. Then he went over to the other body, gave it a cursory examination, and said, "Henry here, on the other hand, is quite dead. He appears to have a hole in his head. I don't need to look in his mouth, I know he wears dentures."

"What the hell are you, a dentist?"

Doc took another pull of his drink and replied, "Yeah, but you don't have to be Doctor Kildare to tell that one of them is warm and one is cold."

"Well, can you bring the live one around?" Just then Stutter recognized the unconscious man. "Wait a minute . . . That's Arnie Chiggerbox. Let's just leave him out as long as we can."

"Sir, if this is a homicide, shouldn't there be a detective here?" asked Newmann.

"You stay out of this, Newmann. I'm still not sure why you're here in the first place. You just clear these people out of here. You," he said, pointing at me, "go find a phone and call the station. Tell them to send an ambulance out, and while you're at it, tell them to send a detective."

I rushed back into the café to the telephone and dialed the operator. I asked for and got the Price Hill police station. I explained the situation as best I could and asked for a detective and an ambulance. The station dispatcher promised both as soon as possible. I hung up the phone and was immediately deluged with questions.

"What's going on out there, Corky?"

"Hey Corky, was old Hairless Hank really bumped off?"

Corky was my Ideal Café nickname. If you were a regular at the Ideal, you were usually given a bizarre nickname. Mine, as opposed to most of the others, was arrived at in a fairly logical way. McCorkel had the word *cork* in it, therefore, Corky was my Ideal nickname.

I ignored the questions and went to the bar. "Give me a Smile, will you, Charlie?"

"Sure, Corky." Charlie handed me a popular orange soda called Smile. "What's going on out there? Do you think I should give Walt a call?"

Walt was the owner of the Ideal, and he was also Charlie's son.

"I don't have any idea what's going on, but I think you better call Walt. I know he wouldn't want to miss this."

"Hey, what's going on?" Walt, the owner of the Ideal, came bursting through the front door. "Why didn't somebody call me?" Walt lived right down the street and couldn't have missed hearing the sirens.

"Take it easy, son, I was just getting ready to give you a call. The phone's been busy, what with calling the cops, the detectives, and the ambulances."

"Why are the police here and why does the backyard look like a battleground?" Walt was now at the back, looking through the ruined screen door.

"Let me through, stand aside," said a burly newcomer as he tried to get past Walt in the doorway. Walt picked him up under the arms and sailed him out into the weeds, causing further damage to the screen in the door and pulling out the remaining hinge. The newcomer in the weeds pulled a gun, and Officer Newmann lunged with his night stick.

"Stop, stop," cried Sergeant Stutter, "that's Detective Andy Clements."

Stutter managed to calm everyone down. Clements put his gun away but glared at Walt, who had grabbed a baseball bat that he kept in the kitchen. Walt glared back at the rumpled detective. Clements put his gun away, still glaring at Walt.

"Get everybody out of here," screamed Clements. Actually, the only ones left in the yard were the three policemen and the two figures on the ground. Walt and I were watching through the door.

"Uh, sir, we're all part of the team. I'm Sergeant William Stutter and this is Patrolman Newmann. The gentleman in the blue suit, over there is the deceased and that guy over there is Officer Chiggerwood, a fellow policeman, who apparently rendered himself unconscious while rushing to the scene of the crime. If indeed there was a crime," he added.

While they were staring down at the fallen officer, he started to regain consciousness. "Where am I? What's going on, and where's my gun?"

"Now just take it easy there, soldier," said the detective, helping Chiggerbox to his feet. "Officer Newmann is holding your gun. He'll return it to you later. You'll be fine in a few minutes." He called toward the back door, "Could someone bring this man a glass of water?"

"Make it a shot and a beer," countered Chiggerbox, "I'm not on duty. Give me back my gun."

Sergeant Stutter said, "Give the gun to me, Officer Chiggerbox, you can pick it up at headquarters."

Chiggerbox sneered at Newmann and said, "And why ain't you in the Army, you young snot?"

This last remark hurt young Joe Newmann deeply. He had tried to join all branches of the services, but had been turned down. During a session in the police academy's pistol range, a freak accident had ruptured his eardrum. Chiggerbox, who didn't have many friends to start with, had just made himself another enemy. Clements sent Chiggerbox into the bar for his drink and asked Joe if he would take notes as he and Stutter dictated.

"Yes, sir," replied the young officer, whipping out a notebook and pencil. "Ready when you are, sir."

Clements started, "We have a white male, in his sixties."

"He has a hole in his head, sir," Stutter added.

"I know that, I would have gotten to it. Put down that he has a hole in his head, Officer Newmann. His hat is lying near the body and has six holes in it."

"Probably caused by three bullets, one in and one out, second one in and out, and so on," piped up Stutter.

"I know that also, Sergeant. Please allow me to finish my observations. To continue, Newmann, six holes in the hat, probably caused by three bullets, and a revolver lying close to the deceased's right hand."

Detective Clements bent down and rolled the body over. "There is a large yellow stain on the dead man's shirt."

"What about the red rag sticking out of Henry's coat pocket?" I asked, while watching the proceedings from the back porch.

"He is going to get around to that," said Stutter.

"No, actually I attach no importance to a piece of red rag the poor man probably used as a handkerchief."

"Well then, could I have it?" I asked. I don't know what made me ask for the rag, but I was thinking of it as "Material Evidence." I think I read about that in a Philip Marlowe book.

"Are you some kind of a morbid ghoul who collects souvenirs from the scenes of tragedy? Give him the red rag, Stutter, quench his macabre temperament."

Stutter gave me the red rag as Clements straightened up and brushed his hands off. "I think that about does it," he said. "Newmann, you guard the body until the ambulance gets here."

"Uh, sir, you didn't mention the strange smelling mud on the shoes and trousers of the victim," Stutter said cautiously.

"I don't find anything unusual about mud on a body that was discovered in the middle of a horseshoe court," countered Clements. "As I said, Newmann, guard the body. Sergeant Stutter and I will go inside to ponder."

I followed the two policemen inside and stood at the bar finishing my orange soda as they commandeered a table and ordered two shots and two beers. They sat with their heads together for some time, consumed three more shots and two more beers apiece, and finally Detective Andy Clements stood up. I turned towards their table.

"Sergeant Stutter and I have considered all aspects of this case and we have decided, unless an autopsy proves otherwise, that this is clearly a suicide."

Everyone in the bar echoed the words—"A SUICIDE?"

THE BAR REGULARS HAD BEEN KEEPING AN EYE ON THE PRO-
ceedings in the backyard and they all were pretty astounded by the
pronouncement of suicide. I just shook my head and turned back to
face Charlie behind the bar.

Old Charlie spoke up, "Like I said before, he must have been
a lousy shot to have missed three times before he got himself.
Holthaus was an old fool, but that doesn't seem possible even for
him."

Cyril Jackson, nicknamed Jake, had come in during the excitement and was standing at the bar. Jake was supposed to be an as-
phalt siding salesman but, as far as anyone knew, he had never made
a sales call. He spent his days at the Ideal with his pal Billy Boy
Hanes. Jake also claimed to be an ex-G-man, and he was my unof-
ficial chauffeur, since I didn't drive.

Jake did a little jig and sang, "Hi diddle diddle, the cat and
the fiddle, poor Henry's been shot in the dome. The cops had a
double and then to save trouble, pronounced the case closed and
went home!"

Detective Clements spoke loudly so that the whole bar could
hear. "I said there would be further investigation. Until then I stand
by our conclusion."

With that, he and Sergeant Stutter took their leave. They left
Patrolman Newmann to guard the body until the ambulance arrived.

I went out to talk to Newmann. "Kinda strange calling it a suicide, don't you think?"

"I don't think at all. If the big boys had called it a hit and run it
would be all right with me. I'm just worried about the guy I popped.
If he remembers what happened I could really be in trouble. This
is the only uniform they're going to let me wear and I would hate
to lose it."

"Don't worry about Chiggerbox. Ever since the motorcycle accident his memory has been a little dim."

Newmann was glad for the company, so he asked, "What happened to him?"

"Well, it was the only time he was ever seen in the Ideal in uniform. He was on his motorcycle, chasing a speeder up Cleves Pike. The speeder turned down Rulison and Chiggerbox tried to take a short cut. He went through the Ideal's front door and out the back. He flew over the three steps and right into a horseshoe stake. The motorcycle stopped dead but Chiggerbox continued on for about twenty-five feet. He's been pretty strange ever since. Of course, he was pretty strange before the accident."

"I just hope he doesn't remember what I did to him this morning."

"He won't. Do you mind if I look around? Maybe I could run over to my office and pick up a camera."

"You really are morbid, but it's O.K. with me, just don't touch anything. You better hurry, that ambulance should have been here by now."

I'm an insurance agent. My office is across the street from the Ideal, on the first floor of the building my apartment is in. I ducked across Cleves Pike. My secretary, Susan Stienle, had opened the office as usual at nine. We stayed open until one on Saturdays. She was looking through the office mail when I came in.

"Where have you been?" she asked. (It really didn't matter if Ed was late, because Susan took care of everything in the office, but she felt that he should at least make an appearance at the office.) "It's almost ten."

"We had some excitement at the Ideal this morning." I gave her a quick rundown on what had happened. "I just came over to get my camera, I have to get back."

"You should stay out of that place, they're going to get you into trouble," she called as I went out the door. (Susan liked Ed a lot, but he didn't realize it anymore than he realized that she ran his business.)

I got to the backyard and took pictures from every angle. I'd just run out of film when I heard a siren. The ambulance arrived and two men got out and took out a stretcher. They lifted the body onto the stretcher, loaded it in the back, and got back in the ambulance, all in about thirty seconds. They watched the ambulance go. "You know," I said, "There sure isn't much blood around."

"I guess not. Hey, I gotta go," said the patrolman. He left and I walked back into the café.

Cyril Jackson was at the end of the bar and went into his little jig again. "Just look at old Cork, he's just Johnny at work. Helped discover our Henry, who's now just a memory." Jackson almost always talked in rhymes.

"You had to reach for that one, Jackson."

"I think my mind going to waste, perhaps if you bought a little taste, it might improve."

I laughed. Jackson was the biggest sponger of drinks I'd ever met, but I needed him from time to time to drive me places and run errands.

"Give Jake and Billy Boy a drink." You never just bought Jake a drink, you always had to buy one for his buddy, too.

"Ah yes, those would be doubles, Walt." Jake would only drink double shots. If his tongue was hanging out from thirst he would refuse a single shot. After all, he always said, he did have some principles.

Walt poured the doubles and set up two beer chasers. I paid him and said, "What happened to Charlie? I thought he was working this morning."

"Yeah, well, he said all the excitement got to him and as long as I was here he thought he would go home and take a nap. He said he would come back about noon. Do you want something to drink?"

"No, I better get over to the office, poor Susan will be a wreck trying to take care of everything." I walked out the door and across the street. I found Susan, far from being a wreck, talking on the phone to a client. I motioned to her to give me the phone but she shook her head. She never let me talk to clients. She thanked the client for his business and hung up the receiver.

"Well, did you and your cronies get tired of discussing poor Henry Holthaus's accident?"

"I don't think it was an accident and I don't think it was suicide, either."

"Suicide? Who said it was suicide?"

"The cops. They said, pending an autopsy, that they thought it was suicide."

"Why would poor Henry Holthaus want to commit suicide? He was a strange old fellow, but he had plenty of money and was in reasonably good health, except for the fact that he was usually pickled. He lived in that big house with his daughter and son-in-law, and she took good care of him. No, I can't see any reason for him to kill himself."

"I don't think it was suicide either. That's why I was nosing around over there. I don't even think he was killed there. I think he was killed someplace else and then hauled over behind the Ideal."

"What makes you think that?" asked Susan.

"Well, I don't think Henry's body would have stayed sitting up on the steps after he was shot. That's the way he was when Charlie found him. The other thing was the blood. There was hardly any. It wasn't a big hole in his head, but it must have bled some."

"This talk is depressing me. If you are going to lunch, you had better go. It's twenty to twelve."

I usually went to lunch between eleven-thirty and twelve-thirty, then I watched the phone from twelve-thirty to one while Susan went home for lunch. (Susan only hoped that no important calls came in while she was gone.)

"Okay, I'll go see if there's anything new. I'll be at the Ideal."

"What's new about that?" remarked Susan.

I crossed the street and stopped at the grocery to pick up a can of tomato soup and a piece of American cheese. "Quite a little excitement next door," said the clerk as he got the soup off the shelf.

"Yeah," I said, and gave him a short version of what had happened.

The clerk shook his head and said, "I seen where some girl from Texas won the Miss America thing last night." He was young, his attention span was limited. He took my money, and counted out change from the register.

Walt was still tending bar when I got there. "You're still here."

"Yeah, but I hope Charlie shows up soon. I have to be in Cheviot in ten minutes. I'm supposed to meet some guy at the Gay Nineties. He wants me to fly him down to Lawrenceburg to take aerial photos of the distillery." Walt was a pilot and flew whenever he could get enough gas and could borrow a plane.

"The guy got an extra ration of gas for the job and Tyrone said I could use his plane." Tyrone owned the Mobil station on Relleum and had a two-seater plane that he kept out at Hugh-Watson Airport on Colerain Road.

Charlie walked in and Walt said, "I'm outta here," as he sailed through the front door. I went back to the café's small kitchen. The back door was shut. I resisted an urge to open it and look out. Instead I got a can opener out and opened the soup, put it in a sauce pan, and put the pan on the stove. I got out a plate and some crackers I kept in the cupboard, then opened the cheese and put it with the crackers on a plate. I carried the plate out to a table and ordered a Smile from Charlie. The soup was hot by then, so I turned off the gas, picked up a knife, a soup spoon, and a napkin, and carried them along with the soup, still in the sauce pan, to a table. I enjoyed having lunch at the Ideal, but unfortunately the bar did not serve food. Oh, the management kept some boiled ham in the refrigerator along with some buns, just in case a liquor agent came in and demanded some food. The buns could have served as hockey pucks and the ham had a greenish sheen.

The only edible food item that was always available was Crackerjacks. The Crackerjacks were always fresh at the Ideal. Occasionally, Walt would cut a tiny slit in a Crackerjack box and insert a dollar bill. The customers assumed that these dollars were one of the prizes and the sale of Crackerjacks soared every time a dollar was found. After all, a dollar would buy four shots and beer chasers were free.

Because of their limited menu, the management did not frown on anyone who brought their own food. You were expected to clean up any dishes or pans that you used, but you were welcome to use any and all of the facilities. Actually, quite a few Ideal patrons availed themselves of this service. Most just brought their lunch in a brown bag.

When I sat down to eat my lunch, there were three other diners in the place. They were Otis Weber, Sam Callmeyer, and Clyde Kieffer. They were known in the Ideal as Oats, Slippery Sam, and Fang, respectively. All three were mailmen and all three lunched from twelve to three so as not to get back to the post office too early.

"Golly, Cork, you were right in the middle of things this morning," said Fang. He was called Fang because he had no front teeth. "Tell us all about it."

I cut off a piece of cheese and told the mailmen to talk to Charlie. After all, it was Charlie who discovered the body.

"Yeah, and it was Charlie who sailed old Hank off into the horseshoe courts," added Slippery Sam. "Tell us about it, Charlie."

"I'd just as soon not talk about it," Charlie said.

"Don't tell us you're going to miss old Hank," smirked Sam.

"Well, Henry and I were kind of in business together at one time. He would sell a piece of property and I would build a building on it. We did pretty good until the Dodd Building thing."

"Oh, yeah," Oats chimed in, "That's when the bottom fell out of things and Dodd went to Florida leaving you and Holthaus holding the bag."

"That's not quite true. The bottom fell out and John went to Florida all right, but he went to try to save some investments the three of us had down there. He failed, just like everything failed up here, but he tried. We all lost a lot of money and it affected all of us. Henry still had plenty of family money, but the staggering losses got him started drinking, John Dodd didn't come back, and I just gave up. Yeah, I'm going to miss Henry. At one time he was my best friend."

I was shocked. Charlie was a man of few words. Yes, no, or a grunt was the most he usually had to say. This had been the longest speech I'd ever heard him give. I decided I would try not to talk about the episode too much when Charlie was around if it was going to affect him like that.

"Well, Corky, you tell us about it then," nagged Fang.

"Not much to tell, we discovered a body and called the police, they came and said it was a suicide . . . Did you know that Bing Crosby was going to be down on Fountain Square tomorrow?" I decided it was time to change the subject. "He's going to be selling War Bonds."

"Don't change the subject, Corky, we want to hear about this morning," said Otis.

"Yeah, give us the details," Sam said.

I got up and took my dishes and pan to the sink. I washed, dried, and put them away. "I don't know any other details," I told them and walked out.

I went to the office. Susan looked up as I came through the door.

"You're early, nobody over there?"

"Yeah, but I just didn't feel like talking to them. Why don't you go on home. I'll handle things here until it's time to close up." (Susan didn't think too much could happen between now and one o'clock, it was a Saturday after all, so she left.)

I went into my little office and sat down. I thought about the events of the day. I pulled an envelope from my inside coat pocket and looked inside, then I smelled it. After the two senior policemen had decided that Henry had committed suicide, I had scraped some of the mud off Henry's shoes. Since Clements didn't feel the mud was important, Newmann didn't object. The mud was in the envelope.

I put the envelope back in my coat pocket and picked up the Enquirer and turned to Walter Winchell's column. Quentin Reynolds said that he was surprised to see how dark New York's dimout was, almost as dark as London. Clark Gable was still being bothered by the women of Miami, and Milton Berle was going to get twenty percent of the profits from a musical he was going to star in for the Shuberts.

Who cares? I thought, as I paged through the paper looking for Ollie James's column. The phone rang. It was someone looking for Susan.

CHAPTER 3

I WENT UPSTAIRS AND TOOK A NAP. I GOT UP ABOUT SIX, GOT cleaned up, and walked over to the Colonial Inn on Glenway. I ate supper there most nights because the kitchen in my apartment was very small and I was a lousy cook.

The Colonial Inn was convenient, inexpensive, and the food was reasonably good. Frank Dodd ran the place. Frank was the son of the man Charlie had been talking about that afternoon, and the restaurant was in the Dodd Building. Frank was clearing a table near the door when I walked in.

"Hiya Ed, I hear there was some excitement over at Walt's this morning."

"Yeah, it was an interesting morning all right. Okay if I sit over in a booth?"

"Sit anywhere you like, we're not very busy tonight." There were customers at four other tables. I didn't recognize any of them.

"It was kind of a shame," Frank continued. "About old Henry, I mean. He was a nice enough old guy, he was one of my dad's best friends."

"Charlie was telling me a little about that."

Frank laughed, "Old Charlie, John, and Hank—they were something when they were younger. Did you know that they tried to make this area, Covedale, into an incorporated village? My dad was going to be mayor and Charlie and Henry were going to be selectmen. It all fell through when the city annexed us. It was just like most of their schemes, they never quite pulled them off."

"I'm sure learning a lot of history today," I said.

"Well, history ain't going to fill your stomach or my cash register. What are you gonna have?"

"What's good?" I asked.

"We got split pea soup and some nice meat loaf."

"I'll pass on the soup, and I had the meat loaf yesterday."

"How about cottage ham, potatoes, and green beans?" Before I could order, the front door opened and the Prince rushed in.

"I'm glad I caught the two of you together," the Prince said. He was out of breath. "I just came from Western Hills High School. There are Japanese soldiers in a balloon above the school dropping leaflets telling us to surrender." He immediately turned around and dashed out the door.

"The cottage ham sounds all right, and coffee, please."

Frank headed toward the kitchen when one of his other customers stopped him. "Did you hear what that man said? Maybe we're being invaded!"

Frank gently pushed the man back into his seat. "The Prince is a nice enough guy, but he sees things that nobody else sees. Finish your meal, maybe have a piece of pie. If the air raid sirens go off, then we can all panic." He continued back to the kitchen.

The man was still a little shaken. He turned to me and said, "Did you know that the Japs bombed Oregon? I'm not kidding. It was on the radio, I heard it on the radio. A small seaplane with Japanese markings dropped bombs into the woods around some town named Mount something, Emily, I think. Then they saw a Japanese sub about three miles off the shore. They think it launched the plane. One of our planes attacked the sub but they don't know if they got it or not. Honest to God, it was on the radio. Do you really think everything is all right, out to the school, I mean?"

"Oh, I'm sure everything is fine." I enjoyed spinning fabrications, not exactly lies, just good stories. I thought the little man's story about a Japanese attack in the Pacific Northwest was great. So I had to tell him one just as good in return.

"You see, the Prince was an aristocrat in Italy when Mussolini took over. He, the Prince, I mean, not Mussolini, escaped with a small army of the palace guard, and they made their way to Ethiopia. When Mussolini attacked that country, the Prince and his band helped to defend it. When all was hopelessly lost, Haile Selassie personally saw to it that the Prince was spirited away to Trinidad. There, in deep despair, the Prince fell victim to an evil drug that is smoked on the island. A nice Italian family from Cincinnati was vacationing there and discovered the poor wretch. They brought him home and treated him as if he was their own son. They helped him get over the addiction to the drug, but his mind was gone. He now lives in a world of his own."

The man paid his check and said, "That certainly is interesting, the poor man. Well, I'd better be getting back to Cheviot. Nice talking to you." He rushed out the door.

Frank brought Ed's food. "You're good. I heard the whole thing, it was almost as if it was one of the Prince's own. Yeah, you're good, but I bet that guy eats at the Gay Nineties for awhile."

I just smiled, and finished off my meal, I asked Frank what there was for dessert.

"We got this great new pie, it's called fake apple pie. It's made with Ritz crackers instead of apples. It's to help the war effort."

"Frank, why would saving apples help the war effort? I think I'll just have another cup of coffee."

"I don't know about the apples, maybe they slip 'em into them C-rations we been hearing about. But I do know about coffee. It's getting harder and harder to get."

We chatted while I finished my coffee. I paid my bill and left. As I cut across Glenway, I decided to stop at the Ideal for a nightcap before going up to my apartment. I walked in and saw Paddlewheel Benny asleep at a table. Bernie Graham, alias Paddlewheel Benny, was one of the great drunks of the world. If they ever made a Drunkards Hall of Fame, Benny would go in on the first ballot. He had saturated his body in whiskey over the years, and now all he had to do was drink one shot to be falling down drunk. Two drinks and he passed out.

Paddlewheel was the promotion man for an excursion steamboat called the Belle of Avon. He was almost as good a salesman as he was a drunk. He could sell the proverbial ice boxes to Eskimos. That's how he kept his job on the Belle.

He came in the Ideal every morning at a little after eight and had two quick shots of Canadian Club, then passed out. He slept until around eleven, woke up, and went to work. He was back at the Ideal in the evening, drank two more shots of CC, and passed out again. He slept at a table until closing time. He then went home, presumably to sleep. He had never been known to eat.

I passed by Benny's table. Hugo Getz and a stranger were playing checkers at the last table, and Walt was talking to Fionna Rosé at the end of the bar. I went down there. Fionna smiled up at me.

"Gee, Corky, you were a real hero today." Fionna was knockout. She worked as a stripper at a downtown nightclub called The Cat and the Fiddle, but was very quiet and shy when she had her clothes on. She lived a couple doors down on Rulison and usually stopped at the Ideal for a few minutes before calling a cab to take her to work. Her real name was Mitzie Pritzle.

"I didn't do anything heroic, just kinda helped Charlie find old Henry's body."

"Golly," she pouted. "I think it's pretty heroic just being around a dead body."

"Would you like another drink?" I asked her. She drank rosé wine from a special jug that Walt kept in the beer box. She only drank one glass a night, but she liked to be offered another even though she always refused.

"No thank you, but I appreciate your asking."

Suddenly the stranger playing checkers jumped up, knocking his chair over. "You haven't made a move in fifteen minutes!" he bellowed, and then stormed out.

Hugo was asleep . . . Benny was asleep . . . Fionna called her cab. It was peaceful in the Ideal. I asked for a Seagram's Seven and ginger ale. I wasn't much of a drinker. Walt put it down in front of me as Fionna went out to her cab.

"How'd the picture-taking go today?" I asked, remembering that he had flown a photographer down to Lawrenceburg to take pictures of the distillery.

"It was pretty funny," Walt laughed. "I came in kind of low off the river and everyone in town must have panicked. They turned on the civilian defense sirens and were running around like chickens with their heads cut off. Seems like there is rumor going around that a Jap plane is flying off a sub and bombing little towns in the U.S.A."

"Hey, I just heard that story at dinner over at the Colonial Inn. I thought the guy was nuts."

Walt continued, "I think it's just a silly rumor but they were sure upset down in Indiana. Either I flew around longer than I should, scaring the Hoosiers, or the guy I was flying didn't get as much gas as he promised. We ran out of gas and I had to glide for about a mile and a half. Just missed some electric wires, but we made it. The guy with the camera was a little green when we landed, though."

A vintage Studebaker pulled up out front. An old fellow got out and came into the bar.

"Hoombdy mffcordness!" he exclaimed. It was Mr. Sellers, who was very old and mumbled when he talked. Walt was the only one who seemed to understand him.

"It sure is," answered Walt. "What'll you have tonight?"

"Ibll friken gerbellatey."

"You want a glass or a stein?"

"Flubbergust!"

Walt filled a stein with draft beer and put it in front of him. "Doggleberrysnide," Sellers mumbled.

"You're welcome," Walt said as he came back towards me.

"Isn't Mr. Sellers a carnation grower?" I asked. Neighboring Delhi was reputed to be the carnation-growing capital of the world, and many of the growers came in the Ideal.

"Yeah," answered Walt, "one of the best in his day."

I pulled out the envelope full of mud that I'd taken from Henry's clothes that morning. "Do you think he would know what this stuff is?"

"Ask him."

"Will you stand by and translate?" As I started down the bar, Hugo Getz suddenly lurched to his feet and staggered out into the night.

"Good night, King William," Walt called. Hugo was a cigar salesman and got his nickname from the most popular brand he sold.

"Good evening, Mr. Sellers," I shook the old man's hand.

"Grabbedy gibberde leak."

"He said it's nice to see you again," Walt translated.

"Would you care for another beer?" I offered.

"Prod slikums ma cumby."

"He said," Walt translated, "No thank you, one a night is his limit."

"Mr. Sellers, I wonder if you could tell me what this stuff is." I handed him the envelope and he shook it out into his hand. He looked at it carefully, rubbed it between two fingers, and then he smelled it and tasted it.

"Itz shit!" he exclaimed, taking a drink of his beer.

"He says it's fertilizer," said Walt.

"Flavber necco doliescebt derororoes, glaven abody tredklollar."

"He thinks some of the growers use it. The best person to ask is Al Heller, he can probably identify it."

Heller was one of the biggest carnation growers in Delhi. He was a regular customer at the Ideal and a nice guy. I made a mental note to talk to him the next time we met.

"Hey, can somebody bring me a beer?" came a voice from the back door.

"Who was that?" I asked Walt.

"It's Earl Klopp," Walt answered as he drew a beer and carried it to the back. Then he walked back behind the bar, threw a dime on the register, and continued. "I threw him out of here about two months ago, but he still comes around and drinks a beer on the back steps. I think Charlie lets him in."

"Hey Walt, did Zesta happen to stop in today?" came the voice from the back.

"No, I didn't see her."

"Zesta was his wife, wasn't she?" I asked.

"Yeah," replied Walt. "She ran off with some gangster about five years ago but he still asks after her."

"Thanks, Walt," came Klopp's voice from the back. "Your glass is on the step."

"Mirna swervedort," called Sellers as he went through the front door.

"Yeah, good night, and thanks for the information." I turned back to Walt. "Are you going to have any trouble getting rid of Benny?"

"No, he's no trouble." Walt and Benny were good friends. Nobody could understand why, but they were. Walt walked over to the table where Benny was sleeping. He kicked the table leg. Benny snapped right up. He cleared his throat a couple of times, looked at the clock and said, "Look at the time, I gotta go. Night Walt, night Corky," and out the door he went.

"That's my cue, Walt. I'm going home, too. Good night."

"So long, Corky."

By the time I got across the street, the Ideal was dark.

CHAPTER 4

SUNDAYS ARE PRETTY DULL AROUND DODD'S CORNER. Nothing is open. The Flop House, that's the Overlook Theater across the street, opens at one, but that's about it. I had finished off the box of cookies in my apartment and come down to my office with my thermos full of coffee. On the way I picked up a Sunday Enquirer at the corner.

I sat at my desk, drank my coffee and read the paper. It was all war news; some was good, some bad. The sports page was all news about the Reds, once again, some good and some bad. Finally I turned to the comics.

Terry was definitely falling for Rouge. She danced, and the way he was watching, you knew he wanted to try something, but she cooled him down and told him to get some sleep. Buzzard's jeep died and Skeezix caught up with him. Skeezix would probably fix the jeep. He was such a nice guy, but sometimes not too bright.

I had just finished the last of my coffee when Susan unlocked the front door and came in. She had a lady with her. I realized that the woman was Marge Baker, Henry Holthaus's daughter. I'd met her a few times before and knew that she was married to the barber who owned the shop next to the Ideal, Fred Baker. Susan said that she had run into Mrs. Baker after mass at St. Clarisa's, and started to introduce her.

I interrupted her. "Yes, we've met before. I'd like to express my heartfelt sympathy to you. It's very sad about your father."

I wondered if she had come in to check on an insurance policy. Susan had already looked yesterday and had found nothing. "If you've come about insurance, I don't believe we carried a policy on him."

"Thank you for your kind words. I didn't come about insurance. I know my father didn't have any. Ever since he lost all that money, over ten years ago, he hasn't trusted any institution. He won't even go in a bank. We have money stashed all over our house. It will be months before Fred and I find it all."

"If it's not about insurance, how can we help?" asked Susan.

"Mr. McCorkel, I don't believe my father committed suicide. Oh, he drank too much and he seemed a little strange, but I know ... I knew my father. He loved life too much to end it. Besides, they found his car yesterday afternoon out at Whitsken's Dairy, back by the pond. I don't think he would have parked out there and then walked to the Ideal to commit suicide. I want to hire you to find out what really happened to him."

"Me! Why would you want to hire me?"

"Your sign says you do private investigations. Doesn't that mean that you're a detective?"

Once more one of my little jokes had backfired. When I was younger, I had sent for a correspondence course on private investigating through an ad on the back of a comic book. I had diligently read all the information and had filled out all the tests and sent them to the school. In due time, I received a mimeographed diploma from the Ace Detective Academy.

Years later, when I was having the windows of the insurance agency lettered, I asked the sign painter to add "PRIVATE INVESTIGATIONS" at the bottom of the glass. I only did it because I thought it added spice to an otherwise humdrum business. No one else had ever taken it seriously either—no one had ever even asked me about it before. Not even Susan had ever mentioned it.

"Gee, Mrs. Baker, I haven't had much experience. Don't you think it would be better to let the police handle this?"

"You saw what the police did yesterday, and it was them that called it a suicide. No, I don't think the police will find out anything. I need someone who will really look into things and I think that someone is you."

"I appreciate your confidence, Mrs. Baker, but I don't know. I don't think I can find the time."

"I'll make sure your schedule is light, so you'll have plenty of time," piped up Susan. (This looked like a great way to keep him out of the office so she could get a lot of work done.)

"You must help me. I'll pay you twenty-five dollars a day, plus any expenses, does that sound fair?"

"Yes, but Mrs. Baker ..."

"No buts, it's settled. You start immediately, and please call me Marge." With that she turned and headed out the door.

"Let us know about the services for your father," Susan called after her. "This is wonderful," she chirped as she turned back to me. "You've had nothing but this shooting thing on your mind since it happened. Now you're officially investigating it."

(Susan was delighted, she didn't think he could get into too much trouble, and it would certainly keep him out of her hair for a couple of days at least. She liked McCorkel—make that loved him—but it would be nice to get him out from under foot for awhile.)

"I have to go," Susan said as she followed Mrs. Baker out the door. "Mom is waiting for me out in the car. I'll see you tomorrow."

I decided to go upstairs and see if I could find that correspondence course. It wouldn't hurt to bone up a little. I looked in the bookcase in my living room. This was the most logical place to find them, but I knew it wouldn't be there, and it wasn't. Next I pulled a big trunk out of my closet. If the correspondence course was going to be anywhere, it would be there. I found books, old dog-eared books on how to sell insurance, books on civilian defense, an emergency first aid book, textbooks from some night classes I took at the university, comic books, and a yearbook from Hughes High School, but no correspondence course.

I pulled out everything in the trunk, found my old baseball letter sweater with the red "H" and finally, in the very bottom of the trunk, I found the diploma. It was dusty and crumpled, but it was all that remained of my private investigation course. I blew the dust off, tried to smooth it out.

I went back down to my office and stayed there all afternoon reading bits and pieces of some of the detective novels I had in my bookcase. I hoped that I might get some ideas on how I should proceed with my own investigation. I couldn't stop thinking about the events of the morning. The incident at the Ideal, that was how I thought about it. I actually thought of it as "AN INCIDENT AT THE IDEAL." All caps and in quotes. Maybe even in italics, *"AN INCIDENT AT THE IDEAL."* That gave me an idea, when it was all over I might write a book about it. That would make a great title, "AN INCIDENT AT THE IDEAL."

No, "AN IDEAL WAY TO DIE." That's what I'd call the book, that was a lot catchier. While I was thinking, I pulled an old briar pipe out of my desk drawer. I didn't smoke, but I did like to hold a cold pipe in my mouth while I pondered.

I'd tried to smoke a pipe. I thought it looked debonair. Unfortunately, I could not keep one lit, and if I did manage to keep one going for any length of time it made me sick. So I just chewed on the pipestem contemplatively now. I sat back in my chair and thought about what happened that morning.

I also wondered why the death of a poor old drunk interested me so much. Sure, I knew him, but Henry Holthaus hadn't been a particular friend of mine. I guessed it was probably because I had been there when it all started, almost "in on the kill." No, bad choice of words.

I glanced at the clock on the wall. It was almost six. I thought I had better start thinking about supper. Everything around here was closed. I decided I would go down to the Trolley Tavern, so I called Checker Cabs and went into the office restroom, washed up, and combed my hair. When I came out, I heard the taxi tooting outside, so I put on my jacket, locked the door and got in the cab.

"Where to, Mac?"

I had never seen this guy before so I assumed he called everybody Mac and was not using the diminutive of McCorkel. "Trolley Tavern, please."

We took off down Cleves Pike to Anderson Ferry Road and were at River Road in just a few minutes. The cab pulled up in front of the tavern.

"Ninety-five cents, Mac," the driver said.

I gave him a dollar and told him to keep the change. He yelled thanks as he drove off.

I walked in and looked around . . . Fatty Hindenberg was seated at a corner table. He motioned for me to come over.

"Why don't you join us?" He was with Arnold Mix, a Delhi carnation grower. "We haven't even ordered yet. You know Arnold, don't you?"

Mix stood up and stuck out his hand. "We see each other at the Ideal all the time, probably never been introduced, but we speak to each other." I recalled that Arnold told everybody who would listen that he was the cousin of Tom Mix, a famous cowboy movie star who had been killed in a freak automobile accident recently.

Fatty ran a bookmaking establishment. Bookmakers around here had nothing to do with printing and binding books. Bookmakers took bets on horses. It was apparently a very lucrative profession, albeit illegal. The laws that prohibited it were pretty much ignored, if the bookies were not too blatant about their operations.

Fatty claimed that that was his real first name. His nickname was Bingo, because any time he answered in the affirmative, he said "Bingo." This habit caused quite a stir one night when he was helping out at the bingo game at St. William's church hall.

Mix handed me a menu. "We're both having the Pork Chop Special."

I put down the menu. "That sounds good to me."

A waitress came to our table. Fatty told her that we all wanted the Pork Chop Special, then he hesitated and looked at us, "With . . . coffee?" We nodded and he turned back to the waitress, "And coffee all around."

"Just put it all on one, we can split it three ways," Fatty said.

The waitress left and Arnold said, "Corky, tell us about what happened at the Ideal yesterday."

I gave them a run-down on yesterday's events. Just as our food arrived, I told them that Mrs. Baker had asked me to investigate.

"Wow," said Fatty, "I didn't know you were a detective . . . I've got a couple of missing clients I would like you to find."

I explained why Marge Baker had called on me, and that I didn't think I was going to be able to help a lot, and that I was pretty sure that I wasn't going to take on any other cases.

While we finished our meals they kept asking questions about the happenings of yesterday. I answered as best I could. Fatty offered to drive me home and as we were leaving the restaurant.

As we walked out to the parking lot, Arnold asked me what I had done so far in my investigation. "Research," I said. "I spent the day doing research."

Fatty gave me a ride back to my place.

CHAPTER 5

IT WAS A LITTLE BEFORE NINE THE NEXT MORNING. I HAD just finished my coffee and paper. The story I heard the night before was apparently true. It was right there in the *Enquirer*, with a bold headline, no less.

JAP PLANE FIRE BOMBS OREGON FOREST AFTER LAUNCHED BY SUB

The article went on to tell how a crater was found in the woods where there were bomb fragments with Japanese markings. The fire that was started was put out by a forest ranger. Later a Japanese submarine was spotted about three miles off the coast and was bombed by American planes. There was no official report of the sub's destruction.

I mentioned the bombing to Walt, who had opened up the bar this morning. He was looking out the window, watching the kids, still wearing little summer dresses and short pants, hurrying to school. Through the same window, I saw Susan walk up to the office, unlock the door, and walk in.

"See you later, Walt, I'm going to work." He was filling the bottle box and didn't answer.

I met Patrolman Newmann as I walked across the street. He followed me into the office and I introduced him to Susan. She said that she had seen him, from time to time, around the corner.

Newmann turned back to me. "Mr. McCorkel, I don't know if I'm strictly following procedure here, but I thought you would like to know, the autopsy report came in. It shows that Mr. Holthaus died as the result of a single shot in the head. The bullet was from a .22-caliber rifle or pistol."

I was flabbergasted. "The pistol that was lying near his hand was a .38-caliber."

"Right," said Newmann. "Kinda rules out the suicide theory, don't you think?"

I told Officer Newmann about the visit from Mrs. Baker and that I was going to investigate the case for her. Newmann seemed pleased and offered any help he could provide.

"Like I said, I'm not in on this officially, but this is my beat. I want to find out what happened yesterday. Yeah, and you should stay away from Stutter and Clements." He wished me luck and left.

Before I went back to my office, I asked Susan if she would like to go over to the Colonial Inn for lunch. I wanted to tell her about all the research I had done yesterday. (Susan liked going to lunch with Ed. She enjoyed being in his company in a social situation. Unfortunately, she got so nervous and excited that she threw up as soon as they returned. Usually she tried to eat very little, so as not to waste food, and then got a couple of candy bars in the afternoon to tide her over.)

"I couldn't find any of the correspondence course books, but I did find my diploma." I showed her the dog-eared scrap of paper.

Susan looked at it. "Did you notice the motto of the Ace Detective School?" she asked.

"Sure. 'Follow the Clues.'" Susan said that it sounded like good advice to her.

"Okay, I'll follow the clues, but after lunch."

Susan did the things she did to make the business run smoothly, while I browsed through a few more novels. Soon it was time for lunch. When we got to the Colonial Inn, it was pretty crowded. Most of the merchants around the corner ate lunch there. It was either eat at the Colonial or brown bag it at the Ideal. There was Wimpie's, but the school kids hung out there. Dow's Drug Store had a fountain, but they only served sandwiches that tasted like cardboard.

Frank found us a booth in the corner and took our orders. I was thinking that this investigation was going to take some time and I should talk to Susan about the extra burden it was going to put on her while I looked into Henry's death. Then for a moment I was honest with myself. It wasn't going to put any burden on Susan; she ran the business anyway. She only let me think I was doing it. In fact, this would be a good time to make her a partner. It would eliminate her salary, and we could split the profits and still make plenty each, the way she ran the operation. I looked up at her as I considered this move. She sure looked pretty sitting over there. A pretty partner couldn't hurt the business. I'd have the windows repainted. Make it "McCORKEL AND STIENLE." Have that silly "PRIVATE INVESTIGATIONS" taken off.

"Hey, is anyone in there?" Susan brought me out of my musings.

"I'm sorry, I guess I was day dreaming." I resolved to talk to Susan soon about the partnership.

"Thinking about becoming another Charlie Chan or Nick Charles?"

"No, I'm not inscrutable enough to be Mr. Chan, and if I were Nick Charles I would need a Nora." Susan blushed.

Their food arrived then. Frank put it on the table and said, "I hear you're officially investigating Henry's death."

"It's unbelievable how fast news gets around this corner, but it's not really official, Marge Baker just asked me to look into it."

"Golly, what do you plan to do?"

"Just follow the clues, Frank, just follow the clues."

(They ate their lunch in relative silence. Being this near Ed always flustered Susan into silence, and he was thinking about the Holthaus case, and about how to broach the idea of a merger to Susan. He decided to wait for a better time to bring it up and she was already beginning to feel a little sick.)

When we returned to the office, Susan went directly to the bathroom. I waited until she came back and asked her if she was feeling all right. She said she was okay so I told her I was going to start following the clues.

"And what better place to start than the Ideal?" she said.

I walked across the street to the café. I was not surprised to see that Jackson and Billy Boy were there. I needed a ride and Jake would be glad to help me.

Walt was still tending bar, and I said to him, "A couple of drinks for Jake and Billy Boy, if you please."

Jackson buck-and-winged it up to the bar. "Our good friend Cork has arranged this libation, I think he is in need of some transportation."

"Yeah, Jake, I want to go over to Al Heller's greenhouses on Foley."

"That seems a long, hot way to go, for but a single double's worth. Perhaps another drink or so, wouldst bless our journey with much mirth."

"It's only about a mile and a half, so we don't have time for mirth. I'll buy you another drink when we get back."

"Let us stand not upon the order of our leaving, et cetera, et cetera," emoted Jackson as he led me and Billy Boy to his car. I got in the back while Jake got in the front passenger's side and slid over behind the wheel. The driver's door was wired shut. Billy Boy followed him and sat in the front passenger's seat. Almost everyone, including his wife, preferred the back seat when Jackson was driving. The less you saw, the better off you were.

Jackson's car had seen better days, but he kept it in working condition because he drove his wife to work every morning and picked her up in the evening. The car was a 1936 Terraplane. Luckily, it had no third gear. Jake could only make it go so fast, so that when he hit things, he did it rather gently.

Even at the snail's pace Jake drove, it took very little time to get to Heller's place. We pulled into the dirt drive that led to the greenhouses. As we were getting out of the car, I saw Al coming around the corner of a shed.

"Hiya, Corky, Jake, B.B.," he called. "Did you stop out to see my 140-pound fox?"

Heller's wife Rita's maiden name had been Fox and his favorite joke was that he had a 140-pound fox at home. Everybody had heard the joke and nobody thought it was funny, but he persisted in telling it.

"Hi Al," I greeted him. "I've already met your wife, thanks. I got some stuff that Mr. Sellers said you might be able to identify." I pulled the envelope from my pocket and handed it to Heller.

Al poured a little out on his band. He looked at it, he smelled it, then he tasted it. "It's shit."

"Yeah, that's what Sellers told me. Can you be a little more specific?"

"It's a cheap, commercial fertilizer. Only one I know of around here that uses it is Saline's Nursery. Hey, Billy Boy, get away from there!"

"Gee, Mr. Heller," whined Hanes, "I was just looking for a place to take a leak."

"Well, not around that greenhouse."

"What's so special about that greenhouse, Al?" I asked. "You got it locked up like Fort Knox."

"I'm working on a secret that is going to revolutionize the carnation industry," Al replied.

Jake shouted just then. Like Billy Boy, he had gone off to find a place to relieve himself. "If you want to keep people out of there, you ought to fix this broken window over here."

"What!" yelled Heller. He ran over to where Jake was pointing. "Jeez, I think somebody broke in. I got to see if they got anything important." He climbed through the broken window. After a few minutes he climbed back out.

"Somebody was in there, but I think the only thing they took was a bottle of citronella that I use to keep away mosquitoes."

"Come on Al, why would anyone steal that? You can buy it at the hardware store for two bits," I said.

"I don't know, but I'm pretty sure that's all that's missing."

"Al, I'm investigating the death of Henry Holthaus. I don't know if it ties in or not, but I would sure like to know what you're doing behind those locked doors. I promise that it won't go any further."

"It's not that big a secret, really. All the other growers know about it. They just don't know how I do it and that's what I want to keep them from finding out."

"Then what is it, what's the big secret?"

Heller looked around furtively and said, "I've discovered how to grow green carnations!"

I WANTED JAKE TO TAKE ME STRAIGHT TO SALINE'S NURS-
ery, but Jake explained that the Ideal was on the way and they had
best stop to refresh themselves.

As they slowly made their way back to the bar, I thought about
what Keeler had told me about the green carnations. If Al had truly
accomplished what he claimed, the ramifications were staggering.
And if he could manage to keep the process a secret, he would have
a virtual monopoly on St. Patrick's Day.

They finally arrived back at the Ideal and trooped in. Charlie
had taken over for Walt behind the bar. "Fix the boys up, Charlie,
and give me an orange."

I saw Arnold Mix sitting over at one of the tables. I took my
soda and walked over. "Hello again, Arnold, mind if I sit here a
minute?"

"Happy to have you," replied Mix, who had a medium-size
greenhouse operation out in Delhi. Besides his claim to be Tom
Mix's cousin, Arnold Mix was also an almost fanatical patriot. He
was the chief air raid warden in the area, and he drove the Boy
Scouts around on Saturdays to pick up scrap. He helped on bond
drives as often as he could.

I said to him, "I'm surprised you aren't downtown helping Bing
Crosby sell bonds."

"As a matter of fact, I'm heading down to Fountain Square right
now, just stopped for a beer first."

"Arnold, I was just over at Al Heller's place. Do you know what
he's trying to do over there?"

Arnold smiled. "You mean the green carnation thing?"

"So you do know about it. Do you think there's anything to
it?"

"I sure hope so," Mix was still smiling. "It would really be a great
thing for Al and his wife. All the growers know about it and would
love to know how he does it."

"How about you, wouldn't you like to know the secret?"

"I'll tell you, Corky, I sell all I can grow right now. I can't do any more unless I expand, and I'm too lazy to expand. Nah, I'm not interested. If he comes up with a way to grow red-white-and-blue ones, then maybe I'd be interested, but not green. Why are you so interested anyway?"

"Marge Baker asked me to investigate her father's death. I'm beginning to think that it may be connected with some of the growers."

"Henry was a nice enough old guy, so I wish you luck, but I don't think any of the growers would kill anybody for a green carnation."

Jake and Billy Boy were getting a little restless at the end of the bar. "Give 'em another drink, Charlie. But I guess I'd better get out of here while Jake can still drive. Thanks for the information, Arnold."

"Anytime I can be of help, just ask."

I carried my empty bottle over to the bar and corralled Jake and Billy Boy. "Okay, let's go. I want to get out to Saline's some time today."

We piled into the Terraplane, Jake aimed it at Neeb Road, and we were away. When we arrived at the nurseries, Jake pulled into another dirt drive. As we got out of the car a disheveled, red-haired man came towards them. He was holding a pitchfork and as he advanced he shoved it threateningly towards the three of us.

"Get out of here! We don't sell retail and we don't allow no visitors."

"Hey, take it easy, mister," I said, putting my hands out. "We don't want any trouble, we just want to ask a few questions."

Just then a younger red-haired man came from around one of the buildings. "Put up that fork, Jimmy!" the younger man yelled. The man with the fork hesitated.

"Put it up," the young man repeated, "and get on out of here."

The man with the pitchfork looked at the younger man, then he looked at us. He made a menacing motion, then threw down the pitchfork and stalked off. "I'm sorry about my brother, he gets a little excited now and then. How can I help you?"

I told him I wanted to get some information about fertilizer.

"I'm Tom Saline by the way, that was my brother Jimmy. I think my dad could answer any questions you might have. He's out in the big shed, just follow me."

As they followed Tom Saline, I whispered to Jake. "What was the problem with that first guy? Do you know him?"

"Yeah," answered Jake sotto voce. "That's the oldest Saline boy, he just got out of prison. He was sent up for robbery or something."

They walked into a large shed. The first thing I noticed was a strong odor, just like that of the sample of fertilizer that was still in my pocket. The second thing I noticed was a large man dressed in bib overalls sitting in a wheelchair.

Tom Saline said, "Dad, this is . . . sorry mister, you didn't tell me who you were."

"I'm sorry, I'm Ed McCorkel. I run the insurance agency up at Dodd's Corner."

"Mr. McCorkel, I think you come to the wrong place. We sure can't afford no more insurance. We're barely getting by as it is. Can't get no help 'cause of this damn war. Tommy here all pissed off that the draft board won't take him 'cause I need him around here and the other one, Jimmy, worthless as teats on a boar hog since he got out of jail. Sure as rain I need more insurance, but needin' and gettin' is two different things."

"I'm not trying to sell insurance, Mr. Saline, I'm trying to identify some fertilizer. Al Heller thought you might be able to help me."

"Heller sent you, huh. How's his green carnation scheme coming? Heh, heh. Al's a nice kid, a dreamer, but I wish him luck. He used to work for me. His old man didn't want to bother with him so he sent him over here to learn the business. I guess I taught him pretty good, him and his damn 140-pound fox. If he pulls this green carnation thing off, he's gonna be rich, damn rich."

I interrupted the old man. "He told me you might know what this stuff is." He handed Saline the envelope.

"Sure I know what it is, it's shit, cheap shit. This place is full of it, can't you smell it? It's called 'Growzembig.' I use it 'cause it's cheap, all I can afford. It works all right but none of the other growers use it 'cause of the gawdawful smell."

I looked around the shed. The stuff was all over the floor. I noticed a red rag over on a table. He went over and picked it up. It was made of a red toweling material and had been torn. Across the bottom in black letters it said "Herzog's Nurseries." I picked it up and took it over to the old man. "How would something like this get here? It's from Herzog's."

"It's just a rag," answered the old man. "Either somebody from over there dropped it when he was here or someone from here picked it up when he was over there. It's just a rag. The Herzog boys buy fancy ones with their name on 'em, and we cut up old bed sheets. Both kinds work the same way. Bet if you looked hard enough you could find a piece of one of our bed sheets at Herzog's."

I asked the old man if I could have it.

"Like I said, it's just a rag. Things is tough, by damn, but I reckon we can let you have a rag. Specially since it ain't even one of ours."

I thanked the garrulous old man and tucked the red rag into my pocket. I said thanks and goodbye to Tom and saw the other brother glaring at us from behind one of the buildings as I herded Jake and B.B. back to the car.

We drove leisurely back to the Ideal. I was pleased with myself. I had a good afternoon. I was following the clues and they were leading me somewhere. I didn't as yet know where, but I was headed somewhere.

When we got back to the café, I was surprised to see Sergeant Stutter and Detective Clements. I bought the boys two more drinks apiece then walked over to the table where the policemen were sitting.

"We been waiting for you," muttered Stutter.

"We were about to give up," added Clements.

I noticed a full shot and a beer in front of each, and there were some other empty glasses on the table. "Surely not before you finished your lunch."

"Bill and I don't appreciate your humor," the detective said, "I think I told you that before."

"I see you two are on a first name basis. You must be doing a lot of work together on the Holthaus case."

"Shut up and sit down," Stutter growled at him, "We'll be asking the questions."

I sat. "Ask away, you might learn something."

"Was the gun in Holthaus's hand when you first saw him?" Clements wanted to know.

"When I first saw him he was flying into the backyard, I didn't really notice the gun."

"Yeah, that damned old man messed things up by moving the body. What time does he come on? We want to talk to him, too," said Stutter.

"I don't know, their schedule is messed up. If you really want to know, ask Walt," I told him.

Clements asked me if I had found anything out about the red rag he'd taken from the body the day before. I told him it was just a rag. I didn't mention the similar rag I'd found out at Saline's.

"How come you're so interested now, did you give up on suicide verdict?"

"We always knew it wasn't no suicide, that was a preliminary observation," Stutter sputtered.

Clements said quietly, "You can go, McCorkel, but keep your nose out of this thing. We don't need your help."

I stood up without replying. I went out the door and across the street. Susan had closed the office for the day and was gone. "She sure is efficient," I thought. "I'm going to have to talk to her about a partnership real soon."

I didn't bother to go into the office, but went straight up to my apartment. I was so pleased with myself that I decided to go downtown for supper. In preparation for the excursion, I shaved and took a bath. I got into a clean suit and left the apartment. Up at the corner, I waited for a streetcar.

CHAPTER 7

THE STREETCAR CAME IN ABOUT FOUR MINUTES. I boarded, said hello to the conductor, dropped in a dime, and took off. I noticed Betty Horn in one of the seats. She was an occasional customer of the Ideal. She was soft spoken and friendly, a bit of a gossip, but nice. I sat down next to her.

She looked over and smiled. "Hi Ed, how're you doing?"

"Hi, Betty. Are you going to work?" I knew she was a waitress in the lounge of the Price Hill Bowling Lanes.

"Yeah, I have to work 'til midnight. Wasn't it too bad about Henry Holthaus? I always liked him. He was a lush, but he never really bothered anybody. Why would someone want to kill him? At least that's what I heard, that he was murdered. Is that true? Somebody told me you were investigating the case. What have you found out, was he killed on purpose?"

"Whoa Betty, slow down, I am looking into things. Marge Baker asked me to this morning. I haven't found out much, and I don't think the police have officially changed their suicide verdict yet, but it was obviously not a suicide, at least I know that much."

"He'll be laid out tomorrow at Ruebel's," Betty said, "and buried Thursday morning at Old St. Joseph's."

"That's the first I heard about the arrangements. I'll have to try to find a ride to the cemetery."

"You can ride with us," Betty offered. "Peter and I will surely go. Just stop over to the Ideal about nine. Peter won't go to the mass, I'm sure, so just meet him there. He'll pick me up after church and we can go together."

"Gee thanks, Betty. I really appreciate your kind offer."

"That's okay." She stood up. "This is my stop. It was nice to see you. Maybe I'll see you at the funeral home."

"Yeah, I'll look for you. Thanks again."

While I rode the rest of the way downtown, I thought about the events of the day. Things had gone pretty well. I was still pleased with my decision to make Susan a partner. That idea was going to work out very well. I was also very pleased that Marge Baker had asked me to investigate her father's death. I'd made a lot of progress on my first day on the case. I had found the source of the stuff on the dead man's clothes. The red rag found in Henry's pocket had been torn from the rag I found at Saline's. When I'd compared the two pieces, they matched. Henry had definitely been in Saline's shed sometime before he met his death.

I decided that tomorrow morning I'd have Jake drive me out to the Herzog Brothers' greenhouses. Maybe I could find out how the rag got to Saline's.

I looked out the window and realized that I was almost to my stop. The streetcar was just passing the nightclub where Fiona Rosé worked. I waited two more stops then pulled the cord and got off at Fifth and Vine. I walked up Vine to Sixth and entered the Paradise Gardens. This was one of my favorite restaurants. It was large, always crowded, and the waiters bustled around like dervishes. The lighting was low but gaudy and the sandwiches were held together with toothpicks with little frilly tops. It was the only place I'd ever seen anything like them.

I waited a few minutes inside the door. A waiter came up, pointed at a table, and said, "Over there."

Before I could say thank you the waiter was gone. I went to the table and sat down.

Another waiter sailed by and dropped off a glass of water and a menu, then left. I looked over the menu and decided on the Chicken a la King. A third waiter dashed up and asked what I had selected. I told him. The waiter suggested soup. I said no, but asked for coffee with my meal. The waiter vanished.

In a very short time a fourth waiter brought me a salad and some crackers and asked if I would like my coffee now. I said I would, and the coffee was brought. "Cream?" asked the waiter.

"No," I said. The waiter was gone.

The waiter soon appeared with my entree. I noted that it was the same one who had brought the salad and coffee, and for some odd reason that pleased me.

I ate and enjoyed my meal. I'd been finished for about forty-five seconds when yet another waiter picked up my dishes and asked if

I'd like dessert. I told him I'd like a piece of apple pie, if it was real. The waiter allowed that he knew of no other kind. I ordered a piece with cheese.

The waiter who had brought the salad and entree brought the pie and filled my coffee cup. As soon as I finished the pie, the waiter was back. He asked if I'd like more coffee and I asked for about a half cup. The waiter poured it, put a check down beside the saucer, asked if everything had been satisfactory, and before I could even answer, he was gone.

Some people thought that the Paradise Gardens tried to rush people in and out. Not me. I thought they were very efficient. They did rush to get your food to you, but they didn't force you to eat fast. I loved to watch the waiters dodging tables and each other. At least once a night there was a major collision, with crashing dinnerware, but the mess was whisked away almost as fast as it happened.

I was in a pleasant mood when I paid my check and stepped out the door. I stood for a moment looking at the theater across the street.

"ACHTUNG, pay attention you dumkoff! I am a dangerous man."

That snapped me right out of my musings. "You can't just stick up somebody in the middle of downtown Cincinnati."

"Ah, but I haf I haf jussst dat, I am up holding you undt you must do precisely vat I tell you to do Mr. McCrackle."

"It's McCorkel, and who the heck are you?"

"Since you are interesssted, my name iss Franchot Tune."

"Wow! The movie actor?" I asked.

No, no, no, you dumkoff!" The little man started to go berserk. "I sssaid Tune! Tune! Tune! Dat actor'ss name iss Tone, you fool!"

"Hey, take it easy, it was a natural mistake. I'm sorry, I didn't mean to rile you up."

"Eferybody getss me mixed up mit dat sssisssy actor. I'm ssorry I effer picked sssuch a name for an aliass." Franchot was waving his gun around and shouting by this time. I tried to calm him.

"Take it easy, Frank. Why use an alias at all, why don't you use your real name?"

"My real name iss Peter Lorry."

"Oh," was the only reply I could come up with.

"Enouff of diss. Ye vaste time, pleassse valk in front of me undt try nothing funny. My gun vill be pointing at you from my poggit."

I pondered that as we walked deeper into the alley until we came to another alley that crossed it. "Turn left here," ordered Franchot.

When we came to the mouth of the second alley, we were on Walnut Street. Franchot told me to turn right and we continued south on Walnut and across Fifth.

We were in front of the Gibson Hotel when Franchot finally called a halt. "Ve are going into der lobby of diss hotel. Iff you are wery calm undt valk directly to der elevatorsss, you may come out again . . . alive."

"Can I ask you one question before we go in? Are you a German?"

"I am from Ssoud America, you fool, now march."

He propelled me across the lobby and into the elevator. "Eighth floor," Franchot said to the operator.

I quickly said, "Operator, I'm being . . .uh . . ." I felt something hard in the small of my back. "Taken to the eighth floor," I finished.

"Yes sir," the boy replied, "and here you are." He opened the doors.

Tune pushed me out into the hallway. "Dat vass wery foolisssh, my friend. You and dat boy could be wery dead if I vern't ssuch a compassionate man. Down der hall, dat vay," he gestured with his gun. "Ssshtop here."

We were in front of a door marked 850. Tune tapped lightly on the door. "Come," said a muffled voice from inside. Franchot opened the door and pushed me inside.

"AH, GOOD EVENING, MR. McCORKEL, SO NICE OF YOU TO come on such short notice."

There was a very fat man sitting in a large overstuffed chair in the middle of the sitting room of a two-bedroom suite. Standing behind the chair was a dark-complected man in a double-breasted, pinstriped suit. The fat man was wearing a wrinkled white suit and a red fez. It was he who had spoken.

He continued in a low, gravelly voice. "I must apologize for the manner of my invitation, but it was of the utmost urgency that we meet. Franchot did not harm you in any way, I trust."

"I don't know who you are, mister, and I don't care. Just tell this little monkey to let me out of here."

"Shut up, Buster," said the man behind the chair. "We'll tell you when to talk."

"Yes, stay calm, Mr. McCorkel, you have done well up to this point. Just listen to what I have to say and you can be on your way in a nonce."

"Say what you have to say. I'm a pretty even-tempered guy, but I'm becoming exasperated."

"Now then," the fat man continued. "I am Mr. Armbruster, with the Agricultural Bureau of Argentina. I am here, in Cincinnati, to study the methods of your wonderful carnation growers. My associate, Mr. Tune, is also with the Bureau and he is here to assist me in my efforts. Behind me is Mr. Kruger, a fellow countryman of yours, who serves me as interpreter and chauffeur."

"I am pleased to meet you all, I'm sure, but why was I forced to come here? What's this all about?"

"I told you to pipe down, no more questions," Kruger pulled a gun and waved it at me.

"Kruger, put that away, and Franchot, bring the gentleman a chair." Tune brought a chair. "Please, Mr. McCorkel, do sit down."

"That's better," Armbruster continued. "I am a peaceful man, Mr. McCorkel. I like to go out to your little village of Delhi and

47

sit around with those wonderful men who grow the carnations and quietly chat about fertilizers and seeds and whatnot. Just gentle conversation. You have made that impossible, Mr. McCorkel. The growers are agitated. They cannot concentrate. They are concerned about your investigation into the death of that foolish old real estate man. I assure you, sir, these good men played no part in the crime, if indeed a crime was even committed. As I understand it, sir, the police favor a verdict of suicide."

"Yes," I replied, "the police did think it was suicide but further evidence has proven that theory wrong. I am just trying to help a grieving daughter get to the truth. I certainly don't suspect any of the growers of foul play and if they had nothing to do with it, the investigation should not concern them, sir."

"Ah, Mr. McCorkel, I did not mean to imply that the growers were concerned that you might uncover something to incriminate one or more of them in this affair. Ah no, sir, they are just disturbed by your continual harassment. I would like to calm my friends and tell them that you will bother them no more. My government, sir, has authorized me to present you with ten thousand dollars as a gesture of our good will, in the hope that you will leave my friends in Delhi out of your investigation."

"Are you trying to bribe me, Buster?" I was furious. "You can take your money and, and, and . . ." I was at a loss for words.

"Calm down, sir, I am certainly not trying to bribe you. I thought only to compensate you for your time."

"Ssshall I throw him out of der vindow?" hissed Tune.

"No, no, Franchot."

"Let me plug him," added Kruger.

"Calm down, both of you." Armbruster turned back to me. "You see, sir, how easy it would be for you to have an accident. I advise you, Mr. McCorkel, take the money or not, that is up to you. But drop the investigation immediately. Your very life could depend on your decision."

"Are you finished? If you are, tell your trained ape to put away the gun and let me out of here." I was angry. "You've wasted enough of my time."

"Trained ape," Kruger sputtered. He brought his gun up and aimed it at McCorkel. "I'll blow your lousy head off!"

Armbruster moved extremely fast for a fat man. He grabbed the pistol out of Kruger's hand. "I said calm down, we don't want anything to happen to Mr. McCorkel unless he decides not to cooperate." He turned to McCorkel. "Be careful of what you say and do, sir, I may not always be around to protect you. You are, of course, free to go."

I went to the door, and Tune didn't try to stop me. Kruger stayed behind the fat man's chair. I turned the knob and walked out.

"Auf Wiedersehen," called the fat man behind me.

I made it to the elevator and pushed the button. It seemed like forever until the doors opened. I got in and said to the operator, "Lobby, please." When the doors opened on the lobby I sighed with relief. I felt lucky to be alive.

I walked through the lobby and out the doors. I was pretty shaky. I stood on Walnut Street for a minute to get my bearings. Once again I felt something hard in my back and a voice said, "Keep your hands where I can see them."

I was astounded. "I've had enough, Loony Tunes." I swung around, knocked the gun from his hand, and pushed him to the ground. My assailant crawled across the sidewalk, picked up the gun, and said, "Jeez, you're better than I thought."

I was flabbergasted again. I was popular tonight—it wasn't Tune I had sent sprawling. In the light from the neon in the window, I saw Sam Callmeyer rising from the sidewalk, gun in hand. Slippery Sam, the mailman.

"Sam, what the hell are you doing here?" I asked in a quiet but desperate voice.

"If you were half as smart as you think you are, you'd know that I was an undercover G-man, you lousy spy," said Sam, rubbing his knee where his pants were torn.

"Sorry, Sam, I thought you were a mailman. Why do you think I'm a spy?"

A car pulled up to the curb. Sam opened the back door and motioned me in with his gun. Sam got in behind me, then told the driver to get going.

"We've been watching your buddies upstairs for a long time. It finally paid off—look what we caught in our net." The driver took us to the foot of Broadway. I could see the bright lights and hear the calliope of the Belle of Avon down on the river. Passengers were boarding for an evening excursion.

No one said anything until the car was parked. "All right, you lousy kraut, I want to hear some singing." Sam was waving the gun around. The driver reached back and forced him to keep it low, out of sight.

"I don't know what's the matter with you. I'm no more a kraut than Father O'Toole is."

Callmeyer smiled, "I happen to know he's Italian. And don't try to change the subject, tell us what you know about Moby Trick."

I told Sam that I knew absolutely nothing about Moby Trick. I told him that I had, in fact, never heard of it before. I explained that I also didn't know the people in Suite 850, and about how I had been forced at gunpoint to go there and how they had tried to bribe me and threaten me to get me to stop investigating the death of Henry Holthaus. I finally convinced Sam that I was a victim of circumstances and not a spy.

"Okay McCorkel, we're going to buy your story this time, but you would be wise to drop out of this investigation. You can go." Sam pushed open the door.

"Wait a minute, you guys have been pretty heavy handed and I have cooperated with you. Now I've got some questions I would like answered."

"We don't have to answer any of your questions, we're the government," Sam replied nastily.

"That's right, you don't have to answer anything, but you said that you were working undercover. If you want to stay undercover, you better talk to me." I had put up with a lot tonight and I was starting to get a little peevish.

The driver mumbled something. "Okay," said Sam, "I'll tell you what I can. What do you want to know?"

"First of all, who were those guys in the hotel?"

"The fat man is Gustav Schmidt. He's a colonel in German intelligence and a high-ranking Nazi. The little man is Peter Lorry, not the actor, but a Nazi corporal who assists Schmidt. Schmidt uses the name Armbruster, and Lorry's alias is Franchot Tune, again, not the actor. The hard-looking guy with the bent nose is just an American thug. Schmidt picked him up for muscle."

I was puzzled. "If you know who and what they are, why don't you just arrest them?"

"They haven't done anything yet. We're watching them and picking up all their contacts. That's why we grabbed you tonight. Anything else? The Catholic Telegraph comes out tomorrow. I got a big delivery, so I gotta get some sleep."

"Yeah, what have those guys got to do with the green carnations and who is Moby Trick?"

"I don't know anything about no green carnations and Moby Trick is strictly hush-hush, top secret." He swung open the door. "That's all I got to say, now get out."

"The least you guys could do is drive me back to the middle of town." The G-men agreed. They drove me to Fifth and Vine, where I had to wait twenty minutes for a streetcar.

On the ride back to Price Hill, I thought about the events of the evening. I knew I was getting close to something, but I didn't have any idea what it was, just that whatever it was, getting closer to it could be dangerous.

I got off the streetcar in front of the Pay-n-Takit and walked over to the Ideal. Charlie was the only one there and he was getting ready to close.

"Give me a ginger ale and Seagram's," I told him. "Put it in a pop bottle and I'll take it home with me. You wouldn't believe what happened to me tonight. I was surrounded by crazy people!"

"Hmmph," said Charlie. "So what's new?"

CHAPTER 9

I OVERSLEPT.

After the night I'd had, it was understandable. I was looking out the kitchen window, waiting for the coffee to perk, and saw Walt unlock the door to the Ideal.

It was almost 7:30 before I got to the café with my bakery goods and paper. "Morning Walt, hello fellas," I said as I entered. Brownie, the Covedale Building custodian, and Ray Brockelberg were standing at the bar, nursing their beers. They grunted, Walt said good morning.

Brockelberg's nickname was Hock. He was one of five brothers, four of them were plasterers. The fifth, Dinky, was a priest. "What's the matter, Hock?" I asked him. "You look morose."

"Mordock stiffed me yesterday." Morie Mordock ran a book out in Cheviot in a café called Tornadoes. "I called in a bet, the horse won and paid $36.40, and Mordock said he never got the call. Refused to pay me."

As Brockelberg was telling his story, Mick Owens walked in. Mick lived in the same apartment building as me, right across the street from the Ideal.

Mick said, "Practically the same thing happened to me yesterday. I bet a deuce on Go Billie Go in the fifth at Arlington. He won and paid $22.20 and Mordock said I tried to past post him. Wouldn't pay off."

"Why do you guys call Mordock?" asked Walt. "You could call Fatty. He's honest and he's closer."

Fatty Hindenberg's bookmaking establishment was in a place on Crookshank Road. A bookmaker, or a bookie, is a person or place that takes bets on horse races. They receive the results of the various races around the country by telephone, or over the wire if they subscribed to that service. Over the wire means that the results are received from a special radio broadcast.

Mick said, "Bingo has a twenty-to-one limit, Mordock gives track odds." Bingo was Fatty's nickname, I remembered, though

I had never understood why someone whose real name was Fatty needed a nickname.

"Track odds times nothing is nothing," Walt philosophized.

"He can afford to give you a hundred to one if he isn't going to pay off."

"This ain't the first time this has happened to me, and it's happened to Mick and probably a lot of other guys," complained Brockelberg. "We ought to do something about it."

Mike, Mick's horse-playing partner, had come in during the conversation. He added his opinion, "If you're talking about Morie Mordock, he has cheated me a few times too."

"You need to come up with a scheme to take him for a big one, one that is foolproof and one that he can't weasel out of," I suggested.

"Yeah," said Mike, "but if there was a foolproof way to beat the races I wouldn't have to worry about some small-time crook like Mordock."

"Wait a minute. I think the Cork might just have something," Walt said. "You all know that you can't beat the races even if you keep trying, but we should be able to figure out some way to beat just one race. Then take all the money you can get together, go over to Tornadoes and place your bet in front of witnesses. If he reneges then, everybody in Cheviot will chase him out of town."

"I think you guys got the answer." Brockelberg was excited. "We need to form a syndicate, develop a plan, and back it with dough. I'm in . . . how about you guys?"

Mick and Mike readily agreed. Walt said that he thought that Mordock needed a lesson, so he was in.

"How about you, Corky? Are you with us?" asked his neighbor Mike.

" Whoa, fellows," I replied. "I've never bet on a horse in my life and I don't want to start now. I'll help in any way I can, but I don't think I want to be a part of any syndicate."

Mike said, "Okay, you'll be our consultant. We need other people, maybe Barnie Pazic?"

"He would be perfect," said Brockelberg. "He likes to play the ponies and he gets off work at UPS early. Walt, how about Muffin? He could be a big help."

Muffin was Frank Schroeder. He ran a pool room four doors down the street from the Ideal. It used to be his family's bakery, where he worked as a young man, thus the nickname. "I'll get him," said Walt.

"Okay," said Brockelberg. "I got to get out to the shop. Get a hold of Pazic and Muffin, and maybe Harry the Haberdasher too, and try to have them here tonight at seven."

"Ok," Walt said. "I'll see what I can do."

Billy Boy Hanes walked in. He always got there early and waited for his pal Jake to show up. "Hiya Corky, we gonna go anywhere today?"

"Yeah, Billy Boy, we might take a little trip today. Give Billy Boy a beer," I called to Walt. Billy Boy, unlike his partner Jake, was not particular, he would drink anything he was offered.

"Walt!"

"Yeah, I'm sorry, I was thinking about how to put the perfect fix on a horse race. What did you want?"

"A beer for Billy."

"Anybody going to the layin'-out tonight?" asked Brownie.

Walt was the first to reply, "I'm going over early, then I'll come back and relieve Charlie so he can go. I guess we'll both work tonight. We'll probably be pretty busy. We better both be here in the morning, too. There'll be a crowd waiting for their wives to get out of church."

"Is there going to be a party here tonight?" asked Billy Boy.

"It's not gonna be a party, it's called a wake," answered Brownie. "Everybody will go to the funeral home and then come over here, where they'll all drink too much and tell each other what a great guy Hairless Hank was. Frankly, I thought he was a pain in the ass."

As he tossed off the last of his drink, Mick said, "Brownie, you think everybody is a pain in the ass." He headed for the door.

"Well, if the shoe fits . . ." Brownie called after him.

Sergeant Stutter walked in. "I'm looking for the other bartender, the old guy, is he around?"

"He's not around," answered Walt. "He won't be in until about four. What do you want him for?"

"I just want to ask him a couple of question. Do you know where he lives?"

Walt said, "I think you had better wait and talk to him up here. He's probably sleeping and he can be pretty surly when you wake him up."

"Well, tell him I'm looking for him, and I'll be back."

"Wait a minute, Sergeant," I called as he stalked out. "I understand the police found Holthaus's car."

"Yeah, some kids playing by the pond at Whitsken's found it. They told one of the guys that works at the dairy and the guy called us. We checked the license and found out that the car belonged to the dead guy."

"Where's the car now—did you guys impound it?" I asked.

"No, we just called the Bakers and told them where it was. I think they had it towed out to their house."

"Didn't the police even look at it?"

"Look, McCorkel, this ain't what you would call one of our priority cases but we're working on it. And we are going to want to talk to you about it some more, so don't go leaving town or anything."

"Is it okay if I go to Delhi?"

"That's the last place I'd go if I was you," the policeman said and walked out.

"So, are we still going to Delhi, Cork?" asked Billy Boy.

"Sure," I said. "I really want to know what's going on out there."

I read my newspaper. It was all war news and none of it too good. The damn Japs were massing for an all-out attack on the Solomon Islands. The Germans had moved into Stalingrad again. That was the third time they'd tried that in as many weeks. They would move in, and the Russians would kick their butts out. Allied bombers hit Crete. That's good, I thought. As I skimmed through the paper, I was really looking to see if there was anything about Henry's death. All I found was a little piece in the obituaries. It said that Henry had died, was survived by his daughter and son-in-law, would be laid out tonight at Ruebel's Funeral Home, and would be buried tomorrow after a mass at St. Clarisa's.

Just then I saw Patrolman Joe Newmann through the window. I ran to the door and called to him. Newmann stopped and I went out to talk to him.

"Officer, I just wanted to tell you how things are going."

Newmann looked around furtively. "I can't talk to you here, I don't want to be seen with you. In about fifteen minutes I'll be in Dow's having a cup of coffee. Meet me there." He walked off.

I stood there for a minute watching the officer leave. Then I went back into the Ideal.

"Looks like you got brushed off," said Walt.

"It's like everybody wants to get rid of me."

"You're always welcome here."

"Thanks, Walt." I hung around for a few minutes then headed for Dow's Drug Store. When I walked up to the door, I saw Officer Newmann sitting at the soda fountain with his coffee.

"Sit down, Mr. McCorkel," Newmann said.

I sat on one of the stools. "Call me Ed."

"Ed, I'm Joe. I could really get in trouble if I was seen talking to you."

"Why, for heaven's sake?"

"The guys down at the station house are pretty mad 'cause you're sticking your nose in this Holthaus business. They think it's police business and not yours."

"Boy, that makes it unanimous." I ran my hand through my hair. "The carnation growers, the Nazis, the G-men, the police, even the post office want me off this case. Any minute I'm expecting a Boy Scout troop to march up with a banner saying 'Lay Off.'"

"Easy, Ed," Newmann tried to calm me down. "What's been going on?"

I started to give him a rundown of all the things that happened last night, but he said, "Whoa, I'm on duty and I don't have much time right now. It sounds like the whole story might take awhile. I'm going to the funeral home about eight tonight. Why don't we meet a little after that at the Ideal? Then we can go to your office and talk in private."

"That sounds great, Joe. I'd like to talk to someone about what's been going on. I'll see you about eight." I started to leave.

"Wait a minute," cautioned Joe, "let me go first. I don't want to be seen leaving with you."

I waited a few moments before following the patrolman out of the door. This was getting serious. Strangers were pointing guns at me, threatening to throw me out of windows, and giving me some strong warnings. People I knew didn't want to be seen with me. For some reason these people thought I was on to something, but for the life of me I couldn't figure out what it was.

I walked on over to the office. I saw Susan through the window, she sure looked cute sitting there. I have to speak to her soon about the partnership. I went in.

"Hi Susan, anything important I should know about?"

"No," she answered. "Everything is under control. How's the investigation going?"

I pulled up a chair. "Have you got a few minutes?"

She nodded.

I sat down and gave her a detailed account of everything that happened to me. As she sat there listening her eyes got bigger and bigger, and at one point she grabbed my hand and whispered, "Oh, no." When I finished she was almost in tears.

"You've got to stop this investigation immediately, you could be hurt or even killed. Marge Baker would never have asked you if she had known how dangerous it would be."

"I'm not going to stop, at least not until I find out what it is that everyone is so afraid I'm going to find out. I wish I knew a tenth of what they all think I do."

Susan sniffed, "You're crazy—but please be careful."

"I'll be okay, really. Are you going to the funeral home tonight?"

Susan said she had planned to close the office a little early and go over after work. "I have to take Mom to the bingo at St. Bill's this evening."

"I'm going out to the Herzog Brothers' nursery this afternoon. I probably won't be back before you leave. So I'll see you tomorrow."

"Okay, but please be careful," she said as I walked out the door.

CHAPTER 10

I WENT BACK OVER TO THE CAFÉ. IT WAS PRETTY CROWDED now. Brownie was still there, and Jake and Billy Boy were at one of the tables. There were two guys I didn't know and Erma Gerbil was at the end of the bar. When I saw her I tried to duck out again, but it was too late. She had seen me.

"Hey you, McCorkel," she bellowed, "come over here." Erma lived next door to Walt and Charlie. She was a loudmouthed harridan. She didn't like anyone and nobody liked her.

"Come over here," she repeated, "I want to talk to you."

I walked over to where she was standing. I knew if I didn't she would cause a scene. "Yeah Erma, what can I do for you?"

"Well, you could buy a girl a drink," she rasped, holding up a half empty glass of port wine.

"Sorry Erma, I put all the money I had in the flower box," I lied.

"Hmmph, flowers for that old fool, Hairless Hank. He won't see 'em or smell 'em either where he's gone. It'll be too hot. The old goat got what he deserved. He hadn't sold a house in twenty years, all he did was get in the way of the other realtors. It's a wonder somebody didn't shot him sooner."

"Boy, Erma, what put you in such a good mood?"

"Don't be a smart aleck, McCorkel. I hear you're investigating Hank's murder and I want to give you some advice."

"Oh no, you don't," I cried. "I've gotten nothing but advice and from experts no less. I'm not going to listen to anything you have to say." I ducked out of the place.

I went back up to Dow's Drug Store. I hated the food, thought it tasted like cardboard, but I wanted to be alone. I didn't think I'd see anyone in there that I knew. I ordered a double-decker and a fountain Coke and sat at the counter and ate my lunch.

While I was sitting there, a little man in a black suit came in and went back to the prescription counter. When he came back to the front of the store, I could feel him staring at me and I looked up at him. "Aren't you Mr. McCorkel, the insurance man?" he asked with a faintly Italian accent.

I put down the sandwich I was eating and replied, "Yes, I am, can I help you?"

"I am Father O'Toole," the little man said. "I just wanted to tell you to be careful, it can be very dangerous out there."

"Thank you, Reverend," I said, taking a sip of my Coke. "And *arrivederci*."

I finished my sandwich and walked back to look at the magazines. I thought maybe I should pick up a copy of *True Detective*. It might give me some pointers. Nah, all I had to do was put things together. I walked over to the stationery counter and bought a notebook instead. Then I went back to the soda fountain, sat down, and bought another Coke.

I pulled out a pen. I started to put down things that I knew about the case:

#1. Henry is dead.
#2. There are three bullet holes in his hat.
    A. Somebody shot at him four times, hitting him with the last shot.
    B. Maybe somebody was playing a game, and they shot Henry's hat off three times, but then they missed on the fourth shot.

Walt showed off from time to time by shooting cigarettes out of the hands of daring customers. And that girl who came in occasionally, Sailor Summers—I'd once seen her shoot a cigarette out of the Prince's mouth.

CONCLUSION

I wrote that real big in my notebook:

POSSIBLY AN ACCIDENT!
MAYBE WALT OR THAT SAILOR GIRL WERE PLAYING
SHARPSHOOTER AND MISSED!

Then I took my pen and scratched out everything I wrote. If Walt or Sailor had killed Hank, they would have done it in front of an audience. After all, they would have been showing off. There would have been all kinds of witnesses.

I realized I had just been wasting time in hopes that Emma Gerbil would leave the Ideal before I got back. I finished my second Coke and left. When I got back to the bar, I peeked in the window and didn't see any sign of her, so I went in. I was pleased to see that Jackson was there.

"I'm glad Jake is still here, Walt, give the boys a drink."

Walt looked at me and said, "Where else would they be? If they ain't driving you around, then they're here."

The happy boys and I headed for Jake's car. Jake slid in from the passenger's side and Billy Boy followed him in. I piled into the back seat. Jackson started the motor, and away we went chugged in a cloud of exhaust.

"What do you guys know about the Herzogs?" I had to shout to be heard over the engine.

"I don't know nothing about them, I never seen 'em," Billy Boy said. That didn't mean much. Somebody could be standing on Billy Boy's foot, and chances are he wouldn't notice them.

"How about you Jake, do you know anything about them?"

Jackson sang forth, "Hickory dickory doc, they keep their dough in a sock. If you think that they're tight, you might just be right. All their money's hid under a rock."

"Jake, my friend if you have any hopes of getting another drink when we get back, you had better stop with the nursery rhymes and talk to me."

"Oh yeah, right, Ed. Nobody knows much about the Herzogs. I think their father came from Germany, and he started the nursery. In fact I think he started the carnation industry in Delhi. Most of the others began after him. Anyway, the father started it and taught the kids. It's all they ever did, work with the carnations. They never played when they were kids, they never go any place now. All they ever do is tend their damn carnations. They've made a lot of money over the years, but they never spend it on anything but the nursery, buying new land or machinery. Neither one of them was ever married, and I know neither one has ever been in the Ideal."

I smiled. "By golly, Cyril, you can be a regular fountain of information if a person knows which plug to pull."

"Roses are red and . . ."

"Can it, Jake, we're almost there."

We saw a large sign announcing "Herzog Brothers, Growers of the Finest Carnations in Delhi, The Carnation Capital of the World." Hanging below this magnificent sign was a more modest one. In hand-painted letters, it said, "Help Wanted."

Jake pulled the car into a large, well-kept, blacktopped parking lot. He parked near a building that looked like it might be the office. As the three of them were getting out of the car, a large man cane out of the door of the building. He was over six feet tall and probably weighed 300 pounds.

"Ah, gentlemen," he boomed, "Welcome. You must have come about the jobs, yes. I am Grossman Herzog. Please come in to the office and we will talk." He did not have an accent, but he almost did. He stuck out his hand, which Billy Boy shook.

"I'm sorry, Mr. Herzog, but we haven't come seeking employment, merely to ask a few questions. I am Ed McCorkel, the insuran . . ."

Before I could finish, Herzog turned white, then bright red. He dropped Billy Boy's hand like it had bitten him. "You were warned, I mean, you aren't supposed to . . . I mean, I know nothing about that poor man's death. I know nothing about green anything. I mean, I do not wish to answer any of your questions."

"Calm down, Mr. Herzog." My mind was working a mile a minute. Something was very strange here. Herzog did not frequent the Ideal, so he didn't hear anything about all the warnings from that quarter. He must have heard from one of the sources of the warnings. It was unlikely that it came from Emma Gerbil or Father O'Toole, I figured, so Herzog must have known that I had been warned off the case from either the G-men or the Nazis. This was an interesting development.

"Calm down," I repeated. "We mean you no harm, and we don't suspect you of any foul play. We are merely trying to establish the events that led up to the death of Mr. Holthaus. I am working very closely with the police and I could have them come out to question you if you would prefer." Everything I had said was a little short of the truth, so I figured that last big lie wouldn't matter.

"No, no police." My bluff had worked. "I will be glad to answer any questions I can." Herzog had calmed down a little but he was still plainly agitated.

"Okay, that's more like it. Where is your brother? I would like to talk to both of you."

"Talbert is not here, he is working."

That puzzled me. "I thought he worked here," I said.

"Oh no, he has taken a job with the Queen City Barge Construction Company. He is a bilge inspector now."

"Why would your brother take a job with a barge construction company when you are short-handed here?"

"He loves the sea," answered Herzog.

Another warning light went on in my head. There's more going on here than meets the eye, I thought. I went back to my questioning. "Have you had any break-ins or noticed anything strange going on around here in the past week or so?"

"No, nothing unusual has happened."

"Do you know a man named Armbruster?"

Herzog hesitated then answered, "Of course, he is a director of agriculture from Argentina. He and his assistants have been here. We talked of growing carnations. He is very interested in our methods."

"Did you discuss green carnations?" I asked quickly.

Herzog turned a little white again. "I know nothing of green carnations, or of blue ones either, for that matter. I think I have been most cooperative, gentlemen, but we have talked long enough. I must return to my work."

"Thank you for your time, Mr. Herzog. I wish I could have met your brother. Do either of you ever stop at the Ideal Café up on Cleves Pike?"

"That place is like a seedy circus with that oaf Walt as the ringmaster to his customers. A crass menagerie. No, neither my brother nor myself ever frequent that place."

I had one last question. "What do you know about Moby Trick?"

This time Grossman Herzog really turned white. When he regained his composure, he said, "Good day, gentlemen. I really must go." With that, he turned and walked back into the nursery office, leaving us standing alone outside.

Billy Boy went over and pissed on a hedge, then we got into the car and left. As we pulled out of the parking lot I said, "I have to talk to another grower immediately. Who's place are we closest to?"

Jake thought about it. "This here's Neeb Road, it runs into Delhi Pike up by the college. Mix's spread—that's what he calls it, a 'spread'—is on Delhi just on the other side of the college out there. But we ought to be getting back to the Ideal."

"Forget your thirst for once, man, we are on to something. Take me to see Arnold Mix right now."

Jackson turned left on Neeb Road and proceeded up the hill. "There's the college," Jake said. "The Mix spread is just beyond it." He turned right at the school and then left into another dirt drive.

The first thing I noticed was the spectacular view of the river. The second thing I saw was dozens of tents in a meadow behind the greenhouses. I jumped out of the car and started yelling.

"Hey Arnold, where are you? I have to talk to you. Where the hell are you?"

Arnold Mix came running up from between two greenhouses. "Ed, Ed McCorkel—here I am! What's the matter with you? You're scaring my guests."

"I'm sorry, Arnold, I guess I'm just excited. I think I'm starting to get some answers to my investigation. Not the answers I was expecting, mind you, but answers. I've got a question for you. Have you ever heard of a Mr. Armbruster or a Franchot Tune?"

"Yeah, ain't that Franchot guy a movie actor? I think he was in a movie with my cousin once."

"No, no, that guy's name was Tone. These guys are named Armbruster and Tune, and there's another guy, Kruger."

"Golly Ed, I don't know any of those guys."

"That's great, Arnold, at least I got one answer I expected."

"Hey, Arnold," Billy Boy called. "What are all the tents for, are you having a Boy Scout jamboree?"

"No, Billy Boy, they ain't Boy Scouts, they're Mixites, and this is their annual conclave. They come from all over the country to celebrate their annual rites and baptize new members in the river."

I had to ask, "What are Mixites and how come they have their annual camp out here?"

"The Mixites are a religious group. Its full name is 'The Church of Tom Mix, His Older Brother Jesus Christ, and All the Lesser Saints.' They believe that Tom was the second coming of the Savior and that he was cut down before he could do any actual saving. They started coming here last year, a year after Tom's death—he died two years ago now. I guess they came here 'cause I was Tom's only living relative. Anyway, I let them camp out in the field there. Last year there were only 26 of them, this year there's 107. They don't cause no trouble and it's the least I can do for old Tom's memory. I understand there's another group that considers themselves orthodox. They meet every year in Dubois, Pennsylvania."

I said, "Arnold, that was really more than I wanted to know. Thank you for helping me out. I have to get my friends here a drink, so we gotta go. Good luck with the Mixers."

"Mixites," Arnold called after the retreating Terraplane.

As we turned out of Mix's property, I noticed a place on the side of the road where the weeds were all crushed down, as if a car had missed the driveway.

Jake drove as fast as his second gear would allow. He knew there was a drink at the end of the trail. He was coasting down Neeb Road when he had an inspiration. "Hey Cork," he called to the back seat, "why don't we stop in at Five Points? They'd know any gossip about the growers."

"Okay, when you don't try to spout poetry you make a lot of sense."

Five Points was a saloon at Neeb and Foley. Devil's Backbone Road also ran into Neeb at that point, and the angles caused by the streets created five points. That's how the place got its name.

When they walked in, they saw only a bartender and a skinny guy sitting at the bar reading the paper. I walked up the bar and pointed to Jake and Billy Boy. "Give 'em a couple of doubles with beer chasers. I'll have an orange pop, do you have a Smile?" I asked.

The bartender gave me a big grin but said he didn't have Smile, "Would a Whistle do?"

I said I'd try one. He poured the shots and chasers and gave me an orange soda. The boys were already in conversation with the man at the end of the bar.

Billy Boy tipped his shot and said "Thanks, McCorkel."

"McCorkel?" echoed the bartender. "Ain't you the guy that found old Henry's body up at the Ideal?"

"Actually, it was the bartender who found the body," I answered.

"Maybe it was old Charlie what killed him. Seems to me there was bad blood between them two. Charlie has him a temper. Come to think of it, one of Charlie's relatives killed a guy right in this joint, stabbed him with a knife."

"Whitey," the man at the end of the bar addressed the bartender, "you don't know what you're talking about."

"Didn't some guy get killed in here 'bout twenty, thirty years ago?"

"Yeah, but the guy what killed him was Gus Imberhold and he stabbed him 107 times with a fork. He was related to Charlie's wife."

Jake spoke up, "Imberhold, ain't that your name?"

"Yeah, I'm Johnny Imberhold. I work up at Herzog's place. You sure got old Grossman upset, mister. Right after you left he told everybody to take the day off and took off in his car. It ain't like him to let people off this early."

"Got him worked up, did I?" I asked. "I wonder why? Come on, you guys, I need you to take me back to the corner."

"You ain't finished your soda," Whitey the bartender shouted.

"Too many bubbles," I called back to him.

I was a happy man when we walked into the Ideal. I was beginning to put together some answers. The bar was crowded. Everyone was trying to soak up enough courage to make it to the funeral home. Some would soak up too much and never make it at all.

Jake and Billy managed to get up to the bar. Charlie was working, and Brownie was helping him out. I caught Charlie's attention, threw down a five and said, "Fill 'em up."

Al Heller and his wife were sitting over in the corner with old man Sellers, so I made my way over to them. I said hello and asked them if they had ever heard of Armbruster.

Al and his wife both said no, and Sellers said "Snorb," and shook his head in a negative manner. These were exactly the answers that I expected.

I decided to go over to my apartment and get cleaned up before going to the funeral home. I made my way through the crowd. Walt was coming in as I left.

"Let's go over to your office for a minute," he said.

We walked over, and Susan wasn't around, but I found a couple of messages she had left for me. One said that she had left for the day and was going to the funeral home. The second note said that a Mr. Armbruster had called, no message, and the third one said that a mailman had come in with a special delivery and would only deliver it personally. I threw all three messages in the wastebasket.

What's up?" I asked Walt.

He handed me a piece of lined paper with scribbles all over it. "My plan for fixing a race, what do you think?"

I read the notes he had made. "This is nuts, can you really do it?"

"Can you get me the gas coupons?"

"Yeah, that looks like the easy part."

"We're going to be really busy tonight. If you can bring the guys over here and explain what each one has to do, we can pull it off ...I think."

I told him I would do what I could. He slapped me on the back and walked out the door.

I went up to my apartment, where I took off my coat and shoes. I sat at the kitchen table and thought back on everything that had happened, including what Walt had just told me. The scheme was ridiculous, but I said I'd help, so I would present it to the guys tonight.

On a more positive note, I had definitely come to some conclusions. I got up and took out my pen and notebook:

#1. The Herzog brothers are up to something.
#2. Armbruster must have told them that he had stopped me from investigating them.

#3. Grossman was surprised to see me.

#4. He knows a lot about the green carnations.

#5. For some reason, Talbert Herzog is spying on the Queen City Barge Construction Company.

#6. Armbruster, Tune, Kruger, and the Herzogs are tied up in some kind of a conspiracy, and the conspiracy has something to do with "Moby Trick," whatever that is.

This time I didn't scratch out my notes. I laid the notebook and pen on the table and got up. I wanted to take a nap, but I knew I had to get cleaned up and go over to the funeral home before I had to meet with the horse race syndicate. I also had to meet Joe Newmann later.

It was a little before seven when I got to the laying-out. I'd changed clothes and had some supper at the Colonial Inn. When I finished eating, I walked over to the funeral parlor. As I passed the Pay-n-Takit, I saw Arnie Chiggerbox trying to keep the mourners out of the grocery store's parking lot, without much success.

The place was crowded when I got there. I looked over the room. Marge Baker was there, of course. She was standing near the coffin talking to the Prince. More precisely, she was listening to the Prince.

Her husband Fred was off to her left talking to a group that looked like real estate men. Over in one corner I saw Cyril Jackson, all scrubbed up and holding his hat in his hand. The lady with him must be his wife. The cigar salesman, Hugo Getz, and his wife were waiting to speak to Marge. Stutter and Clements, the two police-men, were standing in opposite corners of the room. They were in civilian clothes and were closely surveying everyone in the room. There were quite a few other people that I knew from the Ideal. There were a lot of people that I didn't know at all.

I kept trying to edge my way closer to Marge Baker, but there was always someone talking to her. I felt someone touch me on the elbow. I looked around and saw Fred Baker.

"You aren't going to get near her," said Fred. "There are just too many people. It's a nice turnout for the old boy, isn't it?"

"Fred, I know I'm supposed to say something about how good he looks and all, but he just looks dead to me."

Fred looked over at the body in the casket and said, "Yeah, Ed. He didn't look too good even when he was alive. He'd be embarrassed as hell if he knew he was lying there with his bald head hanging out. He used to wear his hat when we ate."

A little bell went off in my head. Hank would never take his hat off in public. He once heard someone say that if you wanted Henry's hat off his head, you would either have to shoot him or it. Who was it that said it?

Fred continued, "I'll tell Marge you were here. She told me to tell you, if I saw you, that she'd like you to call her Friday afternoon."

"Tell her I will, and tell her that I think I'll have some news for her."

Ray Brockelberg came up behind me. "We still on for tonight?"

I told him that I was holding the meeting at my place and that he should go to the Ideal and gather everybody up. "When you see the lights go on in my office, bring them over." He was a little confused by the change in plans but said he would take care of it.

Just then, Arnold Mix came in with two people in long, flowing, flowered robes. They made their way up to the coffin. The two wearing robes made several hand gestures over the body, then they turned abruptly and headed for the door. As they passed Fred and me, Arnold whispered, "They're Mixites, they wanted to come. I figure old Hank can use all the help he can get."

I nodded to Mix, shook Fred's hand, and turned away, right into Franchot Tune. "You are a foolisssh man, Mr. McCorkel," Tune said. "You could be der next one thessse nice peoples vill come to wisssit." Before I could say anything, the little man had disappeared into the crowd.

Someone on my right tapped me on the shoulder, I turned, and ran right into Sam Callmeyer. "Hail, hail, the gang's all here," I said under my breath.

Sam was looking at the body in the casket. He whispered out of the side of his mouth, "I wonder if this many will come to see you, McCorkel?"

I ignored the remark. "Did you come by my office with a special delivery today?"

"When I have a special delivery for you, buddy, you'll know it," Callmeyer replied.

"One other thing, Sam. When is the last time you delivered mail to the Queen City Barge Construction Company?" From the look on Callmeyer's face, I knew I had struck a nerve. Slippery Sam started to reply but I had moved off through the crowd. I noticed that most of the men were starting to leave.

Then I saw Father O'Toole bouncing up to the coffin. At the same time, Thomas Ruebel, the funeral director, was motioning to me from behind a curtain in the next room. I walked into the room where Ruebel was concealed.

"O'Toole is about to start saying the rosary," Ruebel told me. "He's slower than cat shit. You can sneak out this door if you want."

I took advantage of the side door and found myself in the rear of the building, close to St. Clarisa's school yard. I cut through the playground and walked up to the Ideal. The place was packed. Because of the shortcut I took, I beat most of the others who had been at the funeral home but had left before rosary time. They arrived shortly after me and added to the throng. Charlie and Walt were both behind the bar, Fionna was picking up empties, and Brownie was rinsing out glasses as fast as he could.

I knew I would never get a drink. I had hoped to run into Betty or Peter Horn to make sure I could get a ride to the cemetery in the morning, but they weren't there. I caught Walt's eye, nodded to him, and headed for the door. I had no more than flipped on the lights in my office when Brockelberg and the "syndicate" came bursting through the office door.

"What's the plan!"

"How we going to get that dirty dog?"

"Why ain't Walt here?"

"Who made you the boss?"

They were all shouting at once. "Gentlemen, calm down, as you may have noticed, Walt is very busy tonight. I have the plan and I will explain it to you."

They calmed down a little and some of them draped themselves over Susan's desk. A couple more sat in the only two chairs in the place, and Muffin Schroeder sat on the floor. "Let's hear it," he said.

CHAPTER 12

"I DON'T KNOW ANYTHING ABOUT HORSE RACING, SO I'M NOT sure exactly what everything I am going to tell you is about, but Walt told me you'll understand. If this is going to work, everybody needs to be available by one o'clock tomorrow afternoon."

"Mick and me are taking the day off for Henry's funeral," Mike piped up. "We can make it."

Brockelberg said that his brothers could handle the job they were working and that he would be ready to do whatever he had to. Muffin, Harry the Haberdasher, and Barnie Pazic all said that they could be available, too. When they settled down, I told them that I needed to ask some questions.

"Muffin, you run a little book in the pool room, how much time is there between the finish of race and when it is announced over the wire?"

"I don't know, I ain't got no wire. Lemme use your telephone. I'll call Fatty, he'll tell us."

While Muffin was using the telephone, I turned to Harry. "You go out to the track pretty often, Harry, can you tell me what time the sixth race usually starts?"

"Three-o-five exactly, most of the time."

"What does exactly, most of the time mean?"

"The race goes off at three-o-five, but sometimes there are complications in the earlier races and they get behind."

"Do these complications happen often?"

"Nah, usually things go off like clockwork."

Muffin hung up the telephone. "Fatty says a little over three minutes, and said he didn't want to know why I wanted to know, but to stay out of his place."

"Everything fits," I said. "Here's the plan." They all leaned forward a little.

"Tomorrow, Mick and Barnie will drive out to Coney Island. I'll give you a gas coupon, Barnie. You'll go to the drugstore across the street from the main entrance."

70

He saw Harry feverishly writing this all down. "You don't have to take notes, Harry. I've got written instructions for each team."

Mike said quietly, "You're good, McCorkel—maybe we should go into the horse race fixing business full time."

"This is a one-time deal, Mike, and I still think it is too crazy to work. Anyway, you and Muffin are supposed to go to the drugstore across Harrison from Tornadoes."

"How do I fit into the plan?" asked Brockelberg.

"You and Harry will be in Tornadoes. You'll save a place in the line, if there is a line, for Harry. Harry, when you get a signal from the boys in the drugstore, and then you need to place a bet immediately. You will do this rather noisily so that everyone in the place hears you do it."

"How am I going to know which horse to bet on?"

"Here comes the wild part of the scheme. Walt and I are going to fly in Tyrone's plane to River Downs. We'll watch the sixth race from the air and then fly past Coney Island and signal the winner to Mick and Barnie across the street. They'll telephone the drugstore in Cheviot and pass the winner on to Mike and Muffin, who will signal Harry. Harry will place the bet, hopefully collect the winnings, and then we'll all meet at the Ideal, downstairs in the Jolly Boys Club Room, to celebrate."

"Wow, you are good," said Barney. "How do we know what the signals are?"

"I'm not good—this is Walt's plan and I'm still skeptical about it. You ought to think about how much you are going to bet, and where the money is coming from. You should also allow about thirty bucks for expenses. Walt's got the signals worked out on the instruction sheets for you."

They put their heads together and decided that between them they could come up with nine hundred and fifty bucks.

"How about you, Corky? Don't you want to get in on this?" asked Brockelberg.

"I told you that I am not a betting man, but just this once I'll put in a hundred bucks. That way you can bet a thousand and there will be fifty left over for expenses, so if we lose we'll be able to drown our sorrows." They all laughed at me, collected their instructions, and walked out the door, promising to be ready by tomorrow at one.

I looked at the clock, it was two minutes after eight. Joe walked in, turning off the lights in the office as he entered. "Let's go back in your office where nobody can see us from the street," he said.

I sat behind my desk and Joe pulled up a chair. 'What's going on, Mr. McCorkel? Did the Jolly Boys move their clubhouse?"

"No, we just had a little . . . insurance business to discuss. But call me Ed, will you, Joe. I think I've got a lot of information on the Holthaus case. If you've got the time, I'd like to lay it all out for you. I really need another opinion."

"I got all time in the world so long as nobody sees me here. What's been going on?"

"It all started yesterday morning when I went over to see Al Heller . . ." I told Newmann everything that had happened in the past two days. The patrolman didn't say a thing, but his eyes just kept getting bigger and bigger. When I finished my story, Joe spoke.

"Holy cow, you have really been busy! I've got a couple of questions. First, why would anyone steal a bottle of citronella?"

"I think whoever stole it thought it was the secret green carnation formula."

"Is there a secret formula?" Joe asked.

"I don't know, but I doubt it."

"Who was the G-man? It sounded like you knew him."

I had not identified Sam Callmeyer. "I don't think his identity is pertinent at this point and I kinda promised not to give him away."

"Okay, but who. . .".

"Hold the questions, Joe. Just from what I've told you, what kind of conclusions have you come to?"

"Yeah, well, let me see," Joe pondered. "First of all, Henry Holthaus had been in the Saline's shed shortly before he died. He might even have been killed there."

"That's exactly what I think, Joe. I'd like to get another look at that barn when nobody is around."

Joe continued his speculating. "The Herzogs are probably mixed up in the killing. They're the only growers who are dealing with the agricultural experts from Argentina, and those guys are obviously German spies. The Herzogs might even be spies themselves. They called the Nazis and told them to scare you off the case. That's why Grossman Herzog was so surprised when you visited him."

"You hit the bull's eye again, but what are they after? Surely the Nazis didn't send two of their top spies over here just to kill an old drunken real estate man. And I really doubt that they're interested in growing green carnations."

"Moby Trick, that's the answer," said Joe.

"Yeah, but what or who is Moby Trick?" I asked. "Even Sam didn't know, I could tell."

"Sam?" shouted Newmann. "You mean to tell me that Slippery Sam Callmeyer is an undercover G-man?"

"I didn't say that, I didn't say anything about Sam Callmeyer."

"You said enough, Ed! My God, our country is in more danger than I thought."

"Don't tell anyone, I promised to keep it quiet."

"Don't worry, I'll keep it under my hat."

"Yeah, okay, I think we should go out and try to take a look at Saline's barn right now. My car's parked down on Coronado. You got a flashlight?"

I reached in the desk and pulled out a flashlight. "Right here. What happens if we get caught out there?"

"You've got so many people out to get you that the Salines ain't going to make much difference," Joe said as he headed for the door.

We walked down Cleves Pike to Coronado. Joe unlocked a nice-looking 1939 Ford coupe and we got in.

"Nice car," I said.

"It's great when I can get gas for it."

"Does it use a lot of gas?" I was just talking to hide my nervousness.

"Not a lot, but you don't get much with a 'C' sticker."

We made it to Saline's a lot faster than I had expected. I was surprised at how much faster a car with high gear could go. Joe had turned out his lights and pulled off the road before we got to the Saline's drive. We cut through a small wooded area and found ourselves behind some buildings.

"Which shed is it?" whispered Joe.

I pointed to one of the buildings. "I think it's that one."

We walked around the front and peeked in the window. It was dark inside. Joe pushed on the door. It was unlocked and swung open with a squeak. We pushed the door shut behind us, and I turned on the flashlight.

"Keep it shielded," hissed Joe. "We don't want anyone to see it from outside. Where was the red rag when you found it?"

"Right over there." I pointed to a cabinet against the wall and Joe opened it, revealing a gun on the top shelf, just as we heard someone shout somewhere outside. As quietly as we could, we quickly left the shed, went through the little woods, and got back to the car without seeing anyone or being seen. Joe let the car roll down the hill without turning on the lights until we were well out of sight of the nursery. Then he started the engine, turned on the lights, and drove, rather slowly, back to my office.

I finally broke the silence. "That was close back there." Neither of us had said anything since we had run out of the shed.

"Yeah, but it was worth it." Joe said. "I'm pretty sure we know where Holthaus was killed."

"And I think we saw the gun he was killed with, too," I added. "Probably heard the killer, too, but we still don't know why. And how do the Herzogs fit in? Did the green carnations have anything to do with it? What about the Nazis, and the big question—who is Moby Trick?"

"Take it easy, McCorkel," Joe said. "You've got some of the answers. Keep digging and the rest will come. You are going to put it all together, I'm sure of it now." We had arrived back at the corner. I got out of the car.

"Thanks, Joe. You helped me a lot tonight, in more ways than one. It looks like the Ideal is still open, can I buy you a drink?"

"No thanks, I have to get up early. I'll talk to you later."

I was surprised to see the lights on in the café. It was almost midnight, well past the regular closing time. I walked in. Walt was alone, checking on his liquor supply.

"What a night," he said when he saw me. "Almost as much business as Good Friday." Walt always said that Good Friday was his busiest afternoon. The pastor of the church around the corner thought all the businesses on the corner should close from twelve to three on Good Friday, and he had sent around a notice to this effect several years before. Most of the businesses did close, but not the Ideal. Walt claimed that he couldn't afford to lose the business generated by the husbands who waited there while their wives went to church.

"The place doesn't look too much the worse for wear," I said.

"We didn't do too bad. When Fionna had to go to work, Betty Horn came in and helped out. Between her and Brownie and Charlie and me, we got the place cleaned up right after the crowd died down. My only problem is that I'm out of booze and beer and there will be another big crowd here in the morning waiting for the doings at church to be over."

"What're you going to do?"

"I already called Schoenling Brewery, they promised to have a beer truck here by seven. I guess I'm going to have to borrow some liquor."

"Where are you going to borrow whiskey at this hour?"

Walt headed for the door. "I'm on my way down to the Cat and the Fiddle. Do you want to come along?"

CHAPTER **13**

WALT OWNED A 1941 FORD SEDAN. IT WAS ALL BLACK AND had no chrome. It was one of the last cars made for the public before the factories retooled to support the war effort. Walt had had a 1940 Ford, but it burned up in early August. He had to pull a lot of strings to get the one he had now.

We walked down from the Ideal to Walt's house, where the car was parked in the drive. We got in and took off, taking a quick turn onto Coronado and then proceeding to West Eighth. Walt said it was the back way and quicker than going down Glenway.

"I talked to Muffin," Walt said as we sailed across the viaduct. "He said everything is okay for tomorrow."

"Yeah," was all I could answer. My knuckles were white as I held onto the strap. Walt drove pretty fast and I was used to the sedate pace of Cyril Jackson's Terraplane. It seemed like no time before we were downtown, pulling into an alley off Fifth Street to park. We got out of the car. I calmed down and asked him if he wanted to lock the car.

"Nah," said Walt. "Who'd bother it around here?" He led the way to the front door.

We went through the outer doors. "That'll be two bucks apiece, fellas," a man standing at the inner door said. "Oh, never mind. I didn't recognize you at first, Walt."

"Thanks, Angie, I have to see Aaron. I need to borrow some booze."

Angie said, "The show's on. If he's not on stage he'll be in the rear. Go on back."

"Thanks again, Angie."

When we passed through the inner door, we came to a black curtain. We went through an opening in the curtain and were in a very large, darkened room. On the back wall there were huge paintings of women in various stages of undress. There must have been ten of them, each highlighted by a little spotlight.

As I looked around, I saw a small stage at the other end of the room. It was bathed in a soft pink light. As my eyes adapted to the subdued lighting, I noticed a rather plump blond lady on the stage. She appeared to be completely naked except for two tassels mounted on her breasts. She seemed to be concentrating on making them gyrate in opposing directions.

Walt had gone down the side of the room toward the stage. I hurried after him and caught up with him just as he reached a door at one side of the stage. I followed Walt through the door. It was dark, and I found myself standing in the wing of the stage. I could see the small band at the back of the stage and the blond lady dancing toward the front. Standing behind the curtain, watching the dance, was Fionna Rosé. She was wearing a very transparent robe and apparently nothing else. As Walt walked past, she turned.

"Hi, Walt," she said. When she turned, I noticed that the robe was not closed in front. I also noticed that she was wearing a glittery silver g-string.

"Hi, Corky," she said. "Walt and Corky," she giggled. "What are you guys doing here?"

"I've got to see Aaron," Walt answered. "Wait for me here, Ed." He walked toward the back.

I was embarrassed. Standing next to an almost naked lady while watching another one on stage was a little much for me. In order to avoid looking directly at Fionna, I kept my eyes on the dancer on the stage. On closer inspection I noticed that she was wearing flesh-colored mesh panties and a brassiere of the same material.

"Isn't she wonderful?" said Fionna in a dreamy, far away voice. "That's Norma Sales, a real artiste. I watch her every chance I get. I just hope someday I can be half as good as she is."

I thought the woman was kind of clumsy for a dancer. If Fionna thought she was good, I had to wonder at what her act would be like. Just then, a man in a baggy coat and polka-dot pants walked up to where Fionna and I were standing. There was a girl with him. She was one of the most beautiful young women I had ever seen. She was wearing a tight, skimpy nurse's uniform.

The man spoke to Fionna. "How you doing tonight, Mitz?"

Fionna turned. "Hi Cranny. Ed, I would like you to meet Cranston Blues. Cranny is a comedian and this is Ginny Spruce, she helps him in this skit. She's also a dancer, but you missed her. She opened the show. This is Ed McCorkel, he's a friend of mine from Walt's place."

Cranny nodded. Ginny said hello and told him that it was nice to meet him. Just then, Walt came back to where the little group was standing. They all knew each other and said their hellos. Ginny gave Walt a little kiss on the cheek. Walt turned to me. "Aaron is about to go on stage. I'll catch him when he comes off again.

Just then the music ended and Norma Sales came off the stage to a smattering of applause. It wasn't actually applause—the management of the Cat and the Fiddle supplied all the customers with little sticks with wooden balls on one end. They were called knockers, and the audience beat them on the tables instead of applauding. It sounded like a forest full of woodpeckers.

Norma grabbed a robe from a hanger as she came off. "Hi, Walt," she said, and then to Fionna, "You better go get into your costume, honey," and headed to the back.

"Excuse me Ed, I have to go back and put on some clothes. Stay here and watch the show. I'm on right after Ginny and Cran." She followed Miss Sales to the back.

A little man in an ill-fitting tuxedo with a plaid cummerbund walked on stage then, carrying a violin.

"How about that, folks, Norma Sales! Isn't she a cutie?" He played a few bars of a song on the violin. Everybody laughed. "Listen up out there, you better start ordering more drinks. My sister will be here in a few minutes and the only music that makes her happy is the ringing of the cash register. She can be very unpleasant when she is unhappy."

Everybody laughed. He played a few more bars on the violin. "Take my sister . . . Please, take my sister!" Laughter. More violin. More laughter. "But seriously, folks, the Cat and the Fiddle, Cincinnati's finest nightclub, is proud to present . . . America's favorite funny man, Cranston Blues, with his lovely assistant, Miss Ginny Spruce!"

There was another smattering of knocker noise. Walt left again. On stage, the comedian and Ginny went through a very physical skit full of double entendres and mild profanity. Blues took several prat falls, Ginny's breasts fell out of her dress a couple of times.

The audience apparently found the skit hilarious. I thought it was mildly amusing.

The pair on stage came to the end of their act. The knockers sounded. They took several bows and Blues fell again as they dashed off the stage.

"That was good," I said as they went past.

"Thanks," Ginny called to me. "Nice to have met you."

The little man in the plaid cummerbund was back on stage. He must have been Aaron Coffaro, the person Walt had come to see. He told a few more jokes and played his violin, badly. Finally he introduced Fionna Rosé.

The lights dimmed, a rose-colored spotlight came up, and there she was standing center stage, dressed in a full-length red evening gown with long red gloves and a huge feathered hat. She began her dance, moving sensually back and forth across the stage. Slowly she peeled off one glove and then the other. She danced slower and shrugged out of her long dress.

She stood in the middle of the stage in a strapless short garment that looked to me like a red bathing suit. She had on long black stockings and red shoes. The spotlight dimmed to a more lavender color and the music became faster. She danced faster and faster, threw off her shoes, and went through a series of acrobatic moves.

Somehow, and I wasn't quite sure how, the red garment came off. She was again standing in the middle of the stage, clad only in a tiny black brassiere, a black garter belt, stockings, and the big hat. The spot dimmed a little more and the band swung into a slower tempo. She began to move languorously, sliding her hands up and down her body. She slid to the floor, put her legs in the air, and slowly peeled off one stocking. She threw it over her head. She took the other stocking off, then moved to the side of the stage where I was standing. She tossed me the stocking.

She continued to glide around the stage, and once again without me noticing how she did it, removed the garter belt and brassiere. Again she was center stage but with her back to the audience. The tempo of the music picked up, she grabbed her hat from her head, and then she began to dance, whirling round and round, using the hat strategically to hide certain parts of her anatomy. The music stopped abruptly. Fionna was standing on a little platform, the band played a subtle fanfare, and she flung the hat over her head and threw her arms out. She looked to be completely naked. Knocker noise and applause exploded from the audience. Fionna bowed and the lights went out. She ran off the stage and almost into me. She gave me a little kiss and said, "Well, what did you think?"

I had never seen an act like hers before. I had also never been kissed by a nearly naked girl before. I was nonplussed. Before I could reply, she had skipped past me and run to her dressing room.

Her act had been the last one of the show. The lights came up a little and the band was playing dance music. A few couples were already on the dance floor.

I was still stunned by Fionna's performance. I just stood behind the curtain and stared out over the dancers. Suddenly I was jolted from my reverie. Seated at one of the tables in the club were Armbruster, Tune, and Kruger. They were in earnest conversation with another man. I thought the fourth man looked familiar but couldn't place him. Then it dawned on me. The man looked like Grossman Herzog. It must be his brother Talbert, the bilge inspector.

I darted through the stage door and walked up to the table where the foursome was seated. "Birds of a feather," I said. I realized this was an inane remark, but what do you say to Nazi spies in a nightclub in Cincinnati, Ohio? "You must be Talbert Herzog," I continued, nodding at the man I hadn't met before.

Franchot jumped to his feet, knocking over his chair. I quickly put my hand in my coat pocket and said, "Easy, Frankie boy, you too, Kruger. This time I do have my gat and it's pointed right at your stomach."

The bluff worked, Tune picked up his chair and sat down. Kruger put his hands on the table. The maitre d' came over. "Is anything wrong, gentlemen?"

"A little accident, no one is hurt. Would you bring our friend here a chair?" Armbruster said smoothly.

A chair was brought and I sat. "May I ask the meaning of this intrusion, sir?" asked Armbruster.

"Now I'm gonna kill you no matter what," Kruger whispered.

"How did he know who I am? He's never seen me before," said Talbert.

"Calm down, Kruger, Talbert, I will take care of this."

"I repeat, Mr. McCorkel, why are you bothering us?"

"I didn't mean to bother you, Mr. Armbruster," I answered. "I just wanted to meet Mr. Herzog. I've met his brother, and after all, we are all interested in Moby Trick."

Herzog blanched. "What's going on here, how does he know anything about Moby Trick?"

"Be quiet, you fool," Armbruster interrupted, "he knows nothing."

"I am afraid, Mr. McCorkel, that this is a private party, sir. I would appreciate it if you would leave."

"Sure, Fatman." I was getting pretty cocky, trying to talk like the detectives I had seen in the movies. "Sure, I'm on my way."

I started toward the stage door when Walt came through it carrying two cardboard boxes. I took one of them again. "What's this?" I asked.

"Two cases of liquor," Walt replied. "It's all Aaron could let me have. It'll do." We headed out of the nightclub.

Angie opened the front door for us. "You guys need any help with them?" he asked.

"We can make it, Angie, thanks," said Walt.

We walked back the alley to where the car was parked. Walt opened the trunk and loaded in the case he was carrying. I was standing at the back of the car holding the other box.

"You gonna have a hard time gettin' your gat wit dat box in your hands, McCorkel," came a voice from behind him. "You're a dead man."

I turned and saw Kruger standing in the alley. He was holding a gun pointed at me. Then a figure dressed all in black, wearing a black hat pulled low over his eyes, who came up behind Kruger.

"Drop the gun," the figure in black ordered. Kruger spun around. A shot rang out. Kruger dropped. The mysterious stranger stepped back into the dark alley and disappeared.

"Is he dead?" asked Walt

I knelt down and felt for a pulse. "I don't think he's dead but he ain't moving."

"What's going on here?" Walt asked. "Is this tied up with Henry's death?"

"I honestly don't know—on both counts."

"Who was that guy?"

"Him," I said, pointing at the figure on the ground. "That's Kruger."

"Who's Kruger?" asked Walt.

"A friend of Armbruster's," I replied.

"Who is—no, never mind. But who was the guy in black?"

"I don't know for sure who he was. We better get out of here."

"I only got a glimpse of him, but that little guy in black sure looked familiar," said Walt.

"I really think we should get out of here. Now."

"Yeah," Walt answered, "but are we just going to leave him lying there?"

"He was going to kill me, I'm sure not going to give him first aid. Let's just get going while the getting's good. Somebody else might try to shoot me."

We jumped into the car and backed out of the alley. We went up Fifth to Race, turned on to Fourth, and headed home. Once again we went so fast that all I could think about was holding on. In no time, we were pulling into Walt's drive. The light from the headlamps illuminated something that looked alarmingly like a body on the steps leading to his front door.

It was a little fellow wearing a sailor suit, lying across the steps. I was beginning to think I couldn't go anywhere without running into a body.

"It's Ozzie," said Walt. He shook him. "It's okay, he's not dead. Ozzie, what are you doing here?"

The little sailor rubbed his eyes. "Gee Walt, I just finished boot camp and they gave me a leave before I ship out. I hitchhiked home and when I got there everybody was asleep and I couldn't wake them. So I came over here to see if I could sleep here, but I couldn't wake up anybody here, either, so I just sat down on the steps and I guess I fell asleep."

Ozzie lived behind Walt's house on Relleum Avenue. Walt had known him all his life. He had been known to sleep on Walt's couch on other occasions, too. "Well, come on then, but try to be quiet."

"Wait a minute, Walt," I said. "You'll wake up everybody in the house trying to get him settled. He can stay on my couch tonight. There isn't anyone to be disturbed at my place."

"Okay, Ed, that's a good idea. Ozzie, go with Corky here. He'll take care of you tonight and I'll see you in the morning. Thanks, Ed. Good night."

"Good night, Walt." Ozzie and I walked up the street toward the corner. It had been another long night. Hell, it had been a long day, too.

CHAPTER 14

I AWOKE WITH A START. THE ALARM HADN'T GONE OFF. What woke me? There, there it was again, a noise somewhere in the apartment. It sounded like it came from the kitchen. Maybe the Nazis were still trying to do me in. There it was again . . . I recognized the sound now. It was my coffeepot perking.

Then I remembered that I had brought home the little sailor, Ovie or Ollie. No, Ozzie, it was Ozzie, I had brought him home with me last night. I got out of bed, grabbed my old robe, and walked into the kitchen. The little man was sitting in at the kitchen table, staring out of the window.

"Gosh, I hope I didn't wake you," the sailor said when he saw me. "In boot camp we had to get up every morning at five-thirty. I guess it's become a habit."

I pushed back my hair and looked at the clock. It was a little before six. "That's okay, I wanted to get up early. This is going to be a busy day."

"What's going on today?" Ozzie wanted to know.

"Henry Holthaus gets buried today."

"Gee, is he dead?" The sailor saw the funny look on my face. "I didn't mean that. I meant, I didn't know that old Hank had died. How'd it happen?"

"Somebody shot him." I went on to give Ozzie a very short version of what had happened, omitting my part in the investigation.

"Golly, sounds really exciting. I think I'll hang around for the funeral. If I go home first they'll want me to stay at the house. I'll see them later."

The coffeepot had stopped perking, so I went to the cupboard and got out two cups. I handed one to Ozzie and said, "There's milk in the ice box and the sugar is on the table. I don't have anything to eat in the house. I usually walk over to the bakery and get something."

"That sounds great. I'm dressed, I'll run over and get us something. Anything special for you?"

"Whatever you get will be all right with me. Let me give you some money."

"That's okay, it's on me," the sailor said as he went out the door.

While Ozzie was gone, I started getting cleaned up. I made my bed and got out my good grey suit. It seemed like the thing to wear to a funeral. I had just gone in the bathroom to shave when I heard Ozzie's voice.

"Yoo hoo, I'm back. I got one of them cheesecakes with the bugs in it." The bakery made a cheese breakfast cake with raisins in it, but for some reason everybody on the corner called the raisins bugs.

"I'll be right out," I called. I was dressed in the grey suit pants and a white shirt when I came back to the kitchen. Ozzie had very carefully cut the cheesecake right down the middle and had already eaten his half of it.

"Boy, them things cost a quarter now. They was only a dime when I left."

I reached in my pocket. "Here, let me pay for it."

"Heck no," said Ozzie, "I was just surprised that they went up so much."

"It's the war."

"Yeah, I guess. Oh, I forgot to tell you, there's a beer truck over there trying to get in the Ideal."

"Walt had a big night last night. He sold out of beer. If he isn't there to let them in, I'd better call him." We both looked out the window and saw that Walt had just arrived at the café and was letting the driver in the door.

"As soon as I finish dressing, I'm going over there and see if he needs any help."

"If you don't mind," Ozzie said, "I think I'll go over now. I didn't get much of a chance to talk to Walt Thanks a lot for putting me up last night." Ozzie threw his bag over his shoulder and went out the door.

I ate another piece of cheesecake and finished my coffee. Then I went to the bedroom, picked out a somber necktie, tied it around my neck, slipped on my suit coat, and headed for the door.

Walt and Ozzie were at the end of the bar talking when I walked in the Ideal. There wasn't anyone else there. It was only twenty minutes to seven.

"The calm before the storm," said Walt. "I'll bet Brownie is the first one in this morning.

"I got a buck that says it will be Billy Boy," I challenged.

"Well, my buck says that the first one will be . . ." Ozzie was interrupted by the Prince storming through the front door. "That's who I was gonna say!"

Walt and I both laughed. We each threw him a dollar. The Prince was very agitated. "You must, all of you, listen to me. I have seen strange and wondrous things."

"You always see strange and wonderful things. What's new?" asked Walt.

"Last night I journeyed on the river," the Prince began his tale. "My friend, Mr. Graham, provided me with a complimentary ticket for an excursion on his wonderful steamboat. I took advantage of his hospitality and joined the throng of passengers. The boat was rather crowded, and this served to make me nervous. Soon an orchestra began to play loud and raucous music and the passengers commenced dancing, and this served to increase my anxiety."

"I went to the upper deck to seek seclusion. Here I found many young people doing unspeakable things. I went down to the lowest deck and to the rear of the boat. There I found a coil of rope that served me as a seat, far from the maddening crowd. I sat there for quite some time, watching the river and the phosphorescent wake of the paddlewheel. Suddenly, about a quarter of a mile to the rear of the boat, I saw a huge hump arise. It was a sea monster of gargantuan dimensions. There was one eye, right in the middle of its forehead. It stared at me for the longest time, and then sank back into the river. My heart was in my mouth. I did not know what to do. I was sure it would rise again and devour the entire steamboat. I knew that I should go and warn the captain, but I was too frightened to move. I scrunched down in my coil of rope and waited for the inevitable. I must have fallen asleep, because the next thing I remember is arriving back at the dock. The monster had not attacked."

"That's a great story, Prince," said Walt. "Maybe the monster was put there by those Japanese guys in the balloon that you saw the other night."

"This guy is really weird," added Ozzie.

While the Prince was telling his story, Walt had given him a Vichy. He took it to a table and sat there morosely drinking it. I watched him from the vantage point at the bar. Another one of those bells had gone off my head while the Prince told his strange tale. I walked over to the table where the Prince sat. "Can you describe the monster again for me?" I asked.

"It was big." The Prince was still agitated. "It was big and black and ugly. It looked like an island rising up out of the river. I couldn't see its mouth, but it had one eye and that eye glowed."

"Would you say it glowed like an automobile headlight?" I asked him.

"Yes, it glowed just like the headlight of an automobile. It was fearsome." I smiled to myself. Another piece of the puzzle had just dropped into place.

Brownie and Billy Boy walked in together. Brownie was wearing a shiny blue suit, and the pants didn't quite match the coat. Billy Boy was attired in his usual white polo shirt and grey work pants. Either because of the nip in the air or the solemnness of the occasion, he had added a black vest.

"Is everybody going to the graveyard?" Billy asked. "Jake's taking his wife, so I can't go with him." Billy Boy had a lost look. "He don't like his wife and me together. I think he's afraid I'll let it slip that he drinks."

Charlie walked in, dressed in a brown suit and visibly tense. He walked behind the bar, poured himself a big shot, and drank it down. "I haven't been in a church since Lil got married." Lil was his youngest daughter. "I shoulda said no."

"Too late now," said Walt, "What time do you have to be over there?"

"Twenty to nine." Charlie had been asked to be a pallbearer. He had accepted, but now he was getting cold feet. "Elmer Huber is gonna be one, too. He's supposed to meet me here."

Huber was a retired policeman. He lived on Coronado and generally stopped in the Ideal in the early evening for a couple of beers and to "float his jug," which meant he brought a gallon jug in and got it filled with draft beer, then took the jug of beer home to drink. Actually, most of the floaters would only ask for a half gallon, because Walt and Charlie always gave a good measure. Some would come in three or four times a night for "just a half."

At precisely eight-thirty, Huber came in the door. He looked just as nervous as Charlie. "Gimme a double," he said to Walt.

"Me too," echoed Charlie.

Walt laughed and said, "Old Hank's going to feel right at home with you guys weaving up the aisle with the coffin."

They ignored him and drank their drinks. "Who else is on this committee?" asked Elmer.

"I don't know," answered Charlie. "You, me, and Frank Dodd, that's all I know,"

"Well, where is Frank? We ought to get going."

"He never said to wait for him. I guess we'll meet him at the church. Give us each a single, son, then we'll get out of here."

The bar was starting to fill up. Husbands were dropping their wives off at St. Clarisa's, then either parking in the lot at the Pay-n-Takit or on the street. Then most of the men were coming into the Ideal instead of the church.

Frank Dodd stuck his head in the door. "Let's go, you guys, we're going to be late . . . Hi, Walt. Are they okay?"

"They can make it, but I'm glad you stopped by. Another five minutes and I would have needed a wheelbarrow to get them there."

The three pallbearers left, just as St. Clarisa's bells started tolling to announce the beginning of the funeral mass.

"Gee, they sure looked nice," said Billy Boy.

"Everybody on the corner looks nice today," I said. "It's a pity that it takes a funeral to get them to clean up."

Peter Horn came through the door. "Hello, fellow bereaved. I see we are tipping the mourning cup. Pretty soon someone will break out in a plaintive lament."

He had no more than spoken when a high tenor voice was heard. "Oh, Danny boy . . ."

"Knock it off or you're outta here!" yelled Walt. The voice stilled in midnote.

Peter Horn, husband of Betty, was a big jovial man, a fireman. He had dropped Betty off at St. Clarisa's, and walked up to join the men at the bar. "Gimme a beer," he said. "You still wanna ride to the graveyard with us, Ed?"

"Yeah, I'd like to go. Would it be all right if Ozzie came with us?"

Peter spotted the little sailor. "Why, you little peckerwood, did the Navy throw you out already?"

"Naw, I'm home on leave. I'll be shipping out as soon as I get back. Can't tell you where I'm going, you know, loose lips sink ships. Actually I don't know where I'm going. Look, is it okay if I ride with you?"

"Sure Oz, Betty has always had a crush on you. She'd never forgive me if I didn't bring you along."

Just then Officer Joe Newmann stuck his head in the door. "You guys better get a move on. I'm going up to line up the cars. Mass is about over and I don't want anybody holding things up." He disappeared out the door.

Everybody in the bar finished off their drinks, several got one last shot, and they all headed out the door. Ozzie, Ed, Billy Boy, Peter Horn, Walt, and I were the only ones left in the café.

"I'm going to run over and make sure everything is all right in the office," I said as I ran out the door.

"You want to come with us?" Peter asked Billy Boy.

"Naw, I done did my duty," Billy Boy replied.

I checked in with Susan, thinking about how cute she looked this morning. I made up my mind that today was the day I would talk to her about the partnership. I ducked back across the street just in time to meet Peter and Ozzie coming out of the bar. The bells were ringing slowly and mournfully, signaling the end of the funeral.

"I'm up in the Pay-n-Takit lot," said Peter.

They walked up there and found Betty already seated in the car.

"Let's go, or we're going to be late," she said, "Hi fellas . . . why, Ozzie, when did you get home?"

Ozzie and I climbed into the back seat. "'Lo, Mizz Horn," Ozzie answered. "I just got in last night, got a leave before I ship out."

"You have to come over for supper before you go back."

"Yes 'em," he answered.

"Hey Betty, how was the service?" I asked as we headed out of the parking lot.

"Oh, Ed, it was beautiful. The church was just full of flowers, carnations . . ."

"Probably what the growers didn't sell yesterday," interrupted Peter.

"Shut up, Peter," she continued, "the church was beautiful and the whole choir was singing. It was impressive. It wouldn't have hurt any of you to have been there."

Peter had driven over to the front of the church where Newmann was trying to line up the cars. He waved them in behind Hugo Getz and his wife. They could just see the top of Brownie's head over the back seat, and they could see the Prince's hands going a mile a minute.

"Looks like the Prince has a good story to tell. I bet Mrs. Getz is pleased."

Newmann had things pretty well organized. All the stragglers were in line. Suddenly there was the roar of an engine, and Chiggerbox came riding to the front of the procession on his motorcycle.

"Oh-oh, Chiggerbox is leading this parade. We could end up in the river."

CHAPTER 15

The procession started off with Chiggerbox in the lead. He had his siren blaring. He led the cars down Overlook to West Eighth and eventually into the drive of the cemetery. There were no mishaps in the procession until Chiggerbox ran full tilt into the cemetery gate. Apparently no one had opened it, and when he came up against it, Chiggerbox left the motorcycle abruptly and flew into the closed gate. He didn't appear to be hurt, but his head was stuck between two bars. Two of the cemetery's maintenance men rushed over and got the motorcycle out of the way. Then they pushed open the gate, with Chiggerbox still attached. The cavalcade proceeded through to the grave site.

Everyone got their cars parked and a large crowd was standing at the back of the hearse when the pallbearers slid the coffin out. A sudden hush fell over the crowd. There, lying on top of the casket, was a single green carnation.

The crowd started whispering to each other until it sounded like a hive of bees. Frank Dodd reached up and brushed the flower from the coffin. The pallbearers picked up the casket and the funeral director led them to a hole in the ground. They placed the box on a little stand alongside the hole.

The six pallbearers stepped back. I managed to get between Charlie and Frank Dodd.

"How did the flower get on the coffin?" I asked.

"How the hell should I know?" growled Charlie.

"I don't know either," said Frank. "It wasn't there when we slid the box in at the church."

I backed out of the crowd a little, and standing a little to one side of the mob, I noticed Arnold Mix and about twenty-five people dressed in the flowered robes that the Mixites favored. Almost as soon as I saw them, the Mixites started toward the grave site. They pushed through the crowd, and one by one they each deposited a carnation on the casket, then walked back off to the side. None of the carnations were green.

Father O'Toole appeared at the head of the coffin. He was carrying a black book and had two children with him. The children were wearing long black dresses, as was the priest. The children had on white frilly aprons, the priest did not. He did have a narrow purple scarf around his neck, though. One of the children was carrying what looked like a wine bucket and the other had a cross on a long stick.

The priest took something from the wine bucket and started waving it at the coffin. He inadvertently struck one of the boys on the forehead, and the boy in turn dropped the cross. The boy with the bucket tried to catch the cross, but he slipped on the fresh earth by the grave and started to fall into the hole. He pitched the wine bucket in order to save himself, and managed to keep from falling into the hole, but he did fall on the ground. When he got back up, he had mud all over his white apron. The wine bucket had flown toward the Mixites, spraying them with whatever liquid had been in it. The Mixites screamed, crossed their index fingers over their heads, and ran off in a bunch.

As soon as order was restored, the priest went on with the ceremony, but it was anticlimactic. People began to drift away. The priest said his last amens and everyone left, except the two maintenance men, who stayed to help Henry into his final resting place.

As we drove out of the cemetery, I noticed that Chiggerbox was no longer attached to the gate.

The Horns dropped Ozzie and me in front of the Ideal. The bar was very crowded now. Apparently everyone had come back from the cemetery and stopped in to discuss the bizarre events. I had already had enough for one morning. Morning! It was after eleven already.

I said goodbye to Ozzie and walked over to the office. Susan looked up as he walked in. "How did it go? The funeral, I mean."

"It went strangely," I said. I told her about Chiggerbox's mishap. "And then," I continued, "they pulled the coffin out of the hearse and there was one green carnation lying on it."

"But how'd it get there?" asked Susan.

"Nobody seems to know, but I've got a hunch that I want to check out."

I told her about the rest of the rites at the graveyard, including the Mixites putting more carnations on the coffin and the misadventures of the little boys and the priest, and finally about the hasty departure of the Mixites.

"Gosh, I wish I'd gone. It sounds like more fun than Friday night at the Overlook." The Overlook was the local movie theater. On Friday nights they always showed comedies.

"You're right, the whole thing was like a Three Stooges routine. If you want to go to lunch, I'll be here for a while."

"I don't think I'll go to lunch today," Susan said.

"I could go over to Wimpie's and get some hamburgers if you'd like me to."

"That sounds like a good idea, but what about all the kids?"

"It's early, so maybe I can beat 'em."

"Then I'd like two, no onions, and a bottle of Coke. Wait a minute, I'll get some money." She went for her purse.

"That's okay, I guess I can afford to buy my girl some hamburgers." As soon as it was out of my mouth I nearly bit my tongue. Why would I call her "my girl?" I darted out the door. Maybe she didn't notice.

(She noticed all right, her heart leaped to her throat. She thought she was going to throw up. She sat at her desk and took deep breaths and the nausea passed. What did he mean, "my girl?" As soon as she thought about it, the nausea returned, and she had to take more deep breaths.)

I walked slowly up to Glenway. "Why did I say that?" I thought. "I know she noticed, I could tell by the look in her eye. I'll hit her with the partnership thing as soon as I get back. That☐ will get her mind off what I said."

I got to Wimpie's, and the school kids hadn't come in yet. I chatted with George Sarafan, the owner, and picked up four hamburgers and two Cokes. I walked back to the office. Susan looked at me a little oddly when I came in.

She said she would get some glasses and went back to the restroom. I reached into the desk drawer and got a bottle opener. "As soon as she comes back I'm going to ask her to be a partner," I told myself. I dropped the opener, and it bounced under the desk. I got down on my knees to find it.

Susan walked back into the room. I looked up, still on my knees, and said, "Susan, I have a proposal . . ." But before I could finish, Susan had fainted.

I crawled over to her, called her name several times, and slapped her gently. Finally I got up and went to the restroom. I got a glass of water and splashed some on her face.

"Ohhhh, oh my." Susan was coming around. "Oh my goodness!" She jumped up and ran back to the restroom.

I could hear her being sick. It couldn't have been the hamburgers, they were still in the bag. Susan came out wiping her face with a towel.

"Are you all right?"

"I'm fine, darling," she came over and hugged me. "I'm just delirious with happiness. I never thought you would get around to it. I'm going home now, to pull myself together. This has been a shock. Of course I'll marry you! I've been in love with you since I started working here. You've made me so happy! I'm going home to think about this and talk to mother."

"But, but I . . ." I wasn't at all sure what had just happened. "I, ah, we need to . . ."

"Yes dear, we must talk, and make plans, but oh, I'm so excited. We'll talk all about it tomorrow. Oh darling, I'm so happy!" She kissed me and sailed out the door.

I sat down in Susan's office chair. I said, out loud, "What the hell just happened here?" I was still dazed. "She thinks I was going to ask her to marry me. Actually she thinks I did ask her to marry me. How could she have such an idea? I can't marry her, why, it's ridiculous. How could she think . . . just the idea is . . ." The events of the last few minutes just kept going round and round in my head.

I took one of the Cokes and opened it. The hamburgers were cold greasy lumps, beyond eating. The thoughts in my head continued to whirl: "The very idea . . . well, I guess it's not all that bad of an idea, really. She is awful cute and I wouldn't have to work up the nerve to ask her, I already did that . . . No, I didn't! I was going to ask her to be my business partner . . . . she jumped to conclusions! Getting married, that's about the same as taking on a partner . . . No it's not! She already said yes, so I wouldn't have to worry about her rejecting me . . . but marriage, that's a whole different thing . . . she is cute . . . and I wouldn't have to change the sign to McCorkel and Stienle . . . enough already! I'll get this all straightened out tomorrow."

I got up, poured the Coke in the sink, then went out, locking the front door. I went over to the Ideal to get a real drink. By the time I got there I was pleased that Susan had misunderstood me. I was starting to like the idea of getting married.

"Gimme a Seagram's and ginger ale," I called to Walt.

"What's the occasion? I don't ever remember you having a drink this early in the day."

I looked at the clock, and was surprised to see that it was only a quarter past noon. I raised my glass in a toast to Walt, "I think I'm getting married."

"Son of a gun." Walt pushed my money back at me. "Then this one's on me."

(He didn't have to ask who Ed planned to marry. Everyone except Ed had noticed how Susan felt about him for a long time.)

"I know you're kind of excited," Walt continued. "But don't forget we're going for a plane ride this afternoon. Muffin was in earlier and everything is all set, except you owe them a hundred bucks."

"Holy cow, the race completely slipped my mind." I took a sip of his drink and headed towards the door. "I'm going over to the bank and get the money."

I was back from the bank, just across street, in under five minutes. When I walked in, I handed Walt the money and he made me a fresh drink and said, "I threw the other one out, this one is on the house, too. Did I say congratulations?"

"Thank you." I sipped the drink, becoming more and more pleased with what had happened. Then I looked in the mirror in the back bar and saw Al Heller sitting at a table. My thoughts came crashing back to the murder I was investigating. I went over to Al's table.

"Why did you do it, Al?"

"What are you talking about? Why'd I do what?" replied Heller with a look of complete innocence on his face.

"Don't play games with me, I know it was you that put the green carnation on the coffin."

"You can't prove it was me."

"Don't be stupid, Al. Of course it was you. You got the market cornered on green carnations. If someone else had done it that would mean that they had the secret too, and you would have been very upset. I saw you just after the incident and you didn't look upset. I know you did it, I just want to know why."

"Aw, it was just supposed to be a little joke. I knew most of the other growers would be at the funeral, so I thought it would be the perfect place to show off my green carnation. I knew they would all be as green as the flower—with envy. I gave the driver of the hearse a buck to slip it on the coffin as he was driving. I just wanted a little free publicity. I thought I could introduce the new flower in a big way. I think I got everybody's attention, don't you?"

"You got everybody's attention, all right. Do me a favor, will you? Keep your green carnations under wraps for a while. Don't ask me why, but I think two Nazi spies are after your secret. They are unscrupulous men, and you could really be in danger."

"Come on Ed, what would Hitler do with green carnations?"

"I told you, I don't know why. Just watch your step."

"Hey, Ed," called Oats Weber, the mailman. "I been carrying around this special delivery letter for you since yesterday. Here, sign for it." I signed, and Otis handed me a small white envelope.

I tore open the envelope. There was one piece of paper in it, and it bore the letterhead of the Queen City Barge Construction Company. The message was written boldly in pencil:

For more information call SYcamore 1951.

I went straight to the phone, put in a nickel, and dialed the number. It rang six times before someone picked up, and a voice said, "Who's calling, please?"

"My name is Ed McCorkel, to whom am I speaking?" The voice on the other end of the line said, "Ah yes, Mr. McCorkel, I have been expecting your call."

"Who is this?" I demanded. The voice ignored his question. "I may have some information that would be helpful to you. May I suggest that we meet this afternoon?"

"I want to know who you are," I persisted.

"If you wish to meet with me," the voice continued, "come to the offices of the Queen City Barge Construction Company by 1:30. It is located in the Glenn Building on Seventh Street. Take the elevator to the sixth floor. You will see a young lady seated at a desk. Give her your name and she will direct you to me, and please, Mr. McCorkel—Come alone."

"Just one minute, if you think . . . Uh." I realized I was talking to a dead phone. I hung up at my end. I went back to the bar where I had left my drink. I had a lot to think about. Green carnations, Nazi spies, Henry's death, river monsters, a mysterious priest, G-men pretending to be mailmen, and on and on. And now this thing with Susan. Well, actually, this was more than just a thing with Susan, she expected to marry me.

I knew I had to go to the Queen City Barge Construction Company. It could be a trap, but I had to go. But I was supposed to fly with Walt.

"Hey Walt, something really important has come up. I can't go with you this afternoon."

"I think you're too flustered anyway, so I was thinking about getting Ozzie to take your place. We'll have to cut him in on the action, but that's okay. Do what you have to do."

"Thanks, Walt. Did you happen to read this morning's paper? Was there anything about Kruger getting shot last night?"

"I read it and I looked, very carefully, to see if there was anything about the shooting. There wasn't. Maybe it didn't make the deadline. You ought to check one of the afternoon papers."

"I will, and I'm off. I hope everything works out with the race this afternoon. Good luck."

"Good luck to you too, whatever you are going to do. Try not to get shot." Walt called to my back as I headed out the door.

I ran up to the corner and bought a Times Star. Luckily, a streetcar came right away.

I hadn't had a chance to read the paper this morning, what with Ozzie and the funeral and everything else that had been going on. Walt said that he had seen nothing about Kruger but there might be something in this later paper.

The front page was all war news. The Americans had bombed Kiska Island and dealt the Japanese a devastating blow. Six Jap aircraft had been shot out of the sky. The airfield had been virtually destroyed and not a single American aircraft had been lost, though the American aircraft carrier Yorktown had been officially listed as lost. And the Russians had driven the Germans out of Stalingrad.

I looked through the rest of the paper. There was nothing about the shooting. You would think if there was a shooting in downtown somebody would have noticed it.

One other article did catch my attention, though. Apparently a man had been apprehended running down Third Street last night, carrying a broken fishing pole and screaming, "Save me, Lord, and I'll never molest your creatures again!" The police assumed he was drunk and took him to the station. But they could detect no alcohol in his system or about his person, so they listened to his preposterous story. The man said he had been fishing under the Central Bridge over the Ohio. His bobber went under, so he pulled on the rod. The rod broke and the biggest catfish he ever saw, he said it was bigger than a house, rose up out of the river. It was an ugly thing, only had one eye and it stared at him with that one malevolent eye. Malevolent was the reporter's word, not the fisherman's. The man was running from the horrid fish when the police caught up with him. The police sent the fisherman to Longview Asylum for observation.

Bells were tinkling all over the inside of my mind, but I was trying to give the poor thing a rest, so I went on reading the paper. On the same page, down in the lower corner, there was an article about the gathering of the Church of Tom Mix, His Older Brother Jesus Christ, and Lesser Saints. It told about how the religion had begun and how, in a little over a year, its membership had increased fourfold. The article said that the mass baptism Arnold had told him about was planned for this coming Sunday. The Mixites didn't call it baptism, though; they referred to it as a Spiritual Launching, and it was to take place in the river, near the Anderson Ferry landing, on the Ohio side.

It seemed like everything in the paper was pointed at keeping my mind on my problems. I sighed folded up the paper and lay it on the seat. I looked up and noticed that the car was passing the Cat and the Fiddle. I thought about last night, was it just last night? I remembered Fiona standing next to him in the transparent and her beautiful and sensual dance.

"Stop that," I said to myself. "That's not the way an almost married man should think." Suddenly there was an empty feeling in the pit of my stomach and I had arrived at my stop.

I stepped down from the streetcar and walked two blocks up to Seventh and over a block and a half to the Glenn Building. I looked at the directory in the lobby. Sure enough, the offices of the Queen City Barge Construction Company were on the sixth floor.

I RANG FOR AN ELEVATOR. WHEN IT ARRIVED, I GOT ON AND told the operator that I wanted the sixth floor. The doors opened and the operator said, "Watch your step." Too late. The elevator had stopped about two inches short of the sixth floor. I stumbled into the offices of the Queen City Barge Construction Company and almost fell over the receptionist's desk.

A pretty girl in a blue sweater was seated behind the desk. "Are you alright? That jerk does that all the time. He thinks he's funny. He'd have been fired before now if it wasn't so hard to get help, the war you know."

I straightened myself out, pulled my coat down and said, "I'm okay. I'm also Ed McCorkel, and I think I have an appointment to see someone. I don't know who."

"Yes, Mr. McCorkel, you're expected. Please wait a moment while I announce you."

She walked down a hallway, knocked lightly on one of the doors, and opened the door to stick her head into the room. She backed out, closing the door, and came back to where I was standing.

"Please come this way," she said as she led him down the hall. "May I take your paper?" she asked.

"Sure." I handed her the newspaper.

"Here we are." She opened the door for me. I walked into a large room. There were big framed pictures of boats, tugboats, I thought, hanging all over the room. At the far end was a very large desk. A man was sitting behind the desk holding a pair of glasses in his hand. I recognized him immediately. I'd seen his picture in the paper many times.

"Good afternoon, Mr. McCorkel, so good of you to come." He put the glasses on. It was Lowell Mosley, a noted Cincinnati industrialist and inventor.

"Good afternoon, Mr. Mosley. I knew you were involved with radio and cars and airplanes, but I didn't know you had anything to do with boats, or should I say, barges."

"Ah, Mr. McCorkel, it's this war, this damned war. It's turning all our lives topsy-turvy."

My mind started whirling. If Mosley was in on this, it was bigger than I originally thought. How could he be involved in Henry's murder? Was Mosley the mastermind behind Moby Trick?

"Don't think so much, Mr. McCorkel," said Mosley. "You don't have to think so much, because I'm going to explain it all to you, as soon as we get some coffee. You will have a cup—black, isn't it?"

"Yeah, black," I replied. To myself I thought, how the hell did he know I drink it black?

Mosley pushed a button on a little box and asked for two black coffees. He turned back to me. "I know a lot more about you than how you drink your coffee. I know that you are an insurance agent and only an amateur private investigator. I believe this is your first case. I know that you have lived in Price Hill all your life. You graduated from Hughes High School and took some business courses at night at the University. You started working for Venerable Insurance in 1923, when you were 20 years old. Six years later, you became an independent agent, opened an office in the Covedale Building, and you eventually hired a young secretary named Susan Stienle. Who, basically, runs your business. Congratulations, by the way, on your recent engagement.

"I know that both your parents were killed in a train accident in 1935 and that the settlement from the railroad company allowed you to keep your business afloat during our recent depressing times. You are thrifty, and your secretary, I should say fiancée, has a good business head. So you are—not rich—but financially secure. Shall I go on?"

I was stupefied. "How do you know so much about me?"

"Oh, I know much more. For instance, you are not much of a drinker, and when you do drink, it is Seagram's and ginger ale. Pfah, that is probably why you are not much of a drinker."

"I guess you know the color of my bedroom slippers . . ."

"Grey, fuzzy, right sole almost worn through."

Just then there was a soft knock on the door and another young lady came in carrying a tray with two cups and a pot of coffee on it. She placed it on the desk, Mosley thanked her, and she left. He stood, filled both cups from the pot, and handed one to me.

"As you can see, we checked you out pretty thoroughly. We find nothing in your background that would make us think that you could be a security risk to your country, so I am empowered to disclose certain information that is of a very secret nature."

"Before we go any farther," I interrupted, "I would like to know who the 'we' that you keep referring to are."

"Ah, who are we? Yes, I can see where you might be interested in who we are." Mosley rubbed his chin as if thinking. "For the moment, let us just say that we are certain government agencies that became interested in you when you became interested in Moby Trick."

"Is the G-man who is posing as a mailman, or vice versa, is he on our side?"

"Mr. Callmeyer? Yes, he represents the federal government. He is one of the good guys."

"How about the little priest?"

"I don't know anything about any priests." Mosley put his coffee down on the desk and said, "Why don't you hold your questions until I finish my story?"

"Okay, I'm all ears."

"Well," Mosley started. "First things first. Your involvement began with the death of your friend Henry Holthaus. My people have investigated very carefully and they have determined that the death was simply a frightful accident.

"Last Sunday night, Jimmy Saline, an ex-convict and son of one of the Delhi carnation growers, prevailed on Mr. Holthaus to drive him to the nurseries of Mr. Al Heller. While Holthaus sat in the car, Jimmy broke into the secret nursery, the alleged home of the green carnation, and stole a bottle of citronella, which he mistakenly believed was the formula for growing green carnations. Saline then had Holthaus drive him to see the Herzogs, where Grossman gave Jimmy fifty dollars for the bottle.

"Jimmy and Holthaus then left the Herzogs and went back to Saline's property. Jimmy had hidden a quart of whiskey in the shed, and he and Holthaus proceeded to get drunk in celebration of Jimmy's good fortune. At some point in the evening, Saline told Holthaus to take off his hat. It is a well known fact that, because of his baldness, Holthaus never removed the hat. Saline had a rifle in the barn and jokingly shot the hat from Holthaus's head. As Mr. Holthaus scrambled for the hat, Saline kept shooting it out of his reach, until, alas, the fourth shot went astray and killed poor Mr. Holthaus.

"Saline panicked. He bundled Mr. Holthaus into the car, got another gun, a pistol, which he kept in the barn, and drove to the Ideal Café. He dragged Holthaus around to the back of the building and sat him on the steps of the café, placing the pistol in his hand. He didn't realize that the difference in caliber between the gun in Henry's hand and the bullet in his head would be noticeable. Jimmy then went back to the car, drove to Whitsken's Dairy, hid the car by the pond, and walked home."

"That's more or less how I had it figured," I said. "But there is more to it. I don't think Saline killed Henry."

"No offense, Mr. McCorkel, but my investigators are professionals. It happened exactly as I have said."

"Whatever, but that still doesn't explain the Nazi spies. Why did they come down on me?"

"The Herzog brothers are involved with Armbruster and Tune. When they heard that you were investigating the death of Holthaus, they were afraid that you might stumble on to the fact that they had purchased what they thought to be the secret green carnation formula from Jimmy Saline and Holthaus. They asked the Nazis to scare you off. Unfortunately, you didn't scare very easily. It would have been better for all of us if you had just quit at that time. Instead, you kept poking around and turned up things that none of us wanted you to know."

"Like the secret submarine you guys are building at the Queen City Barge Company's warehouse by the river."

"Yes," answered Mosley. "When did you discover it was a submarine?"

"I wasn't sure until I read an article in the paper on the way downtown. It told about a fisherman seeing what he described as a huge, one-eyed catfish in the river last night, and someone else told me about seeing a monster in the water from the excursion boat last night. The two strange sightings, along with the name of your project, Moby Trick, pretty much gave it away."

"You are very astute, Mr. McCorkel. Yes, it is a submarine, and yes, we were testing it in the river last night. Actually, it is more than a submarine. It is built in the shape of a whale, thus its name. We hope to use it in the waters off the Grand Banks of Newfoundland."

"But Armbruster, Kruger, and Tune, how do they fit in all this? Are they here to sabotage Moby Trick? And why are they interested in the green carnations?" I was wondering out loud.

"We know that Armbruster and Tune are Nazi spies. Kruger is an American thug, hired by the Nazis just for muscle. Apparently he has gone to ground. We've lost his trail and are afraid of what he might be up to. I would suggest that you keep a wary eye out for Mr. Kruger. He can be very dangerous."

"I don't think that Mr. Kruger will bother me. I think that he got out of the business completely. And I'm pleased to know that your sources are not infallible."

"Perhaps not infallible, but we do try to keep up." Mosley seemed amused. He continued, "The Nazis are posing as agricultural experts from Argentina. They are protected by the umbrella of that country. We cannot touch them unless we have positive proof of their nefarious activities here."

"Armbruster, as you probably know, is a colonel in German intelligence. His real name is Gustav Schmidt. His assistant is Peter Lorry, alias Franchot Tune, a truly nasty character. He is a corporal, and an expert torturer. He is highly skilled in hand-to-hand combat and is a trained assassin.

"We're still not sure how they got connected with the Herzogs. Before their association with the Nazis, the Herzog boys were just what they seemed to be, hard-working, clean-living, frugal, church-going Americans. They were not very social, but a lot of people keep to themselves, I suppose. Shortly after Armbruster called on them in his guise as an agricultural expert, Grossman became even more introverted and Talbert went to work for Queen City Barge. We keep a close eye on him, by the way. He won't find out anything we don't want him to know.

"We see it this way—the Herzogs have teamed up with the spies. Talbert came to work for us in order to ferret out secrets about Moby Trick. We believe that Armbruster and Tune have promised to find the mysterious green carnation formula and exchange it for the information acquired by Talbert. We don't think that the Herzogs realize the possible harm they could do to their country. We think they are just overwhelmed with greed.

"Have I left anything out? Do you have any more questions, Mr. McCorkel?" Mosley concluded.

"Without dotting all the I's and crossing all the T's, I had most of this figured out," I said.

"I know, Mr. McCorkel. That's why I wanted you to come in, so I could clear up any misconceptions you might have and ask you to keep everything we discussed to yourself. You must reveal nothing of what we have talked about today to anyone."

"But Mr. Mosley, I've got to tell Marge Baker how her father died. She hired me to investigate and she has a right to know."

"Of course she does, tell her about her father's death, that he was murdered. That you will soon be able to explain it all to her. But tell her nothing about—tell no one anything about—the rest of this saga, until we have caught the Nazi spies red-handed, and have put them away for good. I assure you, Mr. McCorkel, you will not have to keep this under wraps for long, and your silence is in the best interest of this great nation of ours . . . God Bless America!"

I had a strong urge to salute. Instead I stood and stuck out my hand. "You can count on me, sir."

Mosley grabbed my hand and shook it vigorously, "I know I can, my boy. You might tell Walt that you ran into me and that I said hello."

"You know Walt?"

"Indeed I do, he sometimes test flies my new planes."

Mosley once again pushed a button on the little box. A moment later the young woman who had brought me to Mosley's office came in and led me back to the elevator. "Would you like your paper back, sir?" she asked.

"Yes, thank you," I replied and tucked it under my arm as I walked out to the elevator.

It descended. I noticed the difference between the floor of the lobby and the floor of the elevator as we stopped, and so I walked off without tripping.

"Watch your step!" called the elevator operator.

As I walked out of the Gwenn Building, I realized how hungry I was. It was almost five and I hadn't had anything since the cheesecake this morning. I went across the street to a little restaurant and sat in a booth by the front windows. I ordered a B.L.T. and a Coke. As I was eating my sandwich, I noticed someone coming out of the Gwenn Building across the street. At first I thought it was Mosley, leaving his office at Queen City Barge. The man was dressed the same as Mosley had been. He did resemble Mosley, but when I looked again, I realized that it was really only because he was wearing the same clothes as the man I'd seen just a few minutes ago. This man was bald, not wearing glasses, and seemed a little thinner than I'd remembered.

On a whim, I decided to follow the man. I quickly paid my check, dropped fifteen cents on the table, and went after him. I didn't have to follow him very far. The man went around the corner and into the Metropole Hotel.

I waited a few minutes, then went into the hotel and up to the desk. I had my newspaper in my hand.

"Hey, dat guy what jest come in," I said to the clerk in what I thought was an imitation of a cab driver, "Who is he? He left dis paper in my cab."

The clerk looked down his nose at me and said, "That is Mr. Marc Ballerd, the impersonator. He would not like to be disturbed, so just leave the newspaper with me."

"Hey, dat's okey-doke," I laid the paper on the counter and walked out.

"Marc Ballerd," I thought. "I just read something about him in the paper. He's appearing at the Glenn Rendezvous, I think it said. Why would he be coming out of the Gwenn Building dressed like Lowell Mosley? Curiouser and curiouser."

While I was thinking, I was walking, and before I knew it I was at Fifth and Broadway. As long as I was this close, I decided to walk down to the foot of Broadway and look at the river. By the time I walked past Fourth, I could hear a calliope, and when I got to Second Street, I could see the Belle of Avon. She was preparing to leave on a cruise. There was smoke billowing everywhere and whistles were blowing as the steamship pulled away from the dock.

"Whistles and smoke," I thought as the Belle moved down the river. "I think this is the second whistles and smoke show I've been treated to today."

I walked back up to Fifth and grabbed a bus. After meandering through most of Price Hill, I got off on Cleves Pike in front of Walt's house and walked back up to the Ideal.

It was a little after six when I walked in the door. Walt was behind the bar, and Barnie was sitting at a table drinking a highball. There wasn't any one else in the bar.

"Evening guys, how did everything go today?"

"Don't ask," said Walt. "You want something?"

"Give me a Smile."

"I may never smile again." He reached in the box and gave me an orange soda.

I turned to Barnie. "Did something go wrong?"

"Sit down, you shouldn't be standing when you hear this."

I sat. "That bad?"

"Not all bad. Everything went off like clockwork. Walt and Ozzie got to the track a little early. Walt flew around in a big circle out over the river and came over the track just as the horses were headed down the stretch. They could easily see that number nine was the winner."

Barnie took a sip of his drink. "Walt had gotten some cloth strips from the tailor shop next door to the pool room."

I interrupted him. "Yeah I knew that, six different colors so we could signal the winner with different color combinations."

"Right, well—white and blue was the combination for nine. Ozzie bent down and pulled out the right pieces of cloth and the white one flew right out of his hand. Tyrone's plane has open cockpits, you know."

"Oh, boy. What did he do?"

"Ozzie thought fast. He pulled out his handkerchief and held it and the blue piece of cloth over his head."

"Good for Ozzie."

"Yeah, well, I was standing across from Coney watching the

plane through a pair of binoculars. I swear I could not see the white handkerchief."

"So you thought the signal was just blue, you thought the number five horse won." I couldn't believe this.

"Hah," said Walt from behind the bar. "He thought the cloth strip was green. The code for number two."

"The sun was in my eyes," whined Barnie.

"Holy cow," was my only comment.

"Anyway," Barnie continued. "I told Mike to call and tell them it was number two. He called Muffin. Muffin told Mick and Mick wrote the horse's number on a little blackboard he had brought with him. Unfortunately, instead of making a regular two, he wrote the Roman numeral two. He said he thought it would be easier to see and understand. Damn Latin school."

"Naturally," Walt piped in, "Ray saw it as eleven and that's the horse Harry plunked the thousand bucks on, number eleven."

"Holy cow," I repeated. "That's awful."

Barney took his glass to the bar, Walt refilled it. "It gets better," Walt said quietly. "Tell him the rest of it."

"Yeah, right," Barney sat back down. "You want another soda or something, Corky?"

"Get on with it!" Walt and I yelled at the same time.

"Okay, okay . . . There was some trouble at the track this afternoon. Two horses in the second race went down and had to be destroyed. It threw the timing of the other races off."

"The race that Ozzie and I saw from the airplane was the fifth, not the sixth," Walt interrupted. Of course, we had no way of knowing it."

"Who's telling this story?" Walt told Barney that he was sorry, but to speed it up.

" A good story is like fine wine, it cannot be hurried."

"Please Barney," I pleaded, "finish the story."

"Well, when Brockelberg gave the number to Harry, Harry rushed to the window and placed a thousand dollar bet on the number eleven horse, in the sixth race at River Downs, Mr. Melody. He was nonplussed when he heard the start of the fifth race come over the wire."

"He knew something was wrong, and tried to call the bet off." Walt had to interject.

"Mordock laughed at him and said, a bet's a bet, no refunds. The Cheviot police chief and Mayor Gingermix both happened to be in the place at the time and they agreed with Mordock."

"What a mess," I said. "I knew this whole thing was too complicated."

"Harry and Brockelberg went over and sat at a corner table," Barney went on. "Mick and Muffin, wondering what had happened, came in and sat with them. Ray quietly told them what had happened. They were so dejected they didn't even realize that the eleven horse had not won the fifth race."

"Then they heard the description of the sixth race come over the wire," Walt said excitedly. "It was won by Mr. Melody by three lengths. He was the number eleven horse."

I sat there trying to digest all this. "You mean we won?"

"We won!" Barney yelled at me. "Our horse, Mr. Melody, won and paid $38.40."

"Can I make a plan or can I make a plan?" Walt added.

"Yeah," I was a little dazed. "What do you mean by it paid $38.40? We bet a thousand bucks. Do we only get $38.40 back?"

"No," Barney explained. "If you bet two bucks, you get $38.40. We bet a thousand. We won $19,200. We're going to cut Ozzie in for helping us out, so your share will be nineteen hundred bucks."

"You mean I made a profit of eighteen hundred dollars and didn't even do anything?"

"That's about the size of it." Barney smiled.

"Can I make a plan or can I make a plan?" Walt piped up.

"Where is the money, and where are the rest of the boys?"

"They ain't back yet. Muffin told me all this over the phone."

"Mordock is going to renege. He isn't going to pay off that kind of money."

Barney brought a Seagram's and ginger ale over to me. "Have one on me, Cork. Celebrate, with the police chief and mayor of Cheviot as witnesses, I don't think he can get out of this one."

" Can I make a . . ."

Barney yelled, "Okay, Walt, you're a mastermind!"

Walt came over and put his hand on my shoulder. "This was a one in a million shot, Corky. Don't let it go to your head. Don't start playing the horses. You are one of the few people who ever got ahead of the nags. You can't beat 'em. Don't try."

With that bit of sage advice the door burst open. The boys came busting in carrying little Ozzie on their shoulders.

"We found this sailor walking up Glenway and decided to shanghai him!" Mick shouted. "Drinks for everybody." I could tell by their exuberance that they had been paid off.

"What happened, did you get it all?" Walt wanted to know.

We all gathered at the end of the bar. Harry took the floor. "We got it all. Mordock tried to stall, put us off, but with Gingermix and Chief Hastings sitting there, he didn't have a chance. We cleaned him out. He even had to take a couple of hundred out of the bar's cash register. When Rainy came in and found that Mordock had riffled the till, he told him to get out and stay out." Rainy Waters owned Tornadoes. He wasn't a very savory character, but several notches above Mordock.

Brockelberg exclaimed, "I think Mr. Mordock is going to leave town. At least I don't think we will see him in these parts ever again."

Harry the Haberdasher threw a wad of money on the bar. "Split it up, Walt!"

Walt divided the money up according to what each man had put up and gave each his share. When he finished, he had two hundred dollars left in his hand.

"This is for you, Ozzie, for helping us out at the last minute."

"Wait a minute, I didn't do anything, in fact I really messed up, losing that white rag and all. I don't deserve anything. Besides, I enjoyed the plane ride!"

The boys laughed, picked the little sailor up again, laid the money on his chest and slid him down the bar.

CHAPTER  18

I WAS WATCHING THE OFFICE FROM THE WINDOW OF THE Ideal. I drank my coffee and ate part of a donut. I was a little queasy and I had a slight headache. I thought this must be what a hangover is. I had never felt quite like this before.

The "boys" and I had celebrated last night until after 10. I had three or four Seagram's and ginger ales. That was more than I had ever drunk in one evening. I was a little woozy when I got back to my apartment.

I still had the nineteen hundred bucks in my pocket, since nobody would let me buy a drink. I had to get to the bank as soon as it opened so I could deposit it.

Besides being a little ill, I was nervous. I had to talk to Susan. I had gotten a reprieve yesterday because she was so excited, but I knew that she would be calm and collected today. I was nervous.

I had resigned myself to marrying her. No, that wasn't true, I had convinced myself that I wanted to marry her. Still I was nervous, I didn't really want to talk about it. I had too many things clattering around in my head. I had to conclude this investigation before I could even discuss the wedding.

Then there was the strange thing that happened during the celebration last night. Fuzzy as I was, I remembered it. Walt had suddenly come around the bar with his baseball bat in his hand. Everybody in the place jumped a foot.

"You're barred, Klopp, get outta here!" Walt had yelled.

Earl Klopp backed toward the door yelling, "Wait, I just wanna talk to Ed for a minute. "Zesta has disappeared." Zesta was Earl's wife. I remembered Walt telling me she had left him five years earlier.

"Zesta left years ago." Walt stood holding the bat.

"No, you don't understand. I hear from Zesta every month, but not this month. Somethin's happened to her. I'm stone sober. I won't cause no trouble. I just need to talk to Ed."

"Okay, but nothing to drink. You say what you have to say then get out. Understand?" Walt walked behind the bar and put the bat away.

Earl pulled me by the sleeve over to one of the tables by the wall, "Somethin's happened to my Zesta. I thought maybe, you being a detective and all, maybe you could find out what happened to her."

"Earl, that something happened over five years ago. She left you, she's not your Zesta anymore. Don't you understand?"

Klopp was whispering. "She still is my Zesta. It's true, she met another guy and married him, but we never got divorced."

"Then she is a bigamist. She can't be married to two guys at once."

"Well, maybe she is, but it don't bother me none and it didn't seem to bother her. She used to write me once a month to tell me how good she had it and how she hoped I wouldn't upset her apple cart. There was always a couple of hundred bucks in the envelope."

I sat back and stared at him. "You were blackmailing her?"

"No, nothing like that, I never asked her for nothin'. She just sent the money. I am her husband, after all."

"Ok, go on." I was still looking at him dubiously.

"Like I said, every month I'd get a letter and two hundred bucks. About five months ago, she stopped writing the notes, but I still got the money, regular as clockwork. But this month I didn't get nothin'. Something has happened to her, I just know it."

"Where does she live?"

"I got no idea," replied Klopp.

"Didn't the letters have any return address on them?" I asked.

"Nope, no return address on 'em."

"Do you have any of the envelopes?"

Earl reached in his pocket and pulled out a crumpled envelope.

I looked at it. "According to the postmark, this was mailed from Lexington. Were the others the same?"

"I don't know, I never paid any attention to them, but I do have this." He handed me an old creased newspaper clipping. It was from the Dayton Herald and described the wedding of Zesta Schmidt, her maiden name, to Harold Starret. It was dated almost five years ago.

I read the clipping. "This isn't much to go on, Earl. I'm pretty busy right now, and anyway, I'm sure that Zesta is okay."

"No she's not." Earl reached into his pocket and pulled out some crumpled bills. "Look. I can pay. I ain't lookin' for no charity. Twenty-five bucks a day, right? Here's plenty."

If Earl was willing to part with that much money, he must be really worried, I thought, and I was just drunk enough to be pleased that he thought I was detective enough to help him.

I fished out a five and two tens and said, "I'll give it a day, Earl. If I turn up anything, then that's it and we're square. If it takes more time, we'll talk about it, okay?"

"That's Jake with me, Corky." Earl yelled across the room, "Hey Walt, how about a beer for me and my pal here?"

"Get outta here!" growled the bartender.

I snapped out of thinking about last night. Susan had just pulled up. I gave her time to park, open the office, and get settled. I saw her looking out the window. She was expecting me to come over. I was nervous . . . I started through the door as somebody in the bar whistled "Taps."

When I walked into the office, Susan grabbed me and gave me a big kiss. "Well, I guess she hasn't forgotten," I thought.

"I told my mother, she was almost as excited as I was and happy for me. We talked all day and most of the night. We have some ideas about the wedding, if they meet with your approval, of course. We have to talk."

"Of course," I said. "Why don't we talk?"

Susan was absolutely bubbly. I didn't think I had ever seen her so effervescent.

"I think we should have a small wedding . . . I guess I will have to call St. Clarisa's . . . I do want a Catholic wedding if that's okay with you . . . Yes, I really want to get married in church . . . Maybe if I talked to that nice Father O'Toole . . . Gosh, what about a reception?"

She was going on so fast that I didn't have a chance to answer any of her questions, if indeed they were questions. As luck would have it, Officer Newmann walked in at that point. He was in civilian clothes. "I hope I'm not interrupting anything but I've got the day off and a little gas in the car. I thought if you needed to go anywhere, I might save you the cost of a few shots of whiskey."

"Hey, that's great. I do have some running around to do. First let me make a phone call. Oh, Joe, I'd like you to meet Susan Stienle, my fiancée. Susan, this is Joe Newmann."

Susan almost fainted again when I called her my fiancée, but she managed to say, "I've seen you around the corner, Officer Newmann, but I don't think we were ever introduced. It's nice to meet you."

"I'm pleased to meet you, I usually hear most of the gossip around here but I didn't know you two were engaged."

"Well, it's a very recent thing," I said.

"Yes it is," said Susan, "and we really have to talk."

I used the phone on Susan's desk. I called Marge Baker. Her number was written in my notebook. I waited. "Hello, may I speak to Mrs. Baker, please."

"Hi Marge, this is Ed McCorkel."

"Yes, I'm fine. I told you that I would call you today and give you a report. What I would like to do, would be to stop out and see you. Joe Newmann is here and has offered me a ride."

"Yes, that nice young policeman."

"I think he's the only one with any sense, too. Okay, we'll be out in a few minutes."

"Please, don't go to any bother."

"Ah . . . Marge is your dad's car out there?"

"Swell, I just want to take a look at it."

"No, it wouldn't do me any good, I don't know how to drive."

"Yeah, I'll keep my ears open, I might find somebody who would be interested in it."

"Okay Marge, we'll be right out."

"Yeah, right, yeah, okay, goodbye."

"It sounds like it's alright for us to come out," Newmann said.

"Yeah, she's making coffee. Susan, we're going out to see Marge Baker, if we go anywhere from there, I'll call you, okay?"

"Oh Ed, Mom wants you to come to dinner tonight. I'll pick you up about six-thirty if that's okay."

"I'm sure it will be fine, but let me call you later to make sure."

"Goodbye, dear," said Susan. She gave me a little kiss. I gave her a wave and Joe and I walked out the door.

"Golly, you two are really serious. Funny that I didn't hear anything about it. I usually hear about things like that."

"It's really a recent thing. It just happened yesterday."

"I see," said Joe. "Had you been thinking a long time about asking her to marry you?"

"It was pretty much a spur of the moment thing."

"Here's the car." Joe unlocked the door. "Well, you must have given it some thought. It's an important decision." Joe started the car and pulled away from the curb.

"I had been thinking for some time about asking her to be my partner in the business." I finally told Joe the whole story.

Joe was passing a milk wagon and burst out laughing, so loud that it startled the horse. It lunged to the side, causing the wagon to jump the curb and run over a bush.

Joe stopped the car and walked back to be sure the driver and horse weren't hurt. He was still giggling, but the milkman was angry, and the look of amusement on Newmann's face made him madder. He started telling Joe what he thought of him.

Joe held up his hand. "Be quiet," he said, "I am Officer Newmann, Cincinnati Police Department. I only stopped to give you a citation for not having your horse under control and for destroying public property."

The milkman's attitude changed suddenly. He was apologetic for his abusive language and explained that his horse had been particularly unpleasant all day, and that he and his horse were tired and anxious to get back to the dairy. He hoped that the officer would overlook this little accident.

Newmann told the driver that he would let him off with a warning this time, but that he should contact the owner of the bush and offer to replace it. The milkman promised to do just that, thanked Joe for being understanding, and got his horse and wagon back on the street and on the way to the dairy.

Joe watched the wagon pull away then got back in his car. We both burst out laughing.

"Not only did you cause that horse to bolt and destroy Mrs. Oldenburg's bush, you also distressed that poor driver. Do you always misuse your authority?" I asked, still laughing.

"No, I'm usually a pretty good cop, but I remember that guy. He would never give us kids any ice." Joe was also still giggling.

He straightened up and said, "So, why are we going to see Mrs. Baker?"

"I promised her that I would let her know what I have found out so far, but more importantly, I want to look at Henry's car. Stutter and Clements weren't interested enough in it to even go look at it, but I have a hunch it might tell us something. I think it's the next driveway on the right."

We had come about a mile and a half from the dairy and were almost to the country club when we pulled into the drive. We got out of the car and walked to the front door. Marge Baker opened it before they could knock.

"Hi Ed, and you are Officer Newmann. I've seen you around the corner. You helped with the cars at the funeral yesterday, didn't you?"

"Yes, Mrs. Baker, I was there, just trying to keep traffic moving."

"I appreciated your help, and call me Marge. Come on in, I've got the coffee ready."

"Marge," I spoke up, "could we go see Hank's car first? It's kind of important."

"Sure," she said. "Its out in the garage, follow me.

She led us around to the back of the house to a three-car garage that had originally been a carriage house. Marge swung back the first set of doors and showed them the car.

"Do you happen to have a flashlight out here?" I asked. Marge walked over to a workbench against the wall and handed it to me. I thanked her, and then passed the beam over the front fender on the driver's side.

"Joe, do you see those scratches? They look fresh, and look there—just in back of the bumper. That's a pretty deep gouge, all the way through the paint."

Joe looked, then said, "It looks like he could have been driving through some brush. A stone could have made that gash."

"I couldn't tell you when he picked up those scratches," said Marge. "I never paid any attention to his car. He could have gotten them a month ago."

I was shining the flashlight around the inside of the car, particularly around the inside of the driver's side door. "Look at these spots, look right through here, see that stain and these specks on the ceiling? What do they look like to you, Joe?"

Joe looked at the spots. He got his knife out and scraped at one. He smelled it.

"If I had to guess, I'd say it was blood."

I got out of the car and closed the door. I handed the flashlight to Marge. "Now I'd like some of that coffee," I said.

Marge put the flashlight away and led them out of the garage. She closed the door and took then into the house through the back door. "Let's just sit here in the kitchen," I suggested.

Marge poured the three of them each a cup of coffee. She had already put out sugar, milk, and some homemade cookies. "Please, help yourselves," she told them. Ed and Joe each took a cookie.

"These are good." I took a drink of my coffee and continued, "Marge, I haven't finished my investigation, but I think I have some of the answers. The trouble is that every time I think I have an answer, I get two more questions. This investigation has gotten very complicated. The deeper I dig, the less I seem to understand."

"You are pretty certain that Dad didn't commit suicide, aren't you?" asked Marge.

"One thing I do know is that your father did not commit suicide. I think his death was the result of an accident, a bizarre accident, but it was still an accident. I think it happened in a shed on the Saline's property, at least something happened there that led up to the killing, and Jimmy Saline was involved."

"Are you saying that Jimmy Saline accidentally killed my father?" Marge asked.

"That was pretty much what I thought until I examined the car, but now I'm not sure, not sure at all."

"How did Dad's body get up to the Ideal if he was killed at Saline's?"

"I am not really sure of what happened exactly. Jimmy Saline may have driven your father's car with his body in it to the Ideal. I know somebody did. They took the body around to the back of the building and sat it up on the steps, then drove the car to Whitsken's, where it was found. I thought Saline did it, but now I am not sure."

"I'm confused," said Marge. "If Jimmy Saline didn't kill my father, why did he drag his body up there?"

"I'm not sure he did, but if he did, it was because Jimmy *thought* he killed Henry."

"Jimmy Saline thinks he killed my father, but you know he didn't?" asked Marge curiously.

"I don't know for sure. Marge, there's a lot I can't tell you, partially because I'm not sure and also because it involves national security."

"Now you're trying to tell me that my father was involved in something that threatened the security of our country! Come on, Ed, you've been drinking too much of that orange stuff."

"Your dad was not involved in anything more than being an accomplice to the theft of two bits worth of citronella. It's my investigation that opened the can of worms."

Marge turned to Officer Newmann. "Does any of this make any sense to you, Joe?"

"Oddly enough it does, but I think you should trust Ed. It could be dangerous for you to know any more at this time."

"What do you mean dangerous, are you in danger, Ed? Is he in danger, Joe?" Marge was visibly upset.

Joe replied, "He has had several warnings, and one attempt was made on his life."

Marge was almost hysterical. "That's it, you're off the case, go back to selling insurance. I just wanted to be sure that my father didn't commit suicide. You showed me he didn't. Thank you. Now quit."

"Calm down, Marge. I'm not going to get hurt, Joe exaggerates. I'm not in any danger. I've just got to tie up a few loose ends then I'll go back to the insurance business. The person who tried to do me harm is no longer around so there's nothing to worry about."

"I don't want to be the cause of your getting hurt. Please, just get out of this right now. Thank you very much, send me a bill."

"Okay Marge, we have to go. I will back off. But if I happen to hear anything more about this business, I will pass it on. Thanks for the coffee and cookies."

"Yeah," chimed in Joe, "thanks, and don't worry. I talk too much. Ed's not really in any danger."

"You quit, Ed. You quit right now," Marge said as she closed the door.

"Anybody ever tell you you've got a big mouth, Joe?"

"I have heard rumors to that effect. Where to from here?"

Let's take a quick run over to Mix's. I think he knows something that he isn't telling us."

When we got there, the place was full of cars and there were people in various states of undress running around. They were all wearing white cowboy hats.

Arnold Mix walked out to the car and stood by my window. I asked him what was going on.

"They're getting ready for the Immersion tomorrow. But you ain't interested in that. You reckon I know something about what happened to old Hank."

"Do you?"

"Yea, but I was sworn to secrecy. I think Hank's daughter's got a right to know, though, so I'll tell you what I know. That new priest up at St. Clarisa's, he's been coming out here getting messages from across the river. They flash lights at him. I caught him once and he told me that he was a secret agent and that it was my duty not to tell anybody about what he was doing."

"Did he tell you who he was a secret agent for?"

Mix thought a bit. "No. But I assumed he was working for us."

"That might not have been the right assumption."

"Oh yeah? Anyways, the other night he was up here flashing his lights. I could see him from the porch. Suddenly a car came swerving up the road and crashed into the bushes he was hiding behind. I ran up to see what had happened, just as the priest whirled around and shot at them. Then he took off on his motorcycle. The car roared away backwards." Mix paused for a breath. "I think it was Henry's car."

"You *think* it was Henry's car?"

"It was Henry's car. There were two people in it. One was kind of slumped over. Am I in trouble?"

"I don't think so, Arnold. You were just doing what you thought was right, but I wish you had told me this earlier." Mix shrugged and walked back toward the crowd in cowboy hats.

"Wow. This thing is getting curiouser and curiouser," Joe said as we drove off.

"No, Joe. In fact, it's starting to make sense."

I looked at my watch. "It's about twelve-thirty. I'd like to get something to eat. Marge Baker's cookies were good, but I need some lunch."

"How about Five Points? I think they serve lunch, at least they'll have some kind of soup and sandwiches," said Joe.

"That sounds alright. I was there yesterday, or maybe it was the day before. I want to stop at Saline's, but let's eat first. I'll buy. We can run up to Saline's after we finish."

"Sounds good to me," Joe nodded and went on down the hill. When he got to the café, he pulled around the back into their little parking lot.

We got out of the car and went in the side door. It entered into a small sitting room. I looked into the bar and didn't see anyone I knew. There was a different bartender from the other day. I stepped back into the sitting room and sat at a table where Joe was looking at a handwritten menu.

A little round woman came out of the back. She looked like she might be a combination waitress and cook. "You guys ready to order?" she asked us. Before we could answer she said, "Special today is tomato soup and grilled cheese, and the blue plate is jack salmon with macaroni and cheese."

I asked if the soup was homemade.

"Yeah," the waitress answered, "they make it over at Mr. Campbell's house." She started cackling after she said it.

I asked if she had any metts.

"No metts today, it's Friday. I could probably find you a piece of chicken liver back there, but you'd be better off with the fish."

"Okay, I'll have the jack salmon."

"Me, too," said Joe.

The waitress bustled back to the kitchen.

Joe laughed, "You better get used to fish on Friday. Once Susan gets a hold of you, she'll turn you into a mackerel snapper like the rest of Price Hill."

"A mackerel snapper? You mean a Catholic? Do you really think she's going to want me to become a Catholic?"

"Sure, that's what little Catholic girls do, turn perfectly good Protestants into Catholics. It's built into them. The nuns train them from the first grade. For eight years, they indoctrinate them. Then if they go on to Seton or Mercy for high school, they get four more years specialized training. I understand the Nazis have been studying the nuns' methods of instruction."

"You sound cynical. Are you a Protestant?"

"No, I'm Catholic, so of course, I'm cynical. I went to St. Bill's for six years, until my father got tired of dealing with the penguins, as he called them, and sent me to West High. I'm just giving you a little advance warning."

"You want to hear something funny? When I was a kid—a good Presbyterian kid—people would ask me where I lived. I would always say that I lived in St. Clarisa's parish."

"Sure," Joe laughed, "the west side of Cincinnati and New Orleans. They're both divided into parishes."

The waitress popped back. "What do you boys want to drink?"

"I'll have a Coca Cola," Joe said.

"You got Smile orange?" I asked.

"Nah, all we got is Whistle.

"That's too bubbly for me. Give me a Coke."

She got our drinks and plunked then down. Then she went to the kitchen and came back right away with our lunch. "Ya want white or rye bread?"

I looked at Joe and said, "Rye?" He nodded. I told the waitress, "Rye."

She went to the kitchen and returned with about half a loaf of rye bread on a plate. She also brought a bowl of butter and a bowl of tartar sauce.

I took a couple of bites and said to Joe, "This fish is delicious. It's cooked perfectly and there isn't a bone in it. How do they get the bones out?"

"I don't know, but you can get jack salmon this good at half a dozen places between here and the river. Crow's Nest, Trolley Tavern, Stadtmiller's, just to name a few."

"I can't believe I've never had it before."

Joe laughed, "For growing up in Price Hill, you've missed some things."

The waitress came back, "Everything okay, fellas?"

I said, "This fish is delicious, but how did you get the bones out?"

"I took 'em out," she said.

"But how do you get them all out without disturbing the fish?"

"Practice," the woman said, she cackled and walked back to the kitchen. We finished our lunch, I commented several more times on how good it was. Joe was amused, I guess it didn't taste any better or any worse than all the other jack salmon he had eaten in his lifetime.

When we finished the waitress came back. "Can I get them plates out of yer way?"

I said, "Yes, and I'll take the check."

"There ain't no check. It comes to a dollar even, just pay the bartender." She went back to the kitchen.

We each left a dime tip. I went into the bar and gave the bartender a dollar. "Do you have a pay phone?"

The bartender told me that they didn't, but that I could use the one on the end of the bar if I left a nickel in the bowl. I told Joe I was going to check with Susan and went to the end of the bar.

I noticed that the end of the bar was covered with names and figures written in chalk. I laughed, the bartender was running a little book and he probably used the phone to lay off bets. "I better make this a quick call," I thought to myself.

I called and Susan answered. "Where are you?" she asked.

I told her.

She said that Grossman Herzog had called three times and needed desperately to talk to me. She gave me Herzog's number. I thanked her and hung up, then realized that I hadn't said anything about coming to dinner at her house tonight. I would call her back later. We really had to sit down and talk about getting married.

I met Joe in the parking lot and told him about the calls from Herzog. Joe said, "Let's just run up to his place. We're practically there now." We jumped in the car and drove over to the nursery. As we pulled in the lot, Grossman came running out of the office door.

"You must have gotten my message, thank God."

"What's going on, Herzog? How come you're calling me? I didn't think we were exactly friends."

"Please, Mr. McCorkel. My brother and I have been fools, Armbruster and Tune deluded us. They are not interested in carnation growing, and they are not South Americans. They are not nice people. I think they may be Nazi spies. Please, Mr. McCorkel, help my brother and me. We may, unwittingly, have threatened the security of our country."

"Slow down, Herzog, and tell me what happened."

"I'm telling you, my brother and I have been fools."

"We've already been through that. Stop, catch your breath, and tell me slowly just what has you so upset."

"It started last night," Grossman began his story. "Talbert came home from work at the barge company. He was very happy, because he had uncovered the secret of Moby Trick. It was a huge submarine they were building there, a submarine that looked like a whale. He was doubly happy because he believed he could set the minds of Armbruster and Tune at ease since he had learned that the government had no plans to use it in South America. They planned to send it to Newfoundland."

"This morning Armbruster and Tune showed up. We told them about the whale or submarine, whichever. We expected them to be happy that it would pose no threat to their country, Argentina. They were happy all right, and excited. They asked Talbert where the sub was kept, how well it was guarded, and if he knew when it would be moved. They were pleased to hear that it could be reached by water."

"Did they say why they wanted to get near it?"

"No, but they said they would have to talk to Jimmy Saline and asked me if we owned a motorboat."

Joe asked if they did own a boat. "No, but the Salines have a big old outboard motorboat that they keep tied up down by Anderson Ferry for fishing. They grind up what they catch and mix it with that awful fertilizer they use."

"Do you think they were going to talk to Jimmy about borrowing the boat?" I asked.

"I don't know. I've seen them talking to Jimmy. He is scared to death of them, like they might be blackmailing him. If they want to use his boat, he'll let them."

I could think of something the Germans could blackmail Jimmy Saline with. I asked Grossman, "Do you think they want a boat so they can sneak in from the river side and get to the submarine?"

"I have no idea. When they left here, they were talking a mile a minute in German, I remember my father speaking it, but they talked so fast I couldn't understand what they were saying. One word I did recognize was *kaput*."

"Do you know where they were going from here?" asked Joe.

"No, but they drove out of here in the direction of Saline's place." I asked him what kind of a car they were driving.

"It was a Packard, a big, black Packard."

"Where is Talbert now?" asked Joe.

"Talbert went to the barge company, to tell them what he did and to warn them about what we are afraid Armbruster and Tune may do. He may be in jail even as we speak and the police may be on their way out to get me."

"Come on," I said, "you were a little greedy and you trusted a couple of bad guys, but I don't think you're going to have to go to jail. By the way, did Armbruster and Tune give you the secret of the green carnations?"

"That's the biggest laugh of all. They left a big fat folder, telling us that it was the secret. It turned out to be full of old Popular Mechanics articles on landscaping. It would all be very funny if I didn't have this feeling of impending doom."

"It's going to be all right, Grossman, I just know it." I was beginning to like the big jerk. Joe and I headed back to the car. "We'll do what we can for you," I called.

"Boy, this has really been our day for confessions," Joe said. "First Mix, then Herzog. Now to Saline's, right?" said Joe.

"Have you got enough time?"

"I'm off duty until Monday morning." Joe replied. He seemed to be enjoying himself.

"Then let's head over to Saline's."

CHAPTER 20

WHEN THEY GOT NEAR THE NURSERY, THEY SAW A STATE police car and a Cincinnati police car parked out front.

"Uh, oh," I said, "it looks like Stutter and Clements might have put two and two together and come up with Jimmy Saline. Do you want to drop me off so they don't see you with me?"

"Nah, I'm in it now. They're bound to find out sooner or later, and anyway, it's my day off. I can do anything I want to on my day off, can't I?"

I laughed. "Sure you can. Let's go see what the cops are doing here."

We pulled in alongside one of the state cars and walked around to the shed. There was a state policeman standing at the door. "You guys can't go in there, there's a police investigation."

Clements stuck his head out the door. "That's all right, Henderson. That one is a cop and this one is a special friend of mine. Let them pass."

He put his arm around Newmann's shoulder. "Well, well, officer, aren't we a little off our beat?"

"We were just driving by and saw all the cop cars and we stopped to see what was going on. Anyway, it's my day off."

"We're very pleased that you could stop in, you and your friend, Mr. Amateur Sleuth."

"Hello, Clements," I said "I'm pleased to see you here. It probably means you are on the right track."

"We're on the right track, all right. We've solved this one, with no help from you, thank you very much."

As we stepped into the shed, I saw another state policeman, Stutter, the younger Saline brother, and old man Saline in his wheelchair.

"Look what I found prowling around outside, Stutter. It's Sherlock Holmes and Cincinnati's Finest, Dr. Watson. It looks like us professionals are one step ahead of them."

"Yeah, I guess we did get here first, too bad, boys," said Stutter.

"That shows what you know, you son of a biscuit. The insurance guy was out here last Tuesday," cackled the elder Saline.

"It doesn't matter, as soon as we catch up with Jimmy Saline, it will all be over," said Stutter.

"Detective Clements, could you tell us what you discovered? Do you know how Henry Holthaus was killed and who killed him?" I asked.

"Sure, I'll tell you," said Clements. "Holthaus and Jimmy Saline were out here Sunday night having a party. They got pretty liquored up on cheap booze. Saline was playing around with a rifle and shot Holthaus's hat off. When he tried to get it, Saline kept shooting it away from him until he missed the hat and shot Holthaus in the head. We dug one of the .22 slugs out of the floor.

"Then Saline panicked. He put the body in the victim's own car and drove up to that bar. He put the body on the back steps, drove the car up to Whitsken's, and walked home."

"I don't think Jimmy done it," said Mr. Saline. "He ain't no angel, I'd be the first to admit that, an' he ain't too bright, that's easy enough to see, but he liked old Hank. They was buddies, drinking buddies to be sure, but good friends. No, I don't think Jimmy done it."

Clements answered the old man, "I'm not saying it was murder, hell no, I think it was an accident. But it is still manslaughter and we got to pick him up."

"Where'd the other gun come from, the one the victim was holding?" asked Joe.

"He wasn't holding a gun when we examined the body, it was lying beside him," Stutter answered.

"Yeah, well, where did it come from?"

Clements answered this time. "It was another gun that Saline had hidden around here, who knows how many he had?"

I asked where Jimmy Saline was now.

"We don't know, we think somebody might have tipped him that we were coming and he flew the coop."

I leaned against the door sill with my arms folded. "Clements, you've figured out everything pretty well."

"Thank you Mr. Private Investigator," said the detective.

"Except for one thing. Jimmy Saline didn't kill Henry

Holthaus."

"Oh yeah, then why did he run away, huh? Tell me that."

"I don't think he ran away, I think he was kidnapped."

"KIDNAPPED?" every one in the room said at the same time.

Mr. Saline was the first one to speak up. "They can't hope to get any ransom out of me, for two reasons. First of all, I ain't got no money, and second, I ain't so sure I want him back."

"Be serious, Paw," said the younger Saline. "We got to do what we can for Jimmy."

"You be serious, young fella, he's your brother and I guess you still love him, but he's been a real trial to me and . . ." Mr. Saline stopped. "Yeah, we got to do something to get him back." He looked at me and asked, "What can we do?"

I went over and stood by the wheelchair. I put my hand on Tom Saline's shoulder. "I don't think they kidnapped him for ransom. They want him to do something for them and I don't know what it is, but I will sure try to find out, and I'll try to find your son."

"Thank you, Mr. McCorkel," said the old man. "I'll be beholden to you for anything you can do." He reached up and shook my hand.

"Yeah, McCorkel, we'd be beholden too," said Sergeant Stutter. "We would like to put that killer away for a long, long time."

I ignored him and turned to Newmann. "Let's go, Joe."

"Wait a minute," Clements said. "If you find him, or find anything out about him, we want to know. I've got a warrant for his arrest, so stay in touch unless you want to be arrested for aiding a criminal."

"We'll keep you posted. Now let's go, Joe."

We walked out to the car. "Now what, Ed?" Joe asked as we got in.

"I think I want to go to the Herzog's place again, if you have the time?"

"I told you, I'm off until Monday morning."

"Good, let's go visit the Herzogs."

When they got back to the nursery, we saw Talbert and Grossman through the office window. The two brothers were in earnest conversation. Joe parked the car and we walked over to the door. I knocked.

"Come in, it's open," boomed Grossman's voice.

When they entered, Grossman stood up and said, "Ah, my friends, I'm glad you returned. Talbert is back and has a strange tale to tell."

The elder Herzog showed us to a couple of chairs. "Sit," he said. "Tell them, brother, tell them what you told me."

Talbert began to pace, swinging his hands around while he talked. "I think Grossman has already told you of our stupidity and greed, trusting and believing those Nazi pigs, actually thinking that they were from South America. It sounds impossible but we really were deceived. We love this country, and thought we were helping."

"Talbert, they know all that. Tell them what happened when you returned to the Queen City Barge Construction Company."

"Yes, of course," Talbert continued. "I went back to the barge company and sought out my immediate supervisor. I told him that I had turned over the secret of the submarine to Nazi agents."

"He acted like he didn't know what I was talking about. Tried to say I was drunk, and have me thrown out. The ruckus was heard by a higher-up official. He took me into the executive offices, to another man. This man asked me to repeat my story, which I did. When I finished I expected him to call the police and have me arrested. Instead he smiled and thanked me. He called my foreman and he escorted me to the door. As I left, he said, 'See you Monday.' Apparently they didn't even fire me."

I asked him if they were not just a little upset when he had mentioned the Nazi agents.

"No, they were not upset at anything I told them."

"Okay," I said, "I told you guys that everything was going to be all right and it is. You haven't seen Armbruster or Tune since this morning, have you?"

Grossman answered, "Not since they drove off this morning."

"Have you seen Jimmy Saline?"

"No, not for days."

I turned to the younger brother. "Is the barge company open on Saturday?"

"In the morning only, they close down at noon," answered Talbert.

"How well is it guarded?"

"Just a couple of security guards."

"Do you think we could sneak in and get a look at the sub?"

"We could try, but why should I trust you? You might also be a spy. I won't be fooled twice."

"Shut up, Talbert," Grossman spat. "We must trust someone, we will trust Mr. McCorkel."

"We trusted the Nazis . . ."

"Enough. What time do you want to be picked up, Mr. McCorkel, and where?"

"I think tomorrow at one p.m. will be fine. In front of the Overlook Theater."

"Fine, he will be there. Thank you for trying to help us, Mr. McCorkel."

"Call me Ed."

"Do you want me to come along, too?" asked Joe.

"No, I've got something else for you to do. Let's go."

I turned back to see the Herzogs still standing at the door of their office. "Goodbye boys, try not to worry. I'll see you tomorrow at one, Talbert."

We got in the car and drove off the Herzog's lot. "Where to?" said Joe.

"Just drive around some of these roads and stop when I tell you."

Joe drove until I shouted for him to stop. "Pull over on the side there." I got out of the car and walked across a field to an old barn. When I got back, I climbed back into the car.

"Okay, go ahead."

"What are you looking for?" asked Joe.

"There are a lot of old barns and sheds in Delhi, I just had a thought that Jimmy Saline might be being held in one of them."

"Or worse yet, lying dead in one of them," said Newmann. "Look, there's another one. I'll stop." We walked over and looked in. There was nothing suspicious.

"That's what I want you to do tomorrow, check out the barns of Delhi." I pulled out my wallet. "Here's a couple of gas coupons. The home office sends them to me from time to time. They don't know that I don't know how to drive."

"Thanks," Joe said. He put the coupons in his shirt pocket. "You want to check any more barns today?"

"No, let's go back now. Do you think you could check them tomorrow, though? I have to get cleaned up for dinner with Susan."

"Sure," said Joe, as drove up to Cleves Pike, turned right, and headed for the corner. He pulled into the bank's parking lot. We got out and walked across the street to the office.

"I have to make a phone call," I told Joe. With everything else that was going on, I hadn't forgotten my promise to Earl Klopp.

Susan had found the phone number in Dayton I needed earlier in the morning, but I hadn't had a chance to make the call earlier. I just hoped that there was someone still there that could give me the information that I needed.

I tried several times to place the long-distance call. Finally, Joe took the phone away from me and spoke to the operator. He got the number and handed the phone back to me.

"Hello, Herald Tribune? I'm trying to get some information about an item that ran in your newspaper about five years ago . . . the morgue? How do I get in touch with them?"

"You can? Wonderful, sure I can wait."

"Hello, there was a story in your paper . . ."

"A wedding, June 11, 1938."

"Zesta Schmidt and Harold Starret . . ."

"Your paper covered it . . . A fancy affair . . ."

"He was some kind of a big shot gangster, holy cow! That wasn't in the article, though . . ."

"Yeah, I guess he wouldn't want to advertise that . . ."

"You don't think they still live in Dayton . . ."

"No, that's okay, I appreciate what you could tell me."

He hung up the telephone and said, "How about that. Earl Klopp's wife really did marry a big-time gangster. I wonder if a gangster would be listed in the City Directory."

"You say his name is Harold Starret?" Joe asked. "There's a guy named High-Pockets Harry Starret, he operates out of Newport, Kentucky. I'm pretty sure he's a gangster."

"How would I find a gangster in Newport?" I asked him.

"Swing a cat," Joe replied.

Just then I heard a siren and a police car pulled up outside. An officer got out, looked through my window, saw us sitting there, and walked in.

"Now what?" said Joe. "George," he said, recognizing the officer. "What's going on?"

"Hi Joe. Sorry, but I gotta arrest your friend here. You are Edward McCorkel, right?"

"Yes, I am, but I haven't done anything."

"I don't know anything about that, I only know that I'm supposed to bring you in." The officer frisked me as he was talking. "Please put your hands behind your back."

"Hey George, that's not necessary," Joe yelled.

"Okay, just put your hands in front of you. I'm sorry, Joe, but he is under arrest. I got to put the cuffs on him." He snapped them loosely on my wrists.

"My keys are on the desk, Joe. At least lock up for me."

Joe picked up the keys and we all walked out the door. He locked it and put the keys in my coat pocket.

"I'll follow you down," said Joe.

"No, don't, this will probably take a little time, but they can't hold me for anything—I didn't do anything. Just do me a favor, call Susan. Her number is Wabash 1877. Tell her that I won't be able to make it for dinner but I'll call her later. And I'll talk to you in the morning."

George the policeman pushed me into the cruiser and took off with his siren blaring. When we arrived at the Price Hill police station, the officer took me inside and turned me over to a policeman, about my age, wearing sergeant's stripes.

"Here now, me boy," the sergeant said. "You had no need to be cuffin' this foine gentleman. Sure now, Detective Clements would only be wantin' a word with him."

The other officer replied, "I was told to arrest him. When I arrest somebody, I put the cuffs on them. That's what I was told to do and that's what I do."

"Well, there is no need to keep 'em on you now, me boy," he said, and he removed the manacles. He walked over to a closed door and opened it. "You could be waiting for the detective in here, sor, I'm sure he'll be along in two shakes of a lamb's tail."

I stopped by the door. "Didn't you go to Elder? You played on the baseball team, didn't you?"

"That I did, me bucko, and I remember a skinny kid on the Hughes team that cut me down at second when I was trying to stretch a long single."

"Yeah, that was it. If I remember correctly, when you cussed me out you didn't have that brogue."

"With a name like Moran, there are certain expectations put upon a fellow. In you go now."

I walked into a small room. There was a table and four chairs. There were no windows in the room. When I walked in, the door shut behind me. I turned and tried the knob. It was locked. I paced around the room for a little while and then sat down on one of the hard wooden chairs. I didn't know how long they intended to keep me here. I started wishing that I smoked. It would give me something to do. I got up and beat on the door from time but no one ever opened it. I finally put my head down on the table and went to sleep.

I awoke when I heard a key in the latch had no idea how long I had been asleep. The door opened and Detective Clements came into the room.

"I'm really sorry to have kept you waiting, something came up and then, well I just plain forgot about you. Isn't that funny?"

I didn't think it was very funny but I didn't say anything. I didn't want to give Clements the satisfaction of knowing that I was annoyed.

The detective continued, "It's really too bad that you had to be bothered like this. I only wanted to ask you if you knew where Saline was hiding."

I looked at him before answering. "I have no idea where Mr. Saline is, and if I did know I would certainly tell you because I think he is in great danger. I know that Jimmy Saline did not kill Henry Holthaus, but I'm not sure that he knows that. He's frightened and might do something foolish."

"I'll tell you this, McCorkel, if I find out you're lying to me, if you know where that little skunk is hiding, I'll arrest you and throw away the key. I won't be as nice the next time you get brought in here."

"If you're finished, I'd like to go."

"I'm finished and you can go, but mark my words, I'll get you if you are lying."

Clements led me out to where the sergeant was still seated. "It's okay for this one to leave," the detective said, then turned around and walked to the back of the building.

"Do you think I could use your telephone?"

"Why, sure now, me foine fellow, we police, being the public servants that we are, are pleased to assist you, the public, in every way that we can. The telephone is right there." He pointed.

I didn't bother to reply. I dialed Susan's number.

"Hello," I heard her voice.

"Hi, it's me."

"Ed McCorkel, you missed dinner. I came for you and waited and waited but you never showed up. Where were you?"

"Joe Newmann was supposed to call you and tell you I couldn't make it," I said.

"I took mother shopping, so I must have missed his call. But what happened? Where are you now?"

"Listen Susan, I was arrested."

"Arrested! Oh, Ed, what happened? Are you all right?"

"Slow down, I'm okay. I've just been released. I was wondering if you could drive down to the police station on Warsaw and pick me up. I could explain what happened on the way home."

"I'm on my way," she said. I heard the phone click.

I put down the phone, said thank you to the sergeant, and went outside to wait for her.

I sat on the steps of the station and thought about how strange my world had become. I wondered if I would ever get everything straightened out and get back to the well-ordered life I had lived before I started this investigation. Then I wondered if I really wanted to get back to that existence. It was certainly more exciting being a private investigator.

A car pulled up. It was Susan. I got in the car and laid my head back against the seat.

"Are you okay?" she said softly.

"Yeah, I'm tired, that's all."

I sat up straighter and told her again that I was sorry about missing dinner. Then I told her how the investigation was going and about my day and about how I had been arrested and locked in the little room. She pulled up outside my apartment. She reached over and patted my cheek. "You poor thing, are you hungry, do you want to go somewhere and get something to eat?"

"No, I just want to get some sleep."

"Will I see you tomorrow?"

"Joe and I need to check some things out tomorrow. But you and your mom go to church at St. Clarisa's on Sunday, don't you?"

"Yes, we go to eleven-thirty mass. It usually lets out around twelve-fifteen."

"Why don't you pick me up here after you go to church and the three of us can go out to that place in College Hill, the Wigwam."

"That sounds good to me. Now you get upstairs and get some sleep." She reached over and kissed me. "And please be careful tomorrow, whatever you're doing with this case."

I got out of the car and went upstairs. I didn't even bother to look across the street to see if the lights were on in the Ideal.

I DIDN'T WAKE UP UNTIL TWENTY PAST NINE ON SATURDAY morning. The first thing I noticed was that I was starving. I hadn't had anything to eat since the fish at Five Points yesterday. I got dressed quickly and walked over to the Colonial Inn, picking up a paper on the way.

The place was fairly crowded, mostly older folks having a late Saturday morning breakfast. Frank looked out of the kitchen as I walked in and motioned me to the back.

"Sit over there in the booth, I want to hear what's going on while you eat. What do you want?"

"I'm starving, give me pancakes and three eggs."

"I've got some nice ham slices, I'll throw one of them on."

"Okay," I said, "and a couple of biscuits." I sat at the booth and opened my paper. Frank brought me some coffee. I looked at the front page of the paper, but didn't really pay any attention to it. Everything I had done during the past week was running through my mind. I felt I had all the loose ends nearly tied up. There was only one thing that bothered me. I didn't know who to go to with what I knew. That Lowell Mosley character I'd talked to was definitely a fake, I figured that out, although I wasn't sure who'd put him up to it.

I couldn't go to the police; Clements and Stutter didn't trust me and they certainly wouldn't believe me. Maybe it would be better to pass the information to Sam Callmeyer, but it was hard to take him seriously when he was complaining about the number of circulars that Sears sent out.

My food came and interrupted my thoughts. Frank put the plates on the table then sat down opposite me. "Now then, tell me what's going on, Ed. Seems like everybody thinks Jimmy Saline killed Henry, but the grapevine says that you don't think he did."

I was busy eating my breakfast, but between mouthfuls I talked to Frank. "I don't think that Saline isn't the killer, but proving it is going to be difficult. The police think he did it and they think he's hiding out somewhere."

"There's lots of places to hide out in Delhi," Frank said.

"I don't think he is hiding. I think he was kidnapped—but I do think he is being held in Delhi. Joe Newmann is going to be looking around out there today."

"Joe the cop?" Frank asked.

I nodded, I had a mouthful of biscuit. "Joe's okay," I finally managed to say.

Frank poured me some more coffee out of the pot he had brought to the table. "If Jimmy Saline didn't kill Henry, then who did?"

"I can't tell you yet. I don't want to tip him off. I've got a lot of information. I've just been sitting here trying to figure out who to turn it over to."

"Can't you give it to the cops?"

"There's a whole lot more to this than Henry's murder. I don't think the police would know how to handle it any more than I do. Besides, the cops don't like me."

I finished my meal and paid my check. Frank told me to be careful. I walked over to the Ideal and found Walt working behind the bar.

"How's it going, Corky?" he asked. "Have you solved the mystery yet?"

"Yeah, I think I have, I just don't know who to tell about it."

"I guess you should go to the police."

"Well, the police don't like me very much. They arrested me last night."

"Arrested you, for what?"

"Nothing really, I think they were just harassing me. It's over, and it wasn't a big deal."

The phone rang. Walt answered it. "It's for you, Cork."

I walked over to the phone. "Hello," I said into it.

"Oh, hi Joe, how are you doing?"

"No, they didn't do anything to me, just left me sit in a room for a couple of hours."

"A little after nine."

"That's okay, Susan picked me up."

"After I explained it, she wasn't too mad. We made a date for Sunday. Have you checked out any hiding places in Delhi?"

"Are you out there now? You're at Five Points? Well, be careful, if you discover anything it could be dangerous."

"I'll call you tonight, yeah, about eight. Be careful."

I hung up the phone. "Give me an orange, Walt, I'm going home."

I drank my soft drink, but then instead of going to my apartment, I went to the office. I sat at Susan's desk, thinking and dozing. I was surprised to see Talbert Herzog pull up across the street. Was it that late already? I stuck my head out the door and hollered. I then locked the door and ran over and got in Talbert's car.

"Am I early?" asked Herzog.

"No, I was daydreaming and I didn't realize that it had gotten so late."

Talbert wasn't very talkative. We drove, mostly in silence. Herzog did ask what I hoped to find in the waterfront warehouse. I told him that I wasn't sure, but that I wanted to see the submarine if I could.

We got downtown and parked on the public landing, near where the Belle of Avon docked. The boat wasn't at the wharf; I figured it was probably out on a cruise.

Herzog said, "It is better that we walk from here. The guards would notice the car."

We crossed some railroad tracks and an empty area where there were old barrels and refuse laying around. Talbert stopped behind some barrels. I motioned for me to join him.

"You see, one side of the building is right at the river's edge. If we go around the other side, I think we will find an open window and we can climb in. The guards are probably around the front, the opposite end from where we are. Try to stay low and behind things. Let's go."

I took off, running low to the ground, taking advantage of the piles of garbage for cover. I thought that this was awfully easy for something that was supposed to be top secret, but I started for the side of the building, running and dodging, just like Herzog did.

I ran around the building and pulled up short. Herzog was trying to jimmy a window with a piece of pipe he had found, and with a slight squeak, he had the window open. He motioned for me to give him a hand up. He disappeared through the window. Soon his head popped out of the window and he offered me a hand, helping me get in through the window.

We both stood still for a moment until our eyes became accustomed to the gloom. I was amazed by what I saw. The warehouse was actually a huge boathouse. There was no floor except around the edges, instead, a large hole had been excavated in the river bank, and the river had been allowed to flood it. The river side wall was a big door, hinged so that whatever was in the warehouse could be floated out onto the river.

Right in the middle of this huge room was a barge, riding very low in the water. Mounted on the barge, almost completely submerged, was sort of a dome-shaped thing made of hard rubber. Talbert and I walked out on the barge on the river side.

"Look," I said "On a dark night, you could mistake this thing for a whale, but I don't think it's a submarine. I think Moby Trick is a fake."

A shot rang out, and I heard something whiz past my ear. I dove into the water. Herzog dropped to the deck. The front door flew open and four figures rushed in. The man in the lead had a gun in his hand and fired four more shots, then just as I recognized him as Sam Callmeyer, the G-man mailman, he tripped over the mail bag he was carrying and fell flat on the deck.

I swam to the edge of the deck and looked back at the window just in time to see a figure dressed all in black clamber out of it. Then I glanced back at the three figures that were still on their feet. I saw that two of them were security guards and one was Joe Newmann. There was a lot of shouting and running around until finally they all decided that the gunman had gotten away.

Sam Callmeyer had recovered himself enough to get to his feet and run over to where Talbert was lying on the deck. He helped him up; Talbert wasn't hurt. Joe and the guards came over and pulled me out of the water.

One of the guards said, "Hold these two guys. I'll call the police."

Callmeyer pulled his wallet out of his pocket and showed his badge to the two guards. "It won't be necessary to call the police, I'll take care of this. Do you have a blanket?"

The guards found a blanket in the first aid room. They wrapped me in it and I got into Joe's car, which was parked right outside. Callmeyer said he would ride back to the corner with Herzog.

"I'm sure grateful that you were down here, but why were you here? And how come Sam was with you?" I asked Joe while they were driving back to Price Hill.

"I was worried about you. I knew what you were doing and I was afraid you would get into trouble," Joe said.

"Which I did . . ."

"Anyway, I remembered that you let slip to me that Slippery Sam was a G-man, so I grabbed him out of the Ideal and came on down."

"I'm sure glad you did. I know that was Father O'Toole who shot at me."

"Yeah, and I'm pretty sure he knows you know, so he won't quit trying. You had better tell somebody about him."

"Who can I tell?"

"Tell Sam the G-man."

"He was here, so he knows. I'm hungry, you want to get a sandwich at the Colonial?"

"No. I'm having dinner at my mom's tonight. If I don't eat everything in sight, she thinks I'm sick. I have to go with an empty stomach. Anyway, you're soaking wet."

"How about doing me a favor then, drop me off at my apartment and get me a ham and Swiss cheese double-decker. I can take a hot bath, have my double-decker, then go to bed. That way, I'll be good and rested when I have to face Susan and her mother tomorrow." I reached in my wallet and gave Joe a soggy dollar bill.

"Do you want something to drink?"

"No, I'll make coffee."

I got to my apartment and peeled off my wet clothes. I put on a robe and my grey slippers. I looked at the sole of the right one, it was getting pretty thin. I had started the water in the tub and was putting coffee into the pot when I heard a knock at the door. I opened it and Joe was there holding a bag.

"Frank threw in some potato chips, and your change is in the bag. Rest up, now."

"Thanks, Joe. Good night," I said as I closed the door behind him.

CHAPTER **23**

I GOT UP ABOUT SEVEN-THIRTY AND PUT THE COFFEE ON. Sunday was usually a boring day. After the week I had just had, a boring day looked pretty good. There wasn't much I could do about my investigation. Jake certainly wouldn't be available to drive me anywhere, and Joe was at his mother's house for the day. Anyway, I had a date this afternoon for lunch at the Wigwam.

I got my paper, came back to the apartment, drank my coffee, and read the paper. The real reason that Sundays were so boring was because the Ideal Café was closed. I guess I was beginning to realize that the only exciting things in my life were the café and its denizens.

Until this last week. Life had suddenly become very busy and very exciting. On top of everything else, I was apparently getting married. Have to talk about that at lunch. Susan was picking me up after she and her mother got out of church, and the three of us were going to drive out to College Hill for lunch.

After I had cleaned myself up and eaten my sandwich the night before, I had gone down to my office to call Susan and assure her I'd be ready to go to lunch on Sunday when they got out of church.

I didn't tell her anything about what happened at the barge company. She was irritated enough about my involvement with the Holthaus investigation. So I just told her I had gotten home pretty late and was very close to solving the case.

I was—I had most of the pieces, but I still wondered where Jimmy Saline was. I knew that those two Nazis had taken him somewhere. I just hoped that Jimmy was still alive.

I happened to look out the window and I saw someone in the Ideal. It was Walt; sometimes he came up on Sunday mornings to clean up or fill the bottle boxes. Yeah, he was mopping the floor.

I went to get another cup of coffee then went back to the window. Walt was out front now, looking up at my window. He was waving both arms.

I opened the window. "Do you want me?" I called down.

140

"Yeah," Walt shouted, "Arnold Mix is on the phone. He wants to talk to you."

"I'll be right down." I didn't have a phone in the apartment. I thought the one in my office was all that was necessary. I didn't like phones very much anyway.

I turned off the stove and ran down the steps and over to the Ideal. As I went in I asked, "What's he want?"

Walt answered, "I don't know, he didn't say. Don't slip on the wet floor." The warning came a little too late, and I slid across the floor and slammed into the wall by the telephone.

"You okay?" asked Walt.

"Yeah," I picked up the receiver. "Hello!"

"You'd sound funny too if you just ran down three flights of stairs, dodged church traffic to cross the street, then slid across a slippery floor right into a wall ..."

"That's all right, it's not your fault. What's going on?"

"Yeah, I had a feeling there might be something you weren't telling me. You're kidding! Yeah, I'd like to see that, too, but I don't know how I would get out there. Jackson's wife keeps him at home on Sundays ..."

"Wait a minute, I'll ask him."

I held my hand over the mouthpiece and said to Walt, "Arnold's got some more information for me on the Holthaus case. And the Mixites are getting ready to go to the river for their Spiritual Soaking or whatever it is. Anyway, Mix wants to give me his information in person, something about not trusting the party lines, and he invited me to come out and watch the Mixite spectacle from his place this morning. He's got a perfect view of the river from there. You want to go? I need a ride."

"Sure," said Walt, "let's go."

I went back to the phone, "Okay, Arnold, we'll be right out, but I have to be back here by noon, my life depends on it ..."

"Okay, we're on our way. Walt's locking the door. Goodbye."

I went out and Walt did lock the door. We walked down the street to Walt's house, where his car was parked in the drive. We got in and Walt backed out. We took off down Cleves Pike. My head snapped back. I shut my eyes and held my breath. It seemed like no time and we were passing Mount St. Joe College.

I opened my eyes; we were almost to Mix's place. There was a pretty steady stream of cars and trucks pulling out of the drive as we drove up, and we could hear snatches of song.

"...and the antelope play." The Mixites were singing at the top of their lungs.

The last car pulled out and Walt started to pull in, then he stopped. Another pickup truck came roaring out, the passengers singing loudly.

"...is heard a discouraging word," and then they were gone.

Walt looked and then carefully pulled in. Arnold came over to meet us.

"There they go to the river. I hope nobody drowns. They're nice people, I really like them."

"What were they all singing?"

"Oh, that was one of their hymns. Come on over here, behind this shed." They walked around a shed and a beautiful panoramic view of the Ohio River met their eyes.

"Wow," said Walt, "I didn't know you had such a great view. Look, there's the Anderson Ferry. This is beautiful."

Mix managed to pull me aside. "I've got to talk to you." He glanced over where Walt was standing. "Can you come into the house a minute?"

"Sure."

Mix pointed to three wooden yard chairs he had moved from his porch, and a Thermos bottle full of coffee and three mugs on a small table.

"Have a seat, Walt, and help yourself to a cup of coffee. We'll be right back." I followed Mix into the house.

Arnold seemed a little agitated. "That little snake was out here again, early this morning. He got another message and he wrote it down. This time he made a little mistake. He dropped the note and I found it. It don't make no sense to me, but here it is."

I looked at the note. It didn't make any sense to me, either. I stuck it in my pocket and we went out to join Walt and sat in the remaining two chairs on the porch.

"I thought we might as well be comfortable while we watched. They should be getting down there pretty soon."

"This is okay, Arnold," said Walt as he sat in one of the chairs. "You sure know how to throw a party."

I looked at Mix. He was relaxed, sitting back in his yard chair, sipping his coffee. The weight of the world was off his shoulders now—unfortunately, it had landed right on mine and I still didn't have all the answers.

"Arnold, you haven't seen anything of Jimmy Saline, have you?" I asked.

"No, I sure haven't, Ed. And I'm not holding out on you this time. I heard he'd gone missing, since Friday isn't it?"

"Yes, and I'm worried about him. I think he could be in serious danger."

"Look, look there, the 'Straight Shooters' are starting to arrive."

"Straight Shooters?"

"That's what they call themselves. Look, they're pulling in all over the river bank. Oh, look at them all, ain't it a glorious sight?" Mix was absolutely jubilant now.

"What are those things?" asked Walt.

"Those are red rubber inner tubes, ain't they glorious! There's a hundred and seven of 'em."

"What are they going to do with them?" Walt and I said at the same time.

"They'll tie them together with rope, then launch out into the river, hallelujah!"

The tiny creatures on the river were scurrying around like ants. The ferry was on the Kentucky side, and you could see that the Mixites were trying to get their Spiritual Launching completed before it returned to the Ohio side.

The first of the Mixites was into the water, and he was soon followed by another and then another. It was a stirring sight.

"Hallelujah!" shouted Mix again. He was watching the show through a pair of field glasses he had around his neck.

"Wait a minute, what's that?" I yelled suddenly. I pointed down river about fifty yards from where the "Straight Shooters" were launching. I grabbed Mix's field glasses, almost strangling him. Mix managed to pull the strap off his neck and handed the glasses to me.

"Look down there," I said, passing the glasses to Walt, "see that black car? Those three guys, I'm sure that's Armbruster and Tune, and Jimmy Saline is with them. They're loading something into that boat."

"I think that's the Salines' boat," said Arnold.

"Hey, it looks like those are explosives in the boxes they're loading," Walt said, still looking through the field glasses. "Yeah, I can read it on the side of the boxes, they're definitely loading explosives into that boat."

I turned white. "They're going to blow up Moby Trick—and God knows what or who else they might blow up in the process!"

"What's Moby Trick?" asked Arnold and Walt in unison.

"Never mind. We've got to stop them."

"I'd say we're too late. The boat is pulling out."

Arnold Mix had taken back the glasses. He said, "That's Saline running the boat and ... Oh my God, look what's happened with the Mixites!"

The inner-tubed Mixites had spread down the river, one hundred and seven strong, and were blocking the progress of the Anderson Ferry, which was trying to get back to the Ohio side. It was carrying four cars and tooting its whistle furiously.

In the motorboat, Jimmy Saline was trying to get around the ferry and past the inner tubes. He made it around the boat and tried to go through the line of Mixites. His boat snared one of the lines connecting the tubes. Four "Straight Shooters" flew from their rings. Luckily, the ferry was just a little behind the near catastrophe and the crew managed to snatch the hapless four from the river. Saline continued on up river. His forward progress was impeded by the drag of one hundred and seven inner tubes and the one hundred and three people hanging on to them. No, make that ninety-seven people; as they watched, six more Mixites slipped into the river.

The Anderson Ferry was still but a short distance behind the flotilla. The captain must have realized the danger the tube riders were in and he was trying to rescue as many as possible. The ferry crew grabbed the six souls in the water and pulled them to safety.

The strange tableau continued slowly up the river as I watched helplessly from the hillside.

"We have to stop them," I shouted. "They could kill themselves and a lot other peoples, not to mention destroying the sub."

"What sub?" asked Mix.

"Never mind, Arnold."

Walt grabbed Mix and started for the house. "Where's your telephone?"

The three of us went into Arnold's house. He pointed to the phone. Walt grabbed it and dialed a number.

"Benny usually sleeps in his office at the boat dock on Saturday nights. He should be there."

"Hello, is Benny there?"

"Yes, I mean Mr. Graham."

"Go wake him, this is very important."

"I don't care what he will do to you. This is Captain Winger and if Mr. Graham is not on the other end of this phone in two minutes, YOU'RE FIRED!" Walt shouted the last two words.

He held his hand over the mouthpiece. "Whoever I was talking to is going to get him."

He put the phone back to his ear. "Benny, this is Walt."

"I don't care, you can always sleep."

"Yeah, yeah, yeah, is any of the crew there?"

"Is that enough to run the boat?"

"If I wanted Captain Winger to run the boat, I would have called Captain Winger, wouldn't I? Benny, this is important. Do you have enough people to run the boat?"

"Alright, now listen carefully. Don't ask me if I'm kidding, this is the truth."

"Hymie Hermann, the river pirate, is headed up river toward you. He is in a motorboat full of explosives and he intends to rob you and blow up your offices and the dock."

"Benny, I told you not to ask me that. Am I getting through to you? Someone wants to steal last night's receipts and blow up the dock and the Belle too, if you are sitting at the dock. You have to take the boat out and run them down."

"We'll get the police, but they can't get there as soon as we can. You have to slow the pirates down."

"Yes, get her cranked up, roust out what crew you can. Tell them that they'll all be killed unless you get away from the dock."

"You can call Winger if you want, but you'll have to take her out before he gets there. He lives in New Richmond, for Pete's sake."

"Listen to me, Benny, don't panic. You can run the boat. You've watched Cap Winger a thousand times. You can do it."

"One more thing. Listen very carefully, this is very important."

"Ed McCorkel and I are on our way down there. We'll get there long before the motorboat, so don't leave without us. I have a plan that will save the receipts, the dock, and the boat, so remember, do not leave without us."

"Okay, go ahead and get things going. We're on our way."

"Yes, Benny, it is the right thing to do. It's the only thing you can do if you want to save everything. Get going."

Walt hung up the phone. I grabbed it back and handed it to Mix. "Listen carefully, we're going to try to stop Saline. You call the Cincinnati police and tell them to get Sergeant Stutter and Detective Clements to meet us at the Belle of Avon's landing dock. Tell them as much as you have to, but get them there. Also tell them to try to get in touch with Sam Callmeyer. You got all that?"

"Call the police, tell them to get Stutter and, do you mean Sam Callmeyer the mailman?"

"Yeah, I'm sorry, I don't have time to answer any more questions. I know it all sounds crazy, but please just do what I told you to. And one more thing—if O'Toole comes back here, watch out. There's no telling what he'll do."

"Don't worry, Ed, I've learned my lesson. I'll keep my distance from him." Before Mix had finished talking, I ran out of the house and jumped into Walt's car. We sped away before he even had the car door closed.

"What kind of a story was that that you told Benny? Saline isn't going to try to rob the Belle of Avon, and who the heck is Hymie Herzog?"

Walt was already on West Eighth Street, headed for the viaduct.

"Do you think he would have believed me if I told him that Jimmy Saline was going to blow up a submarine in the Ohio River? I'm not even sure that I believe that one. Anyway, I had to make it something personal to get Benny moving fast. He loves that old boat and the money it makes. He'd do anything to keep both safe."

"And Hymie Herzog?"

"I said Hymie Hermann, and he actually was a river pirate. Back in the early 1800s he raided and devastated the little hamlet of Rabbit Hash, Kentucky."

"You could give the Prince a run for his money," I mused.

We soared over the viaduct. Luckily, it was Sunday and there was very little traffic. "You don't think he'll take off before we get there, do you?" I asked.

"No, it takes a while to get the boilers going. They probably had the fires banked, but it still takes a little time to get up a full head of steam. Anyway, Benny needs me to tell him what to do, so he won't go without us."

We made it through town without stopping for a light. The lights weren't always green, but we didn't stop. We spun off of Seventh on to Broadway and down to the dock. As Walt squealed to a stop, we could see smoke billowing out of the smokestacks and the calliope was playing madly.

We ran across the dock and up the gangplank, raced up the grand staircase, and then to the upper deck and over to the pilothouse. Bennie was standing in front of the wheel.

"Walt, I don't think we should do this," Benny said quietly. He was very pale.

Walt shouted, "Belay that, partner, you're the captain! Let's get this tub underway."

Benny stuck his head out the window of the pilothouse, "Cast off all lines."

He then leaned over the speaking tube, pulled a lever back, and said, "Aft, a quarter." Slowly, the big paddlewheel started turning and the boat started moving backward.

"All stop," cried Benny. The paddlewheel came to a stop.

"Forward a half," said newly appointed Captain Graham, while turning the wheel slightly.

The grand steamboat sailed out into the current and started majestically down river while the calliope continued to play in a frenzied manner.

"Why is Larry playing the calliope?" Walt wanted to know.

"Ahead full," Benny said into the speaker, then he turned to Walt and said, "He slept on board last night and woke up with a hangover. He kept trying to help the crew, and getting in the way. Finally I told him to play something and he hasn't stopped."

The Belle had passed under the last bridge and now they were at the outer limits of the downtown area. They still had seen no sign of Saline.

"You don't think he could have gotten past us, do you?" I asked.

"Are you kidding, even if he got rid of the inner tubes, he couldn't be this far yet. There's a good-size bend in the river up here. We'll see him soon, don't worry. Benny, do you have any binoculars?" Walt asked.

Benny didn't answer, but he reached down in a cabinet and handed Walt a pair of binoculars, and then handed me an old-fashioned brass telescope.

I looked through it and said, "I can see them. Saline is still dragging the inner tubes, and it looks like about a dozen or so people are left in them."

Even as I spoke, two more dropped off. The two that dropped off were quickly picked up by the Anderson Ferry, which was still trailing the procession.

"I see them." Walt had walked out of the pilothouse and was standing on the upper deck talking to me through the window.

"Saline doesn't have much control over the boat because of the drag. That's perfect, but I wish there weren't any people in those inner tubes."

Just as he spoke, four more people dropped off the tubes, then two more. They were all picked up. There were only six people left clinging to their tubes.

All the rescued survivors from the inner tubes were standing around the four cars on the ferry's deck. When they made out the Belle bearing down on them, they gave a mighty cheer. The ferry tooted its horn, and Benny reached up and pulled the cord on the Belle's steam whistle.

"BENNY, YOU HAVE TO DO EVERYTHING YOU CAN TO SLOW that boat down, to give the police time to get to the dock!" yelled Walt. "But don't let them get too close. They have explosives on board."

I don't think Benny even heard him. He was running the Belle and he was in his glory . . . by this time, the Belle was just abreast of Mount Echo Park, and the distance between her and the motorboat was rapidly diminishing. Jimmy tried to get away from her. He turned his craft toward the Kentucky side. Benny spun the wheel and headed in the same direction. The motorboat was sluggish, but it was still easier to maneuver than the big steamship.

The big boat was sideways in the river now, heading towards the Kentucky shoreline at a pretty rapid clip. Saline turned his boat and went the opposite way.

Benny yelled into the tube, "One quarter speed," and then he said, "Reverse engines!" The paddlewheel started turning the other way, the steamboat slowed, stopped, then started going backwards.

The six remaining tubers had abandoned ship when Saline had turned toward Kentucky. They were all safely aboard the Anderson Ferry.

"What the hell's that sound?" said Benny.

"It's the calliope," I replied.

"No, it's more like a moaning sound."

Suddenly, Larry stopped playing the boat's calliope. Then they could hear it plainly. The Mixites on the ferry were singing "Nearer My God to Thee." Then Larry picked up the beat and the calliope tooted along with the singers.

Meanwhile, the Belle of Avon was backing rapidly toward the Ohio shore. Saline, having lost the weight of the people on the inner tubes, had a little more maneuverability. He turned again.

Benny screamed, "Forward all engines!" The old girl tried, but there was just a moment's hesitation. Saline was getting away. Benny spun the wheel furiously, trying to head off the motorboat, but Saline was going to make it past them.

As the Belle turned, Saline shot past her and up river, right into the path of an oncoming barge. Saline must have seen immediately that it would be impossible to dodge this next obstacle. He cut the engine and jumped overboard.

One of the Belle's crew threw him a line, and even as they were pulling him in, Benny gave the signal for full speed ahead and raced down river, away from the impending disaster. The ferry boat beat it toward the Ohio shore as the steamboat sailed past.

As the barge lumbered into the Saline's small boat, there was a tremendous explosion. Suddenly, the ferry boat and the Belle were being pelted with small missiles.

"What is that?" asked Benny. "Hail?" He stuck his band out the window.

Walt ducked inside the pilothouse. "No, it's corn. That barge must have been headed for the distillery."

Mercifully, the calliope stopped playing. Larry was running for cover. The Mixites on the ferry were huddled against the cars, trying to protect themselves from the rain of corn.

"The other two guys, Armbruster and Tone, the Nazis, what happened to them?" I shouted.

"I don't know," Walt yelled back. "They must have gone up with the corn. If they were Nazis, I say good riddance."

"Yeah," I said, but I kept scanning the river.

The crew of the tugboat was desperately trying to detach the damaged barge from the other two they were towing. They got it loose just before it started to sink to the bottom. The tow edged the two remaining barges toward the Kentucky shore.

The ferry gave a little toot and headed for its home port. Benny pulled the cord and gave a blast on the Belle's whistle, then he turned her into the current and started back to the dock. He reached up on a hook and pulled down Cap Winger's hat and set it on his head at a jaunty angle.

He said, "Not too bad, if I do say so myself."

Walt patted him on the back, "You really did a good job, now all you have to do now is land this thing."

Benny paled a little, but continued up river. As he neared the dock, he called for "Ahead slow." He gently guided the big boat into shore. "All stop," he shouted. The boat slowed even more. He came even with the dock and yelled "Reverse engines!" as the Belle slammed into the dock and stopped dead. There was a great grinding sound, but there didn't appear to be any major damage.

Walt and I ran down the three flights of steps. The crew had tied up Saline and were holding him.

As the gangplank was being lowered, we could see a welcoming committee waiting for us. Captain Winger was there, right in front. Next we could see Stutter and Clements, along with four other policemen. Behind them were Sam Callmeyer and his partner, and finally there was a well-known city councilman screaming about pigeons and corn. Over on the other side of the dock, I spotted Joe Newmann.

The crew had gotten the gangplank in place and the mob on shore started aboard. Benny's head appeared over the rail of the upper deck. He had obviously gone straight to the ship's bar after docking the Belle, because he was roaring drunk. He waved and called out, "Hail the conquering hero comes!" then fell over the rail. He landed at the feet of the startled assembly, said something about being used to hardships, and passed out.

There was chaos. "Help him up!"

"No, leave him alone!"

"Call a doctor!"

"Call the nut house!"

CHAPTER 25

I TOOK ADVANTAGE OF THE CONFUSION TO CROSS THE PLANK and go over to where Newmann was standing to tell him what I'd found out from Arnold Mix.

"Mix found a note that O'Toole dropped. He thinks it's a message that he got from Kentucky. O'Toole was out at his place early this morning and got a daylight message. That's the first time that has ever happened, Mix told me. Apparently after the priest wrote down the message, he dropped it, then jumped on his motorcycle and sped off. Mix picked up the message and gave it to me this morning."

I handed him the slip of paper of paper. Written on it were a jumble of letters and numbers:

EL GROOVE ARV LUNK 2:45

"What do you make of it?" Joe asked. "It looks like it might be Spanish."

I thought about it. "Groove, that name sounds familiar. It was in the paper recently. I know, a General Groove was supposed to be coming to Cincinnati to confer with Lowell Mosley."

I asked Joe where his car was, and Joe pointed at it parked on the landing. I noticed that Clements and Stutter were coming off the gangplank in our direction.

"Don't ask questions," I said, "but when I say go, run for the car and get us to Lunken Airport as fast as you can. GO!"

We sprinted across the dock, jumped a low fence, ran to the car, and got in. Joe had the keys in his hand, jammed them into the ignition, and we were away. We were flying out Columbia Parkway before the car stopped shaking. The speedometer was past eighty and climbing.

Just then we heard a siren. I looked back, "Oh, for Pete's sake, I think it's Chiggerbox on his motorcycle. What's he doing here? Joe, kick it up so he can't catch us, it's a matter of life and death."

"I don't think that's possible, but I'll try. What are we doing?" demanded Joe.

"I'll try to explain . . . The note that Mix gave me, I think what it means is 'Eliminate Groove, arriving Lunken at 2:45.' Groove is an Army general who is flying into Lunken Airport this afternoon." I paused before telling Joe what I'd figured out. "I also think that Father O'Toole is actually a professional assassin."

"And you think O'Toole is headed to Lunken to kill this guy Groove? Isn't that a little farfetched? I mean, O'Toole is a priest."

"I don't know if he really is a priest or not, but I do know that he's dangerous. He has already killed Henry Holthaus, and he's taken at least one shot at me, maybe two. You saw him yesterday, down at the boathouse."

"Yeah, I think I did, but . . ." Joe slowed a little as he got off the Parkway on to Kellogg Avenue. Another motorcycle went shooting past us and the driver wasn't Chiggerbox—it was a much smaller man, dressed all in black.

"There he is!" I shouted. "It's O'Toole—don't let him get out of sight!"

"Holy cow, he must be doing a hundred," said Joe.

"Just don't let him get away from us." I noticed that yet another motorcycle had joined the chase, another policeman, I thought. I did not mention it to Joe.

Suddenly we started catching up to the priest, but it was only because he had slowed to make the turn into the road to the airport. Joe jammed on his brakes and slid into the airport road. O'Toole had disappeared.

"Pull it right up to the steps," I barked.

Joe slammed on his brakes and slid about thirty feet to the steps. The car went up three of them before it ran into a wall and crashed to a stop. Some pieces of the car flew off.

I was out of the car in a flash with Joe right behind me. We ran through the terminal with Chiggerbox and the other motorcycle policeman right behind us.

I plowed through the door and onto the field. There was an Army plane, painted in camouflage colors, parked on the tarmac. Men in khaki uniforms were coming down the steps. I ran toward the steps, right into a military policeman. I bowled the man over and Joe fell on top of us. Three other military policemen jumped on top of us.

Just then, Chiggerbox saw O'Toole, who had come from around the corner of the terminal and was drawing his gun. Chiggerbox grabbed a piece of metal laying by Joe's car, jumped over the pile of bodies, and raced for the priest. He brought the metal bar down on the priest's wrist. The gun went flying, and unfortunately, it discharged. The bullet went through Chiggerbox's hand and then slammed harmlessly into the ground.

The other police officer, who was right behind Chiggerbox, grabbed O'Toole and threw him to the ground. The priest's arm was badly broken and was bleeding profusely. Chiggerbox was dancing around holding his own bloody hand.

The four military police had untangled themselves. Two of them hauled Joe and me to our feet and were holding us.

The other two roughly pulled O'Toole to his feet. They were not the least concerned about his terribly mangled wrist.

A medic with the Army contingent had gone over to Chiggerbox to minister to his wound when Stutter and Clemments came running out of the terminal.

"Hold 'em, men, 'til we get the cuffs on 'em," said Stutter. He put a pair of handcuffs on me.

Clements was putting a pair on Joe. "McCorkel, Newmann, you're under arrest."

An Army colonel walked up to the arresting officers. "Excuse me gentlemen, but General Groove would like to know what the hell is going on here? He has gone back into the plane and requests that you join him. Just the four of you, you military policemen will not be required, but thank you for your fast action. Please gentlemen, follow me."

He led the way up the boarding steps. We followed into the plane, where the interior was set up like an office and a man wearing a general's stars was seated behind an olive drab desk.

"Gentlemen, I am General Leslie Groove, and I would like very much to hear about what just happened here. I assume someone tried to kill me?"

I shook loose of Clement's grasp and said, "Sir, if I may . . ."

The General nodded for me to continue. I introduced myself and Joe and then reluctantly introduced the two policemen. I told the General the whole story, including how the priest had been receiving messages. I told him about the strange message Mix had found and how I was lucky enough to decipher it.

"Amazing," said Groove, "a killer who thinks he's a priest. But do you reall think this fellow is Tom Mix's cousin?"

Before anyone could answer, he turned to the policemen. "It seems to me that these men thwarted an attempt on my life. I don't understand why you are arresting them."

Clements answered, "Sir, so far today these men have stolen a steamboat, destroyed a motorboat, sunk a barge, and covered downtown Cincinnati with kernels of corn, not to mention driving across town at speeds in excess of eighty miles an hour. We're not exactly arresting them. It's more like taking them into protective custody, trying to protect our town, I mean."

"Well then," said the General, "I'm sure you could remove the handcuffs."

Clements nodded and told Stutter to remove the cuffs. The sergeant did as he was told. Meanwhile, a member of Groove's staff had come onto the plane and was speaking quietly to the general. The general nodded, and the man left. Then Groove continued, "I really appreciate what you, all of you, have done here today. At the very least you have saved my life and I personally want to thank you for that. I know that the Cincinnati police will want to prosecute that man for shooting a police officer, but Army Intelligence really needs to question him. I don't believe that he will ever be returned to your jurisdiction when we finish with him."

"I am told that the officer who was shot will be all right. He is being taken to the hospital. I will have Army Intelligence make a complete report on this incident and a copy will be sent to your department. I hope that will be sufficient."

"That will have to do, sir," said Clements, but I thought he looked relieved that he didn't have to write up the report.

The General saluted. "I thank you again. Colonel Webb will see you out."

The colonel who had led us in now showed us out.

"I'd be surprised if the boss doesn't put you all in for medals." He left us at the bottom of the steps.

The second motorcycle policeman was still there. He came over to the four of us and said, "Who was driving the Ford coupe out on the front steps?"

"I was," said Joe.

"You're under arrest," the officer told him. "Let me see your driver's license."

Detective Clements showed his badge and interrupted, "I'm sorry, officer, I already have this man under arrest. I will include the speeding and reckless driving charges in my report."

"Thank you, sir. May I be excused? I would like to return to my post."

CHAPTER 26

Detective Clements told the officer that he was free to leave, and the foursome walked out of the terminal. Joe's car was still on the front steps.

"Looks like I got a busted shock," said Newmann.

"Just leave it here," Clements told him. "I want you guys to ride back with us. When we get back, Sergeant Stutter will make arrangements to have your car and Chiggerbox's motorcycle towed back to the precinct. You'll do that, won't you, Sergeant?"

"Yes, sir," said Stutter as he opened the back door of his cruiser to let Joe and me get in. Clements got in the front seat, then Stutter went around to the driver's side, got in, and drove away.

"Let's wait till we get back to the precinct before we talk about the things that happened today." The detective leaned his head back and shut his eyes. "Let's just be quiet and think about everything that happened so that we can sort it all out when we get back."

"Good God, what time is it?" I asked.

"It's about four-fifteen," said Joe.

"Oh boy, I was supposed to meet Susan at noon." I sank back in the seat and closed my eyes, too.

It took about forty-five minutes to get back to the station house in Price Hill. As soon as we walked in, I asked to use a phone. Stutter pointed to one on a desk.

"Make it snappy. We got a lot to do and I want to get home for supper."

I dialed Susan's number. The phone only rang twice before she picked it up.

"Hello?"

"Hello Susan, it's Ed."

"Ed, where are you?"

"I'm down at the police station."

"Oh, Mom," I heard her cry, "He's back in jail!" The phone was dead for a couple of seconds.

"Susan!"

"I'm still here, what did you do this time, blow something up?"

"Well, kinda. But that's not why I'm here. I'm not under arrest or anything, I'm just trying to straighten things out."

"You had better straighten things out with me. Arrested or not, you will be in the office at nine in the morning. We will lock the door and not answer the phone. You will not sneak over to the Ideal. We will talk. Do you understand?"

"And," Susan continued, "Mom and I went to the Wigwam without you. The hot slaw was delicious. The service was exceptional. I left a two dollar tip. You owe me eleven dollars. Nine o'clock tomorrow, understood?"

"Yes, dear," he said meekly. She had already hung up.

I walked over to where Joe was standing. "I think she is peeved."

"I hope you can straighten things out with her," was Joe's reply. "Do you think I'll get kicked off the force?"

"For what? You heard the general, you're a hero. You're even going to get a medal. You'll probably get a promotion, too."

"I don't know, I think I'm in trouble."

Stutter walked in just then. "Yeah, I'll say, boy, you are in trouble. I made arrangements to have your car towed in, but you are probably going to have to pay for the tow and the damage to the airport steps."

Joe's head sunk lower. Detective Clements came and took us back to that little room and sat down, motioning to us to do the same.

"Let's start with O'Toole and Mix."

I spoke up. "Mix told me that O'Toole had convinced him he was working for the Army and needed to use Mix's place to receive those Morse code messages. Mix is such a patriot, he jumped at the chance to be a part of something top secret.

"But O'Toole wasn't working for the Army, I know that much. He's on the other side, and whatever training he's had has given him lightning-like reflexes.

"While he was out at Mix's receiving one of his messages, Jimmy Saline and Henry were out driving around. They were both drunk, and Jimmy was driving. Somehow he lost control of the car and crashed into a tree, startling the priest who was hiding behind it. The priest whirled around and fired three times, then took off on his motorcycle.

"Jimmy threw the car in reverse and took off backwards. Mix thinks he saw somebody get up from under the car at that point. It looked like he fired at the passenger side window and then stumbled off.

"Arnold Mix saw the whole thing from his porch. He thinks that O'Toole killed Henry and that Jimmy panicked and set up the body at the Ideal's back door. Then he dropped Henry's car off at Whitsken's and walked home from there. Talk to Mix—he's willing to testify against O'Toole. I guess that's all."

"But what about the rest of it?" asked the sergeant. "The steamboat and the explosion, and all that?"

"National security is involved. I don't think I can discuss any of that."

"Do you really think I'm going to let you out of here without an explanation?" shouted Clements.

"I'm sorry, I guess you will have to lock me up." I thought it might be nicer being locked up for a couple of days than meeting with an irate Susan. "But please let Joe go, he doesn't know anything about it."

"Aawww, I'm not going to hold either of you. What's the point? This is all so crazy, it could take weeks to sort everything out anyway. Maybe by the time we've figured out what we want to know from you, the war will be over and you'll be able to talk without worrying about national security. Give them a ride home, would you, Bill?"

"I might as well, it's almost seven. I already missed my supper."

"We haven't had anything to eat, either," said Joe. "Could we stop at the bowling alley? It's the only place open on Sunday night."

"Sounds good to me, let's go," said Stutter as he led the way out the door.

After we ate, Stutter took me home. As I went up stairs, I wondered if I was still engaged, and what Susan was going to have to say to me tomorrow.

CHAPTER 27

IT WAS A GLOOMY MONDAY MORNING. CHARLIE HAD OPENED up the Ideal, and we were the only two people in the place. I drank my coffee and read the paper. It was full of the news from yesterday.

DRUNKEN SALESMAN STEALS
STEAMBOAT AND BLOWS UP BARGE

Sunday, September 16, 1942

The promotion manager of the Belle of Avon, the local excursion steamboat, decided to go for a joyride on the river. It is believed that he was inebriated at the time . . .

The story went on to tell how he had guided the boat up river in a peculiar manner, forward and backward, this way and that, and how he caused a private motor launch to run into a barge full of corn. How the launch and barge had exploded and how the single person in the launch had been rescued by the crew of the steamboat.

The paper then reported that the culprit, Mr. Benjamin Graham, 49, had then returned to the dock, where he attempted suicide by jumping off the upper level of the boat. The article said that he had survived the fall and was taken to the hospital in police custody.

Poor Benny, he was a hero, and look at the shabby treatment he got from the newspaper.

There was another article on the front page about the happenings at the airport. It was almost as confusing and inaccurate as the first story. It reported the attempted assassination of General Groove and that Officer Chiggerwood was the hero of the affair, and said he had been sorely wounded and was also in the hospital.

The third article was buried in the inside of the paper. It simply told of the heroic measures the Anderson Ferry crew had employed to rescue 107 members of a crazy religious cult. The paper's reporters hadn't realized that story was related to the one about Benny's unauthorized excursion on the Belle of Avon.

I was relieved to see that Joe, Walt, and I were not mentioned in any of the stories, but neither were Armbruster or Tune. I wondered what had happened to them.

When I finished reading the paper, I noticed that it was about twenty of nine. I decided I had better get over to the office to wait for Susan.

"See you later, Charlie."

"Grunt," was his reply.

I left the paper on the table. I didn't think Susan needed to read about what had happened, at least not yet and not this version. Just before nine, Susan came in. She locked the door behind her. She took off her sweater and hung it up, then turned to me.

"Sit down, and don't answer that phone if it rings. We are going to talk."

I meekly sat. "I can explain everything . . ."

"Be quiet." I could tell she was a little miffed. "Do you love me?"

I started to stammer out some sort of inane excuses about what had happened the day before.

"Just answer, yes or no."

I thought about her question.

"Stop stalling and answer me."

"Yes," I finally admitted.

"Do you still want to marry me?"

This time I didn't hesitate. "Yes."

"Will you stop playing detective?"

I didn't have to think about this one too long. I had all the pieces together. I had done a good job. And I like investigating. "No," I said.

"Well, two out of three isn't bad. We'll talk about your detective work later. Right now we're going to talk about getting married, okay?"

'Yeah, sure, let's talk."

"Mom and I have been making some plans. Since you have been so busy, we made them without you, but you have the right to make any changes you want to." She said this in a tone of voice that told me that I should only make changes at the risk of my neck.

She continued, "November 29 is a Friday and it's the day after Thanksgiving. FDR changed it to the fourth Thursday again."

"Yes, the merchants were complaining, and . . ."

"Hush!" Susan stopped me in mid-sentence. "We think that would be a good day for the wedding. Then that night we would have a small reception at the Wigwam. We both like that place. We could close the office down the first week of December and have some kind of a honeymoon. Do you want to make any changes to the plans?"

"Good," she said before I had any chance to reply.

"As I told you, I would like to have a church wedding. We have an appointment to see Monsignor Williams, the pastor of St. Clarisa's, at ten this morning. We will make the arrangements with him. Agreeable so far?"

"I, ah, I don't have a lot of luck with priests." I said, thinking about Father O'Toole.

"Hush," she said. "We have to do this. It will be all right."

At ten of ten, we locked the door of the office and walked over towards the church. We turned in at a house that was next to the church on Glenway Avenue. "Why are we going in here?" I asked her.

"This is the rectory. It's where the priests live." I guess I never thought about where priests lived. I guess I never really cared.

We got to the door and Susan rang the bell. She waited a little and rang again.

Suddenly the door flew open. "You needn't keep ringing the bell. I got here as fast as I could. Doorbells work on electricity and electricity costs money. You young people, always in a hurry. What do you want?"

I was ready to run away. The old woman at the door looked like someone Dr. Frankenstein might have manufactured. She was tall and slatternly. She wore an old colorless house dress with a huge grey apron over it. Her dirty grey hair was braided and coiled around her head like a snake. She had a large, hooked nose with a wart on one side of it.

"What do you want?" she screeched again.

"We're here to see the Monsignor," Susan said meekly. "We have an appointment at ten."

"What's that? Speak up!" the old woman screeched.

"I said, we have an . . ."

"I heard you the first time. Come in and mind you wipe your feet. Follow me."

We did as we were told and were led to a little office.

"I thought Dorothy melted her," I whispered.

Susan poked me in the ribs.

"In here," the woman said. The good father will be with you shortly. You can sit if you want." She left us.

We sat. "It seems to be going well so far," I whispered to Susan. This resulted in another poke.

We sat there in silence for about ten minutes. Finally a short, very fat, bald man walked in. He was wearing a long black dress, like the one O'Toole wore to the funeral.

Susan jumped to her feet. The fat man told her to sit down and asked what we wanted to discuss with him.

Susan stood up again. "We want to get married. My fiancé is not Catholic, but I would like a church wedding."

'Not a Catholic, eh, have you ever been baptized, Mr. . . ., uh, Mr. . . ."

"Oh, I'm sorry. This is my fiancé, Edward McCorkel."

"I repeat, have you ever been baptized Mr. McCorkel . . . McCorkel? Were you involved in the Holthaus funeral last week?"

"Well, I did attend."

"Attend, attend!" The little priest started to turn beet red. "You are the one who brought those heathens who made incantations over the deceased," he sputtered. "And that evil little foreign man, the one that knocked poor old Mrs. Bonhue down as he ran out. You are a friend of that pagan who owns the bar on Cleves Pike!"

"Walt's a friend of mine, but . . ."

"And," he interrupted me. "You caused that policeman to ruin the gate at the cemetery. The parishes have to pay for the maintenance there. That gate is going to cost us a great deal."

He was getting redder and redder as he continued, "You were the cause of the acolyte dropping the cross in the mud, a sacrilege, and the members of that cult of yours, running off in all directions.

You make a mockery of organized religion. Marry you . . .in the church . . . Ha! I just wish you were a Catholic so I could have you excommunicated!"

I tried to explain that I had nothing to do with those events, but he was sputtering and had turned an alarming purple hue.

"Get out! Get out!"

We got out and went back to the office. Susan had her handkerchief to her face and seemed to be sobbing. I sat her in a chair and ran back to the restroom to get her some water. When I got back she took the handkerchief away and was laughing so hard she was hiccupping. She drank a little of the water and controlled the hiccups.

She looked up at me, still giggling, and said, "I think that went well, don't you?" Then she burst out laughing again. When she finally gained control she said, "Oh Ed, that man is a maniac. I know you couldn't have caused all those things. Could you? But I wish I had been there to see it all!"

"You're not mad at me?"

"Of course not, you didn't do anything wrong, but I think we are going to have to make some new plans. I'm going home and tell Mom about this morning. Why don't you just close up for the rest of the day? The morning has all ready been wasted." She kissed me and left.

I decided that she would make a good wife. She sure had a sense of humor. I locked the front door and walked over to the Ideal.

OLD CHARLIE WAS STILL TENDING BAR, BUT WALT WAS IN the kitchen repairing the screen door. I got an orange soda and dragged a barstool back to where he was working. I told him about the morning's adventures. He laughed almost as much as Susan had.

"That old guy over there is something. He's been after me for years. I think it's because I won't close on Good Friday. You want to know what his favorite trick is? Whenever some bum comes to his house . . ."

"They call that a rectory," I interjected.

"Whatever, whenever some bum asks him for a handout, he sends them over here. Tells them that I'll give them a sandwich. I always give them a shot and a beer. Makes me feel like I'm getting the better of the good father. But what are you going to do about the wedding? Is there an alternate plan?" Walt asked.

"I guess Susan will come up with something."

"Let me make a telephone call. I might just be able to help you out."

He went in to the telephone. I just sat there and drank my soda, thinking about how well Susan had handled this morning's fiasco.

Walt came back. "I may have a solution for you. Can you and Susan be in your office at eight tonight?"

"Sure, I'll call her and tell her to come up. What's up?"

"Just be there."

We talked about the events of yesterday and I told him that I wish I knew what happened to the two Nazis.

"And not to change the subject or anything," I said. "But you know I promised Earl that I would look into his problem, and I haven't done much about it with all the other stuff that has been happening. I did find out that the other guy Zesta married really was a gangster, like you said. How would I go about finding a gangster in Newport?"

and decided my best bet was to keep sending it. I had somebody mail it from a different city every month.

"Then I got things straightened out, so I stopped. I thought I could let Zesta drop out of his life too, but obviously that was a mistake."

I asked, "How much money was there in her name?"

"A sizable amount. Enough that Mr. Klopp might have to have an accident. You could be in danger, too."

I laughed. "Mr. Starret I've been threatened lately by some pretty impressive villains, so don't try to scare me. It doesn't work, threatening me." I was getting pretty good at this bluffing game. "But maybe I have a solution to your problem."

"I'm listening."

"As I see it, the money is rightly yours, and Earl would only get into trouble with it anyway, but he should get something out of this."

"I'm still listening."

"I suggest you continue sending his allowance every month. Maybe knock it down to a hundred and have postcards sent from various places, from Zesta, of course. Earl doesn't have to learn about her demise, and he won't cause you any more trouble."

"You're a reasonable man," said Starret. "I'm glad you won't have to have an accident, but what's in it for you?"

I thought for a moment. "I think you should pay my fee for the investigation I carried out for Earl."

"That's agreeable." Starret reached into his pocket and pulled out a wad of bills. "Does a thousand dollars sound fair?"

"No, twenty-five dollars is fair, that's all I want."

"You're a decent man, McCorkel , but a sucker."

Starret peeled off a twenty and a ten and handed it to me. "The extra five is for cab fare. Tillie down the street called me and warned me you were coming. Said you arrived in a taxi. If I can ever do anything for you, let me know."

I pocketed the money. "Maybe you could do something for me. I'm trying to find out what happened to a guy named Kruger. I think he was from Newport."

"I know Kruger, he fell in with a couple of hard cases, not the kind of guys we want around. I hear he got hurt . . . shot in the arm and later run over by a car, something like that. Word is that he's in bad shape and hiding out with those guys he's been keeping company with, in that big yellow house, looks like a barn, in Constance. You know, down by the ferry."

I was excited. I might have just learned where Kruger, Armbruster, and Tune were hiding out. "Just one more thing, could somebody call me a cab? I need to get back to the Ideal."

"The Ideal? In Price Hill? Do you know Walt?"

I told him that I did.

"Son of a gun, tell him I said hello. Haven't seen him in a long time. Nice meeting you, McCorkel."

My taxi came and took me back to the corner. I walked into the café and saw Sam Callmeyer. I took him back to the kitchen and told him about the tip I had gotten about the whereabouts of the Nazis. He said he would check it out.

I walked out of the kitchen just as the Prince walked in the front door. "Ed, Ed, the Pope was here, he came to bless the flowers!" he shouted at me, then stormed out. I looked at Walt quizzically.

"It was Arnold Mix," Walt explained. "He has become the 'Supreme Wrangler' of the Mixites. He's selling his place and moving to someplace in Pennsylvania near where his cousin was born. It's become a shrine."

"I've got to get out of here," I said, shaking my head. "If anybody sees Earl Klopp, tell him to come see me in my office."

It was half past six. I walked over to Wimpie's and picked up a couple of hamburgers and a Coke and went back to the office. I had just about finished them when I heard somebody banging on the front door. It was Klopp. I let him in.

"You wanted to see me?"

I knew the corner grapevine was good, but I didn't know it was that good.

I walked into my office with Klopp following. "Sit down, Earl."

"I managed to reach Zesta by telephone," I lied. "She's planning a long trip and was so busy she forgot to send you anything last month. She has made arrangements so you'll get a hundred bucks every month, and she will send you postcards from time to time."

"That's wonderful, Ed." He was visibly relieved. "I'm happy that she is okay and I hope she has a good time on her trip. Do I owe you anything or are we square?"

"Actually, I owe you." I reached in my pocket and pulled out the twenty-five bucks. "It only took two telephone calls to straighten all this out, so you owe me a dime."

Earl stood up, reached in his pocket and handed me a dime, and bounced out the door.

I just sat there at my desk, thinking about the past week. I had it all together now. I'm a pretty good detective, I had to say. Even this afternoon with those thugs from Newport, I had held my own. While I was mentally patting myself on the back, I heard the door open. Susan came in, it was quarter to eight.

"You look like you had a pretty good afternoon," she said.

I went over and gave her a kiss. "You might say I had a miraculous afternoon . . . I raised the dead."

"So, why are we here?" asked Susan. "What's so important that I had to miss 'One Man's Family' on the radio?"

"I don't know, I told Walt about our meeting with the Monsignor, and after he stopped laughing, he made a telephone call, then told me to be here with you at eight."

Susan sat at her desk. "I told my mom about what happened this morning. She didn't find it so amusing. She smiled a little at the part about Mrs. Bonhue getting knocked down, though. Mom never liked her."

"But you know I wasn't responsible for any of those things he accused me of."

"I explained that to her and she understood. She was just worried about Father Williams. He is such a volatile man, she worries about his health."

Just then there was a knock on the door and Walt walked in followed by another man. The man was all dressed in black, just like O'Toole always was.

Walt pulled him forward and said, "I left Brownie behind the bar, so I have to get right back or I won't have any booze left. This is Bob Logan, who is a friend of mine." With that he ducked back out the door.

Susan stood up, so I did too. "Good evening, Father," she said.

"Please, not so formal. Everybody in Price Hill still calls me Bob, or Father Bob, if you prefer."

"Uh, Bob," I kind of stammered. "This is Susan Stienle and I'm Ed McCorkel." I stuck out my hand.

"Yeah, I know. Walt told me that you two want to get married and that you had a little trouble with old Willie over at St. Clarisa's."

"He was a little negative this morning," said Susan.

"I am sure you are being kind, Susan. Walt said he threw you out on your ear."

"Not quite, but he would have if we hadn't been out the door before he could get to us," I said.

"Oh, I know the old boy pretty well. He tried to keep me out of the seminary, said I didn't have the mental capacity to be a priest. Told me I should be a ditch digger . . . but let's get down to this wedding business. You are a Catholic aren't you, Susan?"

"Yes, Father . . . uh, Bob."

"And you, Ed, what are you?"

"I guess I'm nothing. My parents were Presbyterian, and they took me to Sunday school when I was a kid, but after they were killed, I just kinda gave it up. Maybe I'm what you could call a fallen-away Protestant."

"Right, but do you know if you were baptized?"

"Yes, I do know that. There's a baptismal certificate in a file of old stuff about my parents."

"Okay, are you interested in taking instructions and becoming a Catholic?"

Oh, oh, here it comes, I thought. Joe warned me that they would be out to get me to join up. "I don't know. I haven't given it much thought."

"That's okay, Ed, but you would be willing to promise that any children would be raised Catholic?" I hadn't even thought about children.

"Sure," I answered.

"Now then, Susan." He turned to face her. "You would like to get married on November 29, the day after Thanksgiving?"

"Yes, that was the original plan."

"Would a side altar at the cathedral be all right?"

"Wow, that would be wonderful," Susan beamed.

"I just happen to be the secretary to the Archbishop. I think I can talk him into it, but I have a couple of more questions for Ed." I could see how happy this development had made Susan, so I told him to ask away.

"Walt told me that you were involved in that thwarted attempt to assassinate some general that I was reading about in the paper this morning. Were you?"

"Well, yes, I had something to do with it."

"The Archbishop was interested in the story too. When I tell him that you helped to unmask that fake priest, O'Toole, I'm sure he will be more than willing to go ahead with your wedding plans. He might want to perform the ceremony himself."

"There is only one thing, Bob. I don't think O'Toole was a fake priest. I think he was the real thing."

"Holy smoke! I'm sure the Archbishop will be interested in that." Bob said that he would work things out about the wedding and get back to us. "But right now, I'm heading over to Walt's for a beer. Would you two care to join me?"

"Sure!" we both said. Susan hadn't visited the Ideal very often, but she was ready to go now. I locked the door behind us and we crossed the street.

We sat at one of the tables. Walt called over, "What do you want, Susan? I know what those two want."

She said that she would have a root beer. Even she knew that Coke was not available at the Ideal. Walt carried the drinks over to the table, something that didn't happen very often. Father Logan was reaching in his pocket.

"No Bob, these are on me," I said.

"You're wrong, pal. These are on me," said Walt. "Did everything work out, Bobby?"

Susan answered, "They certainly did, and if Ed doesn't ask you to be the best man, Walt, I want you to be my maid of honor."

The priest laughed. "Just what we need, another heathen in the wedding party." The celebration didn't last long, Susan wanted to go home and tell her mother about the new arrangements. Bob had to get back, too.

Before he left he spoke to me. "Ed, I would like you to call me tomorrow." He wrote a telephone number on a napkin. "I'd like to set up an appointment for you with the Archbishop. I know he wants to know more about this O'Toole person."

After they left, I decided to have another drink. It had been another eventful day, and I needed to calm down before I tried to sleep.

Just then Hugo Getz, the cigar salesman, came through the door. "Hey Corky, glad to see you. Could you come out to my car and help me carry something in?"

It was quite unusual to see Getz awake at this time of night. I got up and walked to his car and saw that he had a large bundle wrapped in a blanket tied to the top of his car. We untied it and carried it into the bar. Hugo pulled the blanket off, and there was a full-size Indian standing there. It was made of wood.

"What the heck is that?" Walt came from the bar and looked at it.

"It's a cigar store Indian," said Getz. "Ain't it beautiful? I got it for five bucks at an old store in Addyston."

"Take it back," Walt said as he went back behind the bar.

"You don't understand, Walt. This thing is going to sell more cigars for you. Day and night, this guy can stand out front with cigars in his hand. See, they go right here." Getz pulled some cigars out of his pocket and put them in the hand of his statue.

"Take it back," Walt repeated.

"Just give it a try, I know it will sell more cigars for you. I'll take care of it, and it will . . . it will . . . it'll be a conversation piece. This place will be the talk of the corner."

"Take it back!"

"I'll bet Hartung's would be glad to have it," Getz continued to argue with Walt.

Just then Sam Callmeyer walked in. "Hey Corky, I'm glad I caught you."

Seems like everybody was glad to catch me tonight. "Hi Sam, what can I do for you?"

"Let's walk back to the kitchen," he said. I got up and walked back with him.

"Your tip about the big yellow house in Constance paid off. We nabbed Armbruster, Tune, and Kruger, who, by the way, is in pretty bad shape. We had to take him to the hospital. Plus we got three other guys, they had a shortwave radio and some signaling equipment, the kind that uses a flashing light, I don't know what you call it."

"That's great news," I said.

"We also picked up some records. We think we have the names of a lot of other Nazis operating here in the States. We already picked a bunch in Cleveland. I have to apologize, I really underestimated you."

That made me feel pretty good. "Thanks Sam, I just like to help in any way that I can."

Sam cut me short. "There's a meeting tomorrow, we have a conference room at City Hall. A lot of high muckety-mucks are going to be there. They want—they insist—that you be there too."

"Sure I'll be there. What time?"

"The meeting is at ten o'clock. Why don't I pick you up about nine-thirty?"

"I'll be ready. Don't you have any mail to deliver tomorrow?

"I'm taking a personal leave day." He stuck out his hand. "You did a great job, Ed."

We walked back into the bar. "Hey Callmeyer," Getz called. "Help me set this thing up outside." Apparently he had talked Walt into letting him try the Indian.

"Go home, Ed," Walt said when he saw me. "I want to close before any more nuts come in." I left.

CHAPTER 30

AT EXACTLY NINE-THIRTY THE NEXT MORNING, SAM CALL-meyer pulled up in front of the office and honked his horn. I kissed Susan goodbye and ran out to the car.

"I'm kind of nervous about this morning," I said to Sam, in way of greeting.

"There is no need for you to be nervous, they just want to hear about everything you did and what you know. You're pretty much the central figure in this whole thing."

"Yeah, that's what makes me nervous."

"You know that the city cops still have Jimmy Saline in jail. You said that you know he didn't kill Holthaus. Well, you are going to have to get him off the hook by telling why he didn't do it and who did."

"I think I can do that. I have been worried about Jimmy, and as long as Armbruster was on the loose, I thought Saline was safer in jail. Now that the Nazis have been caught, it's time to get him released."

"The locals still think Paddlewheel Benny stole the Belle and went joyriding. He needs unhooking, too."

"Yeah, as long as he was in the hospital I figured that he was okay."

"And O'Toole," Callmeyer continued, "they are going to want to know about O'Toole."

"Everything is so mixed up and complicated that I didn't really know who to tell it to."

"That's where I'm taking you this morning, to the guys you need to talk to. It's going to work out." We soon arrived at City Hall. Callmeyer pulled through an arched entrance to a courtyard where he parked the car. Then we walked up two flights of stairs, turned a corner, and came upon a table with a coffee urn and boxes of donuts on it. There were a number of men and one woman standing around it. I recognized Detective Clements. He was with a rather stout man in a police uniform.

Sam led me over to them. "Ed, you know Andy Clements, and this is Chief Mecklinburg. Chief, this is Edward McCorkel." I shook hands with both of them.

He nudged me toward a man in a brown suit standing off to one side. "This is Tom Hastings, he's a lawyer. Tom, Ed McCorkel. These three represent the City of Cincinnati and their interest in the case."

We moved over to another group of five men. One of them, wearing an Army uniform, looked familiar to me, and Sam introduced me to him first. "Ed McCorkel, Colonel Avery Webb. He's representing the military." I remembered I had met Webb at General Groove's plane. He gave me a little salute.

"Finally, these four work with me. Tony Ferrate, I think you have met him before." He was the guy who had been driving the car the night they picked me up downtown. I shook his hand.

Sam introduced the rest of them. "This is Art Gravely, Al Tenner, and my boss, Vince Smith. We all work for the government of the United States. Gentlemen, Ed McCorkel."

I was not introduced to the young woman. Apparently she was a stenographer, here to keep a record of the proceedings.

"Would you care for some coffee and a pastry?" asked Mr. Smith.

I declined and Smith immediately asked us all to move into the conference room. I saw Callmeyer grab a cup of coffee and a donut before he followed us.

Mr. Smith sat at one end of a large table and directed me to sit at the other. The city contingent sat on one side and the others sat on the other.

Smith took the floor. "A lot of strange things have happened around here. Some of us know bits and pieces of these happenings, but apparently you, Mr. McCorkel, are the only one that knows the whole story. We hope you can enlighten us. Oh, and don't be afraid of telling us about any thing that you might think is highly secret information, everyone in this room has high government clearance." He sat down. I guessed that meant that I had the floor. I stood.

"This all started the Saturday before last, when old Charlie and I found the body of Henry Holthaus in the rear of the Ideal Café. He was dead, murdered as we found out later. His death was originally considered a suicide."

"Wait a minute . . ." said Andy Clements.

"Please Mr. Clements, hold your questions until Mr. McCorkel finishes," Mr. Smith cut him off.

"Anyway, Henry's daughter was not satisfied with the idea that her father had committed suicide, so she asked me to investigate."

"Sorry, I must interrupt," Smith said. "Why did she ask you to investigate?"

Sam spoke up. "Sir, that could be a long explanation and is not really relevant. I suggest we just go on."

"Long explanation my foot!" Clements exclaimed. "He took a correspondence course when he was a kid."

Smith made a little gesture with his hand and said, "Please continue, sir."

"Some of the things I saw on and around the body caused me to determine that the murder might have something to do with the flower growers of Delhi. I went there to investigate."

"You went to India?"" Colonel Webb asked.

"Delhi is an area just outside the city limits," Tom Hastings interjected. "You're probably thinking of New Delhi, that's in India."

"Please, no more interruptions!" Smith almost screamed. "I would like to get back to Washington before the war ends. Please continue, Mr. McCorkel."

I continued. "One night, during the time that I was investigating the carnation growers, I was abducted by Tune and Armbruster."

"Who is Tune?" Colonel Webb interrupted again.

"He is one of the Nazis. Tune is an alias, you may have heard of him as Peter Lorry."

"The movie actor?" someone said.

"No, this guy spells his name L-O-R-R-Y." This time Smith didn't say anything, he just looked exasperated.

"Anyway, the Nazis tried make me give up my investigation. First, they tried to bribe me and then they threatened me. I had no idea why they were even interested in poor Henry's murder."

"But you didn't quit, did you? The police even tried to get you off the case and still you didn't quit." This came from Clements.

Smith said, "Hold it a minute." He walked outside the room and got a cup of coffee and a donut. When he returned he said, "I wouldn't want to starve to death while this interrogation is going on . . . continue."

"No, I didn't quit, I had discovered some interesting things and I thought I could unravel the case. That's about the time I figured out that two German-Americans were getting some information for the Nazis in return for information about green carnations."

"GREEN CARNATIONS?'" This time it was Smith himself who interrupted me. "Sorry, continue your story," he said in a quieter voice.

"The green carnations are something that Al Heller, a Delhi grower, is working on. The Grossman brothers were trying to discover Al's secret. So they were working with the Nazis, but they didn't know they were Nazis. The Grossmans were duped, and a little greedy, but they are good Americans. When they found out what Armbruster and Tune were really trying to do, they came to me and helped me immeasurably.

"Jimmy Saline, an ex-convict and not too bright, was also trying to discover the secret for the Grossmans. That's how Henry happened to be killed. But first I had better tell you about Father O'Toole and Arnold Mix."

"Who the hell is Arnold Mix, and what the hell does a priest have to do with this?" The police chief blurted out. Smith had given up trying to control the meeting.

"Arnold Mix is the cousin of cowboy movie star, Tom Mix, fairly recently deceased, and Father O'Toole is a professional assassin."

The stenographer threw down her pad and pencil. "Father O'Toole baptized my sister's little girl. I'm not going to listen to any more of this." She stormed out of the room.

Smith said, very quietly, "Let her go. We probably shouldn't keep a record of this anyway."

"Father O'Toole saved my life one night in back of the Cat and the Fiddle. He also tried to kill me at least once. More importantly, O'Toole had Arnold Mix convinced that he was with U.S. Intelligence and he was using a vantage point at Mix's farm to receive messages from across the river. Probably from that yellow house in Constance."

"Where we caught the spies?" This from Callmeyer.

"Yes, but back to the murder of Holthaus. On the night he was killed—Friday, September the seventh—he and Jimmy Saline were drinking and riding around in Henry's car. They had gone to Heller's greenhouses, where Jimmy broke in and stole a bottle of citronella, which he thought was Al's secret formula for the green carnations. They took it over to the Grossmans and sold it to them for fifty dollars. Then they went to Lawrenceburg to get some whiskey, which they took to a shed on the Saline property. They proceeded to get drunk.

"Jimmy got an old rifle out of one of the cabinets, one they used to shoot rats, I think, and jokingly shot Henry's hat off. Every time Henry would reach for it, Jimmy would shoot it again. Finally, Henry grabbed his hat and ran out to his car. Jimmy, in his drunken stupor, thought he might have shot Holthaus, so he ran after him.

"Apparently Henry was not hurt and both men got in the car and took off, with Jimmy driving. I have no idea where they were going but they drove up Neeb Road, turned on to Delhi, and lost control of the car.

"It skidded across the road and ran over a guy named Kruger who was hiding behind a tree at the side of the road. Kruger was there spying on O'Toole, who was receiving a coded message from his cohorts across the river. O'Toole, with a trained killer's lightning reflexes, whirled around and shot at the car, then jumped on his motorcycle and roared off.

"Right then, Jimmy threw the car in reverse to get out of there, moving the car off Kruger, who somehow got up and fired his gun into the passenger side window. Kruger then managed to hobble to where he had hidden his car and drove off. I think it's a pretty good guess that either O'Toole or Kruger killed Henry Holthaus.

"Jimmy panicked. He drove off backwards for about three-quarters of a mile and his heart was pounding. He didn't even hear the motorcycle drive off. He was sitting in Henry's car with Henry dead on the seat beside him. He was scared to death. Finally he drove to the family farm, found an old pistol in another shed, and drove to the Ideal. He put the body on the back steps of the café and threw the old pistol down beside it, hoping that Henry's death would be considered a suicide. Which it originally was."

'That was just a preliminary observation," Clements said angrily.

"Whatever." I continued, "Saline drove the car up to Whitsken's Dairy, where he left it by the pond. Then he walked back to the farm hoping that no one would associate him with Henry's death.

"Arnold Mix had been alerted by the crash, so he walked out on his porch just in time to see the shooting. He will verify what I just told you, but you had better get to him quickly. I understand that he is moving to Dubois, Pennsylvania, very soon."

"Wait a minute," Smith said. "Let's go see if that coffee is still hot, I think we need a break." We went out and drank coffee. Nobody said anything.

CHAPTER 31

We finished our coffee, a couple of the men went to the restroom, and then we filed back into the room and sat down. I stayed sitting while I continued my story.

"It was because of Mix that we were able to thwart the attempt to blow up Moby Trick."

"Moby Trick, what's a Moby Trick?" I don't even know who said that.

"We won't go into Moby Trick right now, it is top secret," Smith replied.

"Oh come on, Smith," I said. "You know as well as I do that Moby Trick was an elaborate hoax to try to capture the spies. It worked, the spies are captured. I think we can let old Moby sail of into the sunset."

"Very well, I guess there is no harm in telling them about it."

"Moby Trick is a huge rubber boat, I guess it is a boat. It could be submerged or it could float but it couldn't go anywhere without being towed. The whole idea behind it was to make the spies think it was a submarine to be used off the Grand Banks of Newfoundland. It had to have been one of the worst-kept secrets of the war and it was a hoax.

"It was because of Mix that I discovered the plot to blow it up. Mix called me last Sunday and asked me to come out to see him, that he had some important information. Walt drove me out to his place."

"Who is Walt?" This time it was Smith himself who interrupted.

"Walt owns the Ideal Café," several people interjected. I noticed one of them was the police chief.

"Mix told me about O'Toole shooting Henry. He had been reluctant to tell me before because he still thought the priest was one of the good guys. As long as we were out there, Mix invited us to watch the 'Straight Shooters' down on the river."

"Straight Shooters?" Smith again.

"Leave it alone," growled Sam.

I continued. "While we were watching the ceremony at the river, we noticed Jimmy Saline, Armbruster, and Tune launching a boat nearby. We could read the writing on the boxes they were loading into the boat and realized it was full of explosives. I knew at once that they were going to try to blow up Moby Trick. At that point I wasn't sure that it was a hoax, so I felt I had to try to stop them."

"I thought you told me that Saline was just confused, not a part of this." This one came from Clements.

"He was completely innocent, but the Nazis were blackmailing him. They said that they would tell the police about him killing Henry. By the time he sobered up, he thought he might have done it, so the blackmail worked. He was helping them to save his own neck, at least that's what he thought.

"I'm sure you all heard about the Belle of Avon causing the motor boat to run into the barge and blow up."

The police chief spoke up, "The mayor is still pretty pissed about all the corn."

"C'est la guerre," I said. "At least we stopped them. Then Mix came through again. He found the note that O'Toole had scribbled when he got the last message. We put two and two together and we were able to stop the assassination attempt on General Groove."

The police chief asked, "What do you mean by 'we'? Was there someone else involved?" he wanted to know.

"Yes sir, one of your own police officers, Joe Newmann. He has been involved in this whole investigation. He is a fine young man, and I think he deserves a commendation. That's about the whole story. Are there any questions?"

Were there any questions—I must have sat there for about two hours answering their questions. Finally Smith called a halt to it. He thanked me for the information I had given them.

Sam rode me home. Neither of us said anything until we got to my office. Then he reached over and shook my hand. He said quietly, "You done good, Corky." High praise indeed, coming from a mailman.

I walked into the office. Susan looked up and said, "Wow, that was some meeting, did everything go all right?"

"Everything worked out just fine, just fine indeed."

She smiled and kissed me. "Father Bob called. He wants us to have lunch with the Archbishop tomorrow. I told him we would be delighted. You have no say, we are going."

"That sounds fine, what time?"

"About one, and you're coming to my house for dinner tonight. I'll pick you up about six. You have no say in this one either, don't get involved in anything."

"I'll be right here waiting for you."

By this time, it was a little after four. Susan said, "I'm leaving, but I'll be back to pick you up. Be here."

I thought about going over to the Ideal, "Nah, why take a chance?" I said out loud. I walked upstairs to get cleaned up and maybe take a little nap.

Susan rang my bell about 5:30. I was waiting for her and ran down the steps to meet her. I opened the door and she kissed me.

"Wow, you actually remembered me this time. Mother was dubious about setting out a plate for you."

"Those other times were not my fault."

"I know dear, I was just teasing you." She threw me the keys to her mother's Pontiac. "Here, you drive."

I handed them back to her. "I don't drive."

"You don't drive." She looked at me in astonishment. "Of course, I noticed that you didn't own a car, but I had no idea that you didn't know how to drive."

"Oh, I learned to drive, back when I was in high school. But I have never felt the need for a car, living right here on the streetcar line."

"That's astonishing," she said. "All boys love cars. That's the first thing they want when they turn sixteen. You are not normal."

"I think I am normal enough, just never cared anything about owning a car. I love you, not your car."

I must have said the right thing, cause she hugged and kissed me right there on the sidewalk. Then she handed me back the keys and told me that I should show her how I could do.

I reluctantly got behind the steering wheel and with great apprehension pushed the starter button. I pulled it into gear and touched the gas pedal with my foot.

"GEERRRAAAACKKKK!"

"The clutch!" Susan screamed, "you've got to use the clutch!"

I started again and managed to get the car moving. We bucked and bounced down Cleves Pike, and by the time I got to Covedale, I had it in high gear. I shifted back into second as I made a rather wide turn. An oncoming car honked his horn at me and drove up on the curb. I pulled over and turned the car off.

"You take it from here," I told her as I started to slide over. She got out and walked around to the driver's seat.

"That wasn't too bad," she said as she made the turn on to Ralph Avenue. "A little practice is all you need."

I could tell she was a little shaken as she drove up to her driveway and turned in. "You just need a little practice and you will do fine, darling." She grabbed my arm and we walked in the house.

"Where have you two been? Supper's getting cold," Susan's mother called from another part of the house. She popped into the living room, took our coats, and put them in the closet. Then she grabbed me by the arm and pulled me to the dining room.

"You show up so seldom that I don't want you to get away this time."

We sat at the table. The two ladies bowed their heads and appeared to be praying. Mother Stienle raised her head and said, "Try that roast beef, Junie Blackhorn got it special for me." Blackhorn was a butcher with a shop up on Glenway.

The roast beef was delicious, as were the potatoes and carrots. I told Mrs Stienle how good everything was and how much I enjoyed it.

"I just got the meat from the butcher. Susan cooked the dinner. You're getting a good cook, Mr. McCorkel," she laughed.

"If this was a sample of her cooking, I am obviously getting more than I bargained for. I will soon get fat."

Her mother laughed and jumped up. "Just wait until you taste her dessert." She went into the kitchen and came back with three little bowls of white frothy stuff.

"This is called Apple Snow. You will love it."

I ate the stuff. It wasn't very good. It was bland, but there was a strange after taste. I didn't like it, but I ate it.

After we ate, Susan told her mother to go in and listen to her radio programs while she did the dishes. She told me that I could help.

While we were in the kitchen cleaning up, she apologized for the dessert. "It comes in a box; all you do is whip it up. It was developed after the war started. It apparently doesn't have any ingredients in it that are in short supply. Mother loves it, but I could tell you didn't."

"After that great meal, you don't have to apologize for some wartime dessert. I loved it."

She whipped her dish towel at me and said, "Liar!"

After we finished the dishes, we went into the living room. Susan's mother turned off the radio and we chatted. I told them a little about my adventures and about Moby Trick. I figured the secret was out of the bag and it wouldn't make any difference.

I left about nine o'clock. Susan drove me back to the corner and kissed me goodbye. I told her that I had a good time and that the dinner was great.

"Even the snowy stuff!" I called to her as she drove away.

CHAPTER  33

O<small>UT THE FRONT WINDOW OF THE</small> I<small>DEAL</small>, I <small>JUST HAPPENED</small> to see Susan unlocking the office door at eight in the morning. That was unusually early for her to be there. I had finished my breakfast, so I laid my paper aside and ran across the street.

"Is something wrong?" I shouted as I went through the door. "Why are you so early?"

Susan was hanging up her jacket. She was all dressed up. "Nothing's wrong, I have been thinking and thinking about our luncheon today, I just couldn't sleep. I decided I would just come on up and get anything done that needed doing so we would be free this afternoon." She walked over and kissed me. "Mom wanted me to apologize to you for last night's meal."

"Apologize for what? The meal was great."

"She said I let the potatoes get lumpy."

"Really, that's the way the potatoes always are at the Colonial Inn. I thought it was the way they were supposed to be."

"Oh darling, just wait until were married and I can start cooking for you. You're going to find out what good food really tastes like."

"If what I read in the paper this morning is true, about the time we get married, food is going to be rationed."

"Oh, pshaw. This is America, we'll always have enough to eat— you are going to change before we go, aren't you?"

I thought the suit I had on looked reasonably good, I had only worn it for a couple of days, but I could see that she didn't think it would do, so I said, "Of course. I am going to wear my good suit. I just had it dry-cleaned."

"Good, why don't you go up now and take a bath and shave and change, so we will be ready to go. We certainly don't want to be late." Every time I decided that married life was going to be great, she pulled something like this.

"I'll go up in a minute, but I would like to ask you about something first. Last night at dinner your mother suggested that after we were married, we should move into the house and that she would like to find a small apartment. Was she serious?"

"Yes dear," Susan said. "She has been wanting to find something smaller for a long time and this gives her a good excuse."

"Do you think it's a good idea? Do you think we should live there?"

"I grew up in that house, I love it. I would like to do a little redecorating, but yes, I would like us to live there."

I had never even thought about where we were going to live. I obviously haven't thought about a lot of things that were going to have to change. "We can't just let her give us the house."

"Why not? Dad left her fairly well off. A small apartment would probably cost her less a month than the upkeep on the house. She really wants to do it."

"How about this, what if I bought the house. I recently came into some . . . what I consider ill-gotten gains. . ."

"The money you won on that horse race?"

"Yeah, how did you know about that? Oh never mind, the Dodd Corner grapevine strikes again. Anyway, that nineteen hundred dollars would make a down payment and the 5/3rd Bank would probably handle a mortgage for us."

"I think that sounds like a good idea. We'll have to talk Mom into it, but she'll probably go along with it if that's what you want to do. Now go upstairs and get ready," she added.

I did as I was told. I went upstairs thinking how well things were working out. I hoped things went as well at the luncheon with Bob Logan's boss.

It was about quarter past twelve when I came back down, all spruced up and shining. Susan was waiting for me. "We should get going, we don't want to be late."

"We have plenty of time," I told her as I helped her into her coat.

We locked up and walked out to her Pontiac and headed downtown. As we drove down Glenway, I said, "I guess this luncheon will be in the bishop's rectory."

"When it's a bishop or archbishop's place, it's called a chancery."

"You Catholics have a language all your own, don't you?" She let that one pass and we rehashed the plans for the wedding and the reception that we had made last night.

She parked the car and we walked around to the side of a huge church, "the cathedral," she told me, to a slightly smaller building. We walked up six steps and rang the bell. The huge carved door opened and Bob greeted us.

"Right on time, come on into the parlor, the Archbishop is waiting for us."

I was very nervous, I thought about the meeting we had with Father Williams.

"What do I call this guy?" I whispered to Susan.

Bob heard me and said, "Your Holiness is the way he is usually addressed, but I think you can just call him Bishop."

We walked into a large room. A tall, thin man rose out of a chair as we entered. He, like Bob, was dressed in one of those long black dresses.

"Ah, Miss Stienle and Mr. McCorkel, so nice to meet you."

He put out his hand. Susan took it, kissed it, and started to kneel down. He took her hand and pulled her up. "We don't need any of that here," he told her, then reached over and shook my hand. I just smiled and nodded.

"Please, sit down. Susan and Ed, may I call you that?" We both just nodded.

"Father Logan has told me of your dilemma and about your meeting with Father Williams. I apologize for your encounter with 'Wild Willie.' He has a rather violent temper, but I assure you not all my pastors are quite as vociferous as he is."

"Thank you, Your Holiness," Susan managed to stammer.

"Father Logan and I have discussed your wedding and I have no objections. Unfortunately, as much as I would like to, I cannot officiate. I am going to visit relatives in Terre Haute over Thanksgiving and will not be here on the date you choose. But I think that Father Logan is rather pleased that I won't be here. He wants to perform the wedding.

"I am sorry I won't be at the ceremony. I particularly wanted to meet his friend Walt. I have heard of his generosity to the downtrodden that Father Williams sends to him."

Just then, just as I almost burst out laughing, a woman came to the door of the parlor and told us that lunch was ready. She was dressed all in black, too. Not at all like the priest's dresses. Her clothes looked like she was wearing a black robe on top of a black robe with a long black shawl over her head. She was also wearing one of those big grey aprons like the housekeeper at St. Clarisa's rectory had on. I figured that the aprons, like the men's dresses, were standard Catholic issue.

"This way," said the Archbishop, leading us to a dining room with a table that would have easily seated sixteen people. Today it was set for only four, all at one end.

When we were seated the Archbishop bowed his head and said a short prayer. When he finished, Bob and Susan said, "Amen." I said it, too, a little late.

The woman in the robes and apron came in and served us all green salads. She went out and then came in with a huge bowl of rice. She went to the Archbishop and sat it down by him. He put some of the rice on his plate and passed the bowl to Susan. We each in turn followed his lead and took some of the rice.

Then she came back in with a bowl full of something that looked like an odd-colored stew, again she put it down by the Archbishop. As he put some over the rice he said, "I think you will enjoy this dish. One of our parishioners is the chef at the Latin Quarter, the nightclub in Newport. He gave us the recipe. It's called 'Shrimp à la Pacific.' I find it delicious."

It was, too. It was shrimp and pineapple and coconut and I don't know what all.

"To get back to the wedding," our host said. "I think you three should get together and work out the details. As long as Walt doesn't bring any of his 'Mixups,' I will approve them."

"Uh sir, they are Mixites, and Walt didn't really have any thing to do with them."

"I was kidding, Ed. But I do really want to talk to you about Father O'Toole. I did some checking, and I have to admit, I was shocked to find out what I did about your friend, O'Toole."

"Hardly my friend, sir. I think he saved my life on one occasion, I also think he tried to kill me a couple of other times."

"Once again, I called him your friend in jest. But seriously, what I found out is hard to believe."

"O'Toole was—is—a priest, a very strange priest. I did some checking on him. It wasn't easy, the Church is reluctant to give out this sort information, even to archbishops. I finally had to call a friend in Rome.

"O'Toole—and that really is his name, by the way—had a nervous breakdown when he was in the seminary." He turned to me. "That's a school where they teach young men to be priests.

"He was suspended for a year. During this year, he studied Church history, especially the parts about how the Church was persecuted. Finally it was decided that he was cured and could continue. After he finished his studies, he was graduated and ordained a priest.

"He was sent to a church in Mississippi where the non-Catholics, which most of the people in the town were, didn't like the Catholics. The attitude of the townspeople made him think that he was being persecuted.

"He snapped. He was sent to a monastery." Once again he looked at me. "That's a place where priests go around all day praying and not talking.

"He brooded in silence, thinking about how he had to save his Church. Finally he escaped from the monastery. Actually, he just walked out. He made his way to California, where he fell in with a bunch of religious zealots called the AVC, Americans for Vatican Control. They were a group of about two hundred people, each one crazier than the next.

"They believe that America should be a Catholic country under the direct control of the Vatican. The Church in no way sanctioned this group.

"The AVC set up a camp in Italy, where they trained seven of their members to be undercover agents, actually to be assassins. O'Toole was one of the seven. He was so taken with Italy that he, as they say, went native. He even affected an Italian accent."

"After he completed his AVC training, he was indoctrinated by the Italian Fascists and further trained to be a spy and assassin. He was sent to this country, as a priest, to blend into the community and be prepared to serve the cause when the need came up.

"O'Toole came to Cincinnati, and with false papers, he managed to get assigned to St. Clarisa's. I suppose I must take the blame for that.

"The AVC heard about something called the Manhattan Project. I don't have any idea what it actually is, but they decided that it was a plot to nationalize all the property in New York City.

"Since a lot of that property is owned by the Vatican, they felt that they had to sabotage the project. The Fascist government in Italy encouraged their efforts.

"Somehow they learned that a General Leslie Groove was going to be named director of the project, and that he was coming to Cincinnati. The AVC called on O'Toole to do his duty and assassinate the General."

"What did they do, just call him up and tell him to shoot this guy?" I asked.

"No, some German agents, realizing that this crazy bunch could potentially cause chaos in the United States, decided to use them. They—the Germans—had a secret radio operator over in Kentucky. The Nazi agents made the operation available to the AVC.

"Messages from the AVC were flashed in Morse code to O'Toole on this side of the river. That is about all I found out," concluded the Archbishop.

"Good lord! Oops, I beg your pardon your Lordship. But that just about fills in the last hole in this mystery."

"I took no offense, Ed, the Lord is good and you can just call me Bishop."

I was so excited I just continued on, "O'Toole had convinced the owner of the property where he was receiving the messages from Kentucky—Arnold Mix—that he was an officer in Army Intelligence on the trail of some Nazi spies. The fact that there really were Nazi spies lurking around was just a coincidence. And it was O'Toole who shot the guy who was trying to kill me."

"Someone tried to kill you? You didn't tell me that," Susan said in alarm.

"It was just a little mix-up, nothing to fret about. But the priest definitely was crazy. He got so caught up in the story he told Mix, about being after the spies, that he believed it himself. He discovered that this gang were really spies and started following them around, and that's why he was in that alley downtown. He had no idea that he was actually working for them.

"Then, when he saw me hanging around at Mix's place, he decided I was a threat. That's when he took a shot at me."

"He shot at you, too," Susan said, very quietly. "You didn't tell me about that either."

"There was no need. O'Toole was a crack shot. I knew he wasn't trying to kill me, he was just warning me to stop my snooping around."

Susan whispered, "Your Holiness, could I use your bathroom?"

Father Logan stood up and called, "SISTER!" The woman who served us came in.

"Could you show Miss Stienle to the bathroom?" Susan followed her out of the room.

"I suppose then he got the message about General Groove from the Nazis and went off to assassinate him," said the Archbishop.

"Yes, and Mix accidentally discovered the note he had written the message on and called Joe Newmann, who was working with me. Between us and a Cincinnati policeman named Chiggerbox, we managed to stop him at the airport."

Susan returned, looking a little pale. We all stood.

The Archbishop laid his napkin on the table. "You are a fascinating man, Mr. McCorkel. I would love to hear about the explosion you caused, but alas, I have another appointment."

He turned to Susan. "My dear, I hope your wedding goes well and that you both have a happy life. When that first baby comes along, I suggest you bypass Father Williams and come to me to baptize him or her. I expect that the child will be brought up as a Catholic . . . good afternoon."

After he left, Susan, Bob, and I went back to the parlor, where we made the arrangement for the wedding.

Susan was bubbling on the drive back. She couldn't stop talking about our luncheon. She didn't say anything about the attempts on my life. Maybe she had forgotten about them.

When we got back, she told me she was going home to tell her mother about our afternoon. There was very little insurance business going on around the office anyway.

CHAPTER 34

AFTER SUSAN LEFT, I DECIDED TO CALL MARGE BAKER AND tell her the whole story of Henry's death. I picked up the telephone and dialed her number.

"Marge, this is Ed McCorkel . . ." This time I was able to tell her the whole story. About Jimmy and Henry and what happened in the shed. How I believed that either Kruger or O'Toole had shot her father, and how the greenhouse owners were involved.

She stopped me from time to time to ask questions. I answered them fully. I explained how the Nazis were involved, about Paddle-wheel Benny and the Belle, and about the Mixites and their part in stopping the attempt to blow up Moby Dick.

I also told her all about Moby Dick and about O'Toole's attempt on General Groove's life. I told her the whole story. Well, I left out the part about watching Fionna dance. I didn't think that was an important part of the story. When I finished, she had a few more questions. Then she said, "Ed, you are a hero."

"No, I'm no hero, I just stumbled around, found things out and put two and two together. If there is any hero, I think it was your father . . . his death, sad as it was, resulted in the capture of a Nazi spy ring, saved the life of someone very important to our war effort, and unmasked that crazy priest. It was also sort of responsible for Susan and me planning to get married."

"Thank you, Ed. You are a very good man. I am so happy to hear about you and Susan getting married."

There was a catch in her voice, she might have been crying. "I'll talk to you later," she said and hung up.

I sat there for a few minutes. Then I decided that I had earned a Smile. I walked across the street.

Outside the door, I noticed the Indian. He had a hand full of cigars and a little sign hung on the cup. The sign read, "Take one and put a nickel in the cup." Just for fun, I took a nickel out of my pocket and put it in the cup. I took one of the cigars from the Indian's hand.

I walked in the bar and got an orange soda from Charlie. "How is the Indian doing?" I asked him.

"Hah," Charlie replied. "Getz was in early this morning, checking up on it. All the cigars were gone, but there wasn't no nickels in the pot. He figured people didn't know they were supposed to pay for them, so he made that sign and hung it around the cup."

Wow, I thought. Charlie is getting garrulous. I handed the cigar to him, drank my soda, and went home.

The next morning, I walked over to the Ideal with my coffee. I noticed that the Indian didn't have any cigars in his hand. The cup was empty and the sign was gone. I was about to ask Walt about it when Getz came in.

"Did you bring the money in?" he asked Walt.

"I didn't touch anything. There were no cigars or money, even the sign was gone."

"Damn," said Getz. He stormed out.

Apparently he walked up to the dry cleaners and got a shirt cardboard. He brought it back, borrowed an orange crayon that Walt found in one of the drawers in the back bar, and made a new, larger sign. He held it up and studied it. "They will be able to see this one, it is sure to work. You'll see, Walt, once we work out the kinks everything will be okey-doke."

The new sign read:

THESE CIGARS ARE FOR SALE. FEEL FREE TO TAKE ONE BUT PUT A NICKEL IN THE POT.

He then borrowed a piece of string and went out and tied the sign around the neck of the Indian. After he left, I told Walt everything I had learned about O'Toole from the Archbishop. I also thanked him for introducing me to Father Bob.

"Did everything work out for the wedding?" he asked.

"Everything worked out great." I told him all about the plans we made. "Walt, I would sure like it if you will be my best man. Susan is going to have to look somewhere else for a maid of honor."

"I would be honored, but what does Bob's boss think about that?"

"I think he liked the idea. He knows all about the game you play with Father Williams and he thinks it is funny."

"How in the heck did he find out about that?"

"I don't know, he said he would like to meet you, but unfortunately, he will be out of town on the day of the wedding. Bob is going to marry us."

"Every thing sounds great, but there's just one more thing. We want to have a party for you and Susan. Something to celebrate your engagement. We want to have it here on Saturday. Can the two of you make it, around two in the afternoon of the twenty-second?"

"Shucks Walt, you don't have to do that."

"Yes I do. You are famous, everybody is going to want to talk to you. I'll be charging for drinks, so I will make a good profit on the day."

"When you put it that way, how can we refuse? I'll go over and tell Susan about it right now."

Susan was on the telephone when I walked in. When she hung up, I told her about the party. She said it sounded like fun.

I sat down and we talked about what had happened the day before, and about the wedding plans and about buying the house. About noon she told me to come with her, to our future home, and have lunch.

We got back a little before one, and I noticed that the Indian was missing. "Excuse me for just a minute," I told her and ran over to the café.

"Where did the Indian go?" I asked Walt.

"I don't know. I didn't even know it was gone."

"Curiouser and curiouser," I said and went back to the office.

Susan and I worked on insurance business the rest of the afternoon. Yes, she even let me help a little. She had gotten a little behind because of all the time off we had taken. Suddenly, the door burst open and Hugo Getz was standing there.

"It's gone!" he shouted. "Somebody stole my Indian! Corky, I want to hire you to find him."

I walked over and put my arm around his shoulder. "Sorry, Hugo, I don't do missing person cases," I told him, hoping he hadn't talked to Earl Klopp recently.

CHAPTER 35

ON THURSDAY AND FRIDAY, SUSAN AND I WORKED ON INsurance business. We straightened out and upgraded the files, reviewed the forms we used, called clients. She re-taught me all the things I had kind of forgotten as she had taken over handling the business. We even rearranged the office furniture and really cleaned the place up.

We worked diligently—well, not too diligently. We found ourselves stopping a few times to talk about our future together.

I also took an occasional break to walk across the street. These visits always took longer than I expected because I kept running in to people who wanted to hear the story about Henry, the spies, the priest, and Moby Trick.

But even with all the interruption we got a lot done. During one of our breaks, Susan brought up the attempts on my life. "I hope you plan to give up this detecting business," she told me. "You know, you could have been killed."

"I was really in danger only one time, when Kruger pulled his gun on me. The good Father O'Toole took care of that one. The rest of the time I don't think I was in any real danger, it was just that they were trying to scare me off the case."

"When I heard about some of your escapades, I was really scared," she said.

"The thing is, I think I am really good at this stuff, correspondence course or no correspondence course."

"You didn't find the wooden Indian."

"I didn't look for it, but I happen to know that Jackson and Billie Boy heisted it and hid it in the garage under Brownie's apartment."

Susan looked surprised. "How did you figure that out so fast?"

"Walt told me . . . he saw them do it."

"Well, I guess you are still a pretty good detective, but you are getting better at the insurance business, too."

"We'll have to talk about that."

CHAPTER 36

BEFORE I KNEW IT, IT WAS SATURDAY AFTERNOON. SUSAN had kept me busy all morning, I didn't get over to the bar even once. Around two o'clock, she and I walked over to the Ideal.

When we walked in, we were surprised. The place was decorated with balloons and crepe paper streamers, all in red, white, and blue. There was food all over the bar, including a small wedding cake, and the place was mobbed. Everybody I ever knew, and some I never met, seemed to be there.

Aaron Coffaro was playing "Yankee Doodle Dandy" on his violin and Jake Jackson was accompanying him by beating a couple of spoons on the bar.

Ray and Dinky Brockelberg were there, along with their three brothers. The syndicate was there, too—Fatty, Frank Dodd, and Muffin Schroeder.

Walt met me at the door, and Charlie and Brownie were behind the bar. Betty Horn and Fionna had on aprons and were acting as waitresses. Erma Gerbil was helping them.

Joe Newmann, Andy Clements, Sergeant Stutter, and Police Chief Mecklinberg were standing with a rather stout, short man in a suit. I didn't know him.

Sam Callmeyer, his partner, Tony, and their boss Vince Smith were peeking out of the kitchen. That wasn't everybody by a long shot, but the rest of the people there I didn't know.

When the music died down, the whole bunch of them gave a mighty cheer. After that, Bob Neighborhouse, the guy who ran the grocery next door, stuck his head in the door to see what was going on. When he saw the party, he stayed, too.

Walt took us to an open space in the middle of the bar. There were two fancy barstools there, something unheard of in the Ideal, and he had us sit there. Then he went to the end of the bar, where there was an overturned beer case.

He got up on the case and said, "Ed, we are all proud of you, and so pleased that you and Susan have finally decided to get married, we knew it was only a matter of time before she hooked you. So we decided to throw you a party."

Shouts and comments came from the crowd, some rather bawdy. But I did make out Muffin Schroeder's voice saying, "I made the cake!"

Walt waved for quiet. "First, my dad has something to say."

Old Charlie got up on the beer case. "Corky, we all want you to know that we are proud to know you." Wow, old Charlie orating.

"We," he continued, "wanted to get you some presents but we didn't know what to get, so we took up a collection and decided to give you the money. For a honeymoon, maybe."

Walt helped him off the case and he came over and laid a wad of bills down in front of us. "Two hundred and forty-eight bucks, no . . ." he reached in his pocket and pulled out two singles, "make that two hundred and fifty."

More cheering!

Andy Clements got up on the box next. "Chief Mecklinberg has graciously allowed me to speak for the Cincinnati Police Department. I have to say that I thought you were a nut. You certainly proved me wrong. We appreciate all you did to help us out. I would like to present you with this Private Investigator's license."

"Oh no," I heard Susan whisper over the renewed cheering.

Clements raised his hand for quiet. "I would also like to tell you that Patrolman Newmann and Officer Chiggerbox will receive commendations, which will go in their permanent files."

More cheering, and I heard Fatty shout "Bingo!"

When the crowd quieted down, Clements continued. "I would now like to introduce the mayor of Cincinnati, his honor . . ." He was drowned out by the cheering.

The stout little man I had not recognized stood on the box. "I have a proclamation declaring today as 'Edward McCorkel Day' here in Cincinnati."

This time the crowd broke out in mild applause. The mayor continued, "Of course, you may be found financially responsible for the damaged barge and the city wide clean up of the corn."

This time there were boos. While the crowd was showing its displeasure at the mayor's last remark, a man came in the front door wearing a tan sport coat and carrying a small box. He went directly to the beer case, helped the mayor down, and stood up on it.

"Ed, I am Lowell Mosley, the real one this time. Walt will vouch for me. And I'm sorry about the little subterfuge I had to employ the last time you thought we met."

"That was Marc Ballerd the last time, wasn't it?"

"Yes, it was, you haven't missed a trick. But to get to the barge that was destroyed, it belonged to my company and we do not expect any restitution.

"And the corn, Mr. Mayor? It is my understanding that the pigeons cleaned that up and Mr. McCorkel can not be held responsible for the pigeons." Cheering.

"I have brought you a present," Mosley continued, "certainly little enough to show you my gratitude," and he handed me the box he had been carrying.

I opened the box. Inside there was a Mosley *Super Deluxe* radio with a little gold plaque on the front that read:

ED McCORKEL
PATRIOT

I thanked him, and Brownie put a glass of beer in his hand. Just then, we heard a loud wail of sirens, and three black cars pulled up outside. Six burly men in brown suits pushed into the crowd, clearing a path to where I was seated. They were followed by a woman in a funny hat and a coat with a fur collar. She came right up to me.

I heard some one in the crowd say, "Eleanor Roosevelt!"

"Mr. McCorkel, I am Eleanor Roosevelt. I was attending a meeting in Columbus, and since I was so close, Franklin insisted I see you personally.

"He is very proud of what you have done here in Cincinnatah. You have helped our war effort immeasurably. I have a medal that the President wishes me to present to you. It is the Medal of Merit for Home Defense.' He said to tell you that you deserved a higher award, but alas anything more auspicious is presented to the military only."

She hung the medal on a long ribbon around my neck. "I suppose if I were French I would kiss you on the cheek now," she said, "but we Americans are not quite so demonstrative."

She paused for a moment and said, "But this is a special occasion." She reached up and kissed me on the cheek.

Thunderous applause . . .

She continued, "I spoke to General Groove before coming here. He sends his heartfelt thanks and this." She handed me a small box with another medal in it.

"This is the General's own Silver Star. You can't wear it . . . but he said you deserve it. And some day, perhaps, if all goes well, and we pray that it does—you will know how important it was that you saved his life."

Just then Walt came up and asked her if she would care for a drink.

"Why yes, a little sherry would be nice."

He looked a little quizzical for a moment, then he reached in the bottle box and pulled out Fionna's special wine. He filled a chaser glass half full and placed it in front of her. I introduced him to Mrs. Roosevelt.

"Oh yes, I have a special accommodation for you too, and others for Officer Joe Newmann, Arnold Mix, and Bernard Graham."

She motioned to one of the brown-suited men. He laid four rolled scrolls on the bar in front of her. She looked at the names on them. She handed one to Walt and said, "With the President's gratitude. Are the others here?"

I called Joe over, and she handed him a scroll.

"Mr. Graham is still in the hospital," I told her, "and Arnold has moved to Pennsylvania, but I will personally see that they get these."

That seemed to satisfy her. She took a sip of her wine and a funny look crossed her face, but didn't say anything. I introduced her to Susan.

"I understand that you two are getting married around Thanksgiving," she said to Susan, and then under her breath, I thought I heard her say, "If Franklin doesn't move it again."

"Yes, Mrs. President," Susan stammered.

The First Lady smiled. "Just call me Eleanor."

"Asheville, North Carolina, is a lovely town," she continued. "And not too far from here. One of my favorite places, the Bosksward Inn, is located there. I will be attending a meeting there myself in late November. I think it would be a lovely place for a honeymoon. Would you allow me to arrange it for you? It would be Franklin's treat, of course."

We both stammered, "That would be wonderful."

She took another sip of her wine and then set it down on the bar. "We will be in touch." With that she sailed out the door with her entourage in close pursuit.

Right about then we heard Earl Klopp's voice calling, "Hey Charlie, can you come to the back door?"

"Son of a bitch!" said old Charlie from behind the bar. "That's how this story started."

I Thought Pigs Could Fly!

Americans Revisited, Vol. 1

Drawing The Big Red Machine

The Collected Old Curmudgeon

Staglieno: Art of the Marble Carver

Sucking It Up: American Soldiers in 2008

Price Hill Saloons and Much, Much More!

Drawing Super Wars: The Early Years of Bengal Football

Cincinnati's Findlay Market - A Photographic Journey, Past & Present

Managing Nonprofit (& for Profit) Organizations: Tips, Tools and Tactics

Remembering Remus in Price Hill

Pre-Victorian Homes

Drawing Pete

Right, Angels!

Body Of Work

Point Of View

Anything Goes

one³

Your Best Shot

Your Best Shot 2010

When Big Artists Were Little Kids

When More Big Artists Were Little Kids

When Big Architects Were Little Kids

Alena and the Favorite Thing

Cincinnati Trips with Kids

Hobo Finds a Home

Cliffie's Life Lessons

Paragon & Jubiliee

The Curious Moog

CPSIA information can be obtained at www.ICGtesting.com
Printed in the USA
BVOW07s1212080914

365441BV00001B/1/P